THE DO-ANYTHING KIDS

CHRISTOPHER GIARRATANO

ISBN: 978-0-5781-8958-1 (sc)
ISBN: 978-0-5781-8959-8 (hc)
ISBN: 978-0-5781-8960-4 (e)

Solarium House
5666 La Jolla Blvd. La Jolla, CA 92037
858-224-2130
Solariumhousepublishing.com

Lulu Publishing Services rev. date: 03/24/2017

THE
DO~ANYTHING
KIDS

CHRISTOPHER GIARRATANO

ISBN: 978-0-5781-8958-1 (sc)
ISBN: 978-0-5781-8959-8 (hc)
ISBN: 978-0-5781-8960-4 (e)

Solarium House
5666 La Jolla Blvd. La Jolla, CA 92037
858-224-2130
Solariumhousepublishing.com

Lulu Publishing Services rev. date: 03/24/2017

1

We've Got Angels That Left
Heaven for the Stage

Starting in the Fall of '98, there were four months when I spent all of my free time with Brody Shaw. We had similar tastes, but he was an adult, whereas I had recently graduated from college. I had a degree in English, and was all set to be a writer of fiction—a.k.a. a bar back living with two other "writers."

Brody taught me everything *he* wanted me to know—about what I couldn't really say. Certainly, not in one word, not even in a few. But then it dawned on me that Brody was a book. He defied logic by living beyond it, because he lived what he called "sacrifice and devotion." Brody ended up challenging every single thing I ever believed concerning myself and others, including the sun, moon, and stars.

For various reasons that I will explain later, I hadn't seen or spoken to Brody in five years. And my life suffered because of it. I'm sure his did, too. Regardless, by the time I sat down with him at Mang's Chinese Restaurant, he was already finishing his meal and lubricated on wine.

Sitting alone in a booth, he was flipping through a weathered copy of *The Great Gatsby.* As I approached, he had the smell of broken on him: I couldn't tell why he was staring so intensely at that book. When I looked closer, I saw that the pages were decorated with notes. Highlighted sections, pencil scribbles, and scores of underlined words.

A Harvard thesis on brain surgery could not have been more annotated. As the Earth revolves around the sun, he revolved around books.

Brody was every bit of thirty-six years old, with a pronounced widow's peak and short sideburns that were rapidly going white. He had recently gained weight, but wore it well. It didn't hurt that he was handsome and tanned, even though he had crooked bottom teeth that were shading yellow.

There were several varieties of humor that suited Brody's multidimensional personality. His latest hobby was taking photos of pigeons' feet. He observed that he rarely saw pigeons with perfect feet. So he figured a photo of them would be a rare find in his "only in New York" collection, which he likened to Heinrich Schliemann's excavations at Troy.

Although he had invited me out to "clear the air," we did not embrace. In the previous five years, he had apparently changed his warm, lovable style into something more remote and cold.

"I came back from Rio three weeks ago," he said.

Clearly, he was eager to pour out his tall tales, which were disconnected and unhinged. But for a guy who had never been hinged to begin with, that wasn't strange. Without fail, he marched into a rant.

"I'm not a numerologist," he said, "but I know about numbers and their inner workings."

Out of nowhere, he started flashing his fingers at me, one at a time for emphasis.

"Eight is the number of renewal. Monday…, Tuesday…, Wednesday…, Thursday…, Friday…, Saturday…, Sunday…, and then Monday again! Seven days of the week. Then the eighth day is really a new first day. It happens in musical theory, too."

I flashed him my squinted eye of confusion.

"*Do…, re…, mi…, fa…, sol…, la…, ti*," he sailed on, "Seven notes building to the conclusion of another *do*. You get the idea but it finds itself in a dramatic way on the periodic table, which is not dogmatic. It's one hundred and sixteen natural elements continually charted out with each discovery. It's set in stone. Each element gets its number on the chart, based on how many protons are in its nucleus. I think I've told you this before."

He flashed his fingers again.

"The first eight are…hydrogen…, helium…, lithium…, beryllium…, boron…, carbon…, nitrogen…, and, in the eighth spot, oxygen."

He launched into another seemingly unrelated flow of thoughts.

"Now, all this talk of eight is adorably strange and intriguing. Like my trip to Rio, now *that* had a feel…, eight people for eight days. I know the difference between cosmic and cosmetic, I cracked that nut in grade school. I know the difference between humility and humiliation. I decoded that during my stay at Bellevue. Maybe there was a time when I needed an elevator to tell me which way was up, but those days are long gone. I've made the transition from lusting after the girls in *Playboy* to seeing the quality of beauty and modesty of the women in *Elle*. I look at the stars and see astronomy, not astrology. And it's worth pointing out that *no* astronomer has *ever* reported a UFO, because they *know* what *they're* looking at!"

While I was trying to weigh the validity of that last sentence, Brody never stopped.

"To know the difference between artifice and genuine spiritual matters has always been left in the hands of the men and women who trained and disciplined themselves in the art and science of living supernaturally. Most of the ones I met go by another handle, which is known as 'Followers of The Way.' And wouldn't you know it? When good ol' Confucius started his thing, he called it following the Way'! Even though he came five hundred years *before* Jesus!"

Brody banged his hand on the table to punctuate his passion. The other patrons in the restaurant immediately knew there was a loose cannon among them.

To *not* know Brody meant that you would presume that he had a glorious life-changing experience every three seconds. To *know* him meant that he had an experience every ten minutes, which may or may not have been life-changing.

Brody always had a repertoire of short rants at his disposal, which he would break out at inopportune moments. For instance, when he met acquaintances from outside Manhattan, he always threw out this grenade: "You're rank amateurs concerning earthly things if you didn't grow up in the land of the freaks and home of the brazen! The underground? Think *underneath* the underground. The mountaintop? Try a penthouse in a skyscraper. They don't give those away in a Cracker Jack box!"

Brody was a library of unique observations. "Ask anyone," he would say, "where the best slice is in the city, and they'll always tell you the one downstairs from the place they live."

He also behaved like an urban compass.

"Uptown is the most irrelevant place on Earth. Don't head uptown! That's what you'll hear on Fifty-fourth Street. That makes Seventy-eighth Street uptown. But you can bet, and undoubtedly win every time, that on Seventy-eighth Street they'll tell you the trouble is really uptown. Don't head uptown! To them, that's Ninety-sixth Street. And so on."

When the waiter brought the fortune cookies to the table, Brody finally shut up. Ignoring his cookie, he went straight to his fortune. After he read it, he placed the paper on his tongue. Then he closed his eyes and hummed aloud.

That gave me my first chance to get in a word, so I made a formal toast: "To my old friend Brody, may our ships dock for the evening as we give praise to all things beautiful!"

Brody asked the waiter for some tea, and remained quiet long enough for me to listen to all the other chatter around us. Trite, vapid, vague, robotic, and—worst of all—fake. I realized once again what I had always known: I was sitting across from the realest person I knew. I was glad to see him in *any* condition.

That night at the restaurant was long as Brody described what he called "the finest trip ever invented…. It should be packaged."

Brody was married to hyperbole. Although he never went fishing, you could always count on him to come up with a story about landing a shark. But the story wouldn't end *there*. Brody went in for *massive* hyperbole. In his story, he would ride the back of the shark down to the ocean floor, where he would meet a fisherman with a gambling problem, and bet the guy that he could cure him before they ran out of breath. That would be a typical Brody-gone-fishing tale.

As I was paying the bill, Brody went solemn, muttering, "Few people realize how a new and different scientific paradigm subsumes the prior one. But they know innately when something is ascending or descending. Everything that April thought about herself went under a knife and got cut out. But many people made the grave mistake of believing that I was the surgeon. Truth be told, I only showed her the light."

And therein lay Brody—an unrelated thought that at a much later time would be tied together. He was a human roller coaster.

When we left Mang's, we moved to a nearby after-hours spot for a few drinks.

This evening, like all times with Brody, really started deep in the past. However, there are days, and then there are *days*—brief moments that sear your heart, forever changing you.

On March 15th, 2003, Brody was in Brazil, a country rich in perverted poverty *and* colorful celebration. There he saw Orion's Belt for the first time, but it had to be pointed out to him. Then he stared at it intently as he floated in a pool beside a house at the edge of a mountain rainforest overlooking the South Atlantic. He almost forgot the blood orange martini in his hand.

Rio de Janeiro was the first place that Brody ever drew a breath of fresh air. Every gasp before that was the ad hoc electricity of New York. That's what was inside of him—ad hoc electricity. He took it everywhere he went. When you met Brody, you might not see it, or hear it, or taste it, or feel it, or smell it, but it was there. It might be invisible until he spoke words into fragmented sentences, and then linked them to abstract thoughts that he hoped made sense, because halfway through, he forgot what he was talking about.

Speaking of which, the number eight followed him like a disheveled down-and-out detective trying to solve an incredibly stale story of love gone amuck.

"Orion's Belt was not an overwhelming sight," Brody said to me. "I'm sure, though, with binoculars, it's jaw dropping."

But the sight that really blew his mind was April Graves.

"Now *she* was a vision," he said. "An impossibly beautiful face. A flawless concoction of a breathtaking physique, a soothing voice, an intoxicating personality, and a naturalness that blended absolutely in the rainforest. It hid her cunning character perfectly."

In addition to April, there was Paige Brentwood, his old friend. Paige had been April's roommate at Vassar.

"Everything was being rationalized by the number eight. It was the frequency in which God spoke to me."

Brody sounded like that both drunk *and* sober. The night went on that way till we shut the place down. It was good to see Brody. I had become accustomed to writing down his stories as soon as I got home. This latest story was so far out that I didn't *have* to write it down. Instead I had a few friends over for dinner and repeated it back to them over a juicy brisket and couscous. Here's what Brody told me:

Paige's parents, Darius and Lesley Brentwood, commercial real estate tycoons, had decided to celebrate her twenty-first birthday by orchestrating an all-expenses-paid trip to Rio. Brody had a healthy respect and a genuine love for the Brentwoods, who represented everything he wanted to see unfold in his own life—mainly money and children. He had met them at an esoteric Bible fellowship in Manhattan when Paige was twelve years old.

Brody said of their first evening in Brazil, "The night was falling upon us. The sky was filled with diamonds. I was tranquil. Several benzos were traveling in my blood. Traveling in my mind was euphoria. LSD wishes it could take you that far. I was the X marking the spot. The exotic locale had taken on a life of its own. I could smell flowers forty feet away…, hear waves crashing hundreds of feet below. The bananas falling off the trees were a variety I had never tasted before. We must've been eating pure potassium. Which, by the way is nineteen on the periodic table. I thought they were making my heartbeat syncopate against the tide."

Brody had known Darius, he said, for nine years without their ever having had a conversation of importance concerning money or kids. Where Brody was demonstrative, Darius was concise.

"When I was in that pool," Brody said, "looking up at Orion's Belt, Darius came out with a cognac and a lit cigar. His face was warm with majestic confidence. Everyone was under his authority. This was *his* trip. He had considered everything. He was a walking conductor. No one was going to play out of tune or time. 'An ignorant style,' he told me, 'has people lighting the cognac to warm it. Do they realize they're burning away the alcohol?' He said this as if it were one of the great injustices of the world. What kind of life was that man living that the burning of cognac sounded like abuse? So, I said to him, 'Darius, perhaps the world where the burning of cognac is a problem may not be a bad place to be."

That sent the proverbial chill up Darius's German spine. He was a hard-working immigrant, who had materialized the American Dream. Nothing had been handed to him. He had even changed his last name from Brandt to Brentwood after learning that there are several affluent places in the U.S. with that name.

When Darius bid goodnight, he left Brody sitting by himself at the edge of the pool, content to look up at the deep dark sky. Upstairs, knocked out from the travel, was Brody's wife, Midori. He once said, "If Frank Lloyd Wright made women, he would have made Midori."

As Brody was counting stars, the loveliest one strolled in—April Graves, the definition of poetry in motion. Later, she would claim to be a virgin, but there was nothing virginal about her. Brody seriously doubted that she walked like *that* in Wyoming. In her innocence and her sheltered upbringing, she hadn't even known that people like Brody existed.

He was breathing slowly, inhaling and exhaling with purpose. Even the cigar in his hand could not overwhelm the magnificence of this oxygen.

April sat down next to him, with her feet in the water. It was obvious that she was wearing some sort of *en vogue* celebrity-endorsed perfume. She was also unnecessarily wearing makeup, the type seen on the women at Chateau Marmont. It didn't interfere with her looks, but it did make for a jarring appearance in a jungle. Without asking, she grabbed the cigar from him and took a drag.

As she handed the cigar back to him, his thoughts were less important than the feelings that surged through his body.

Sixteen hours earlier, he told me, they were all in an airport in the early morning, on little or no sleep, to catch a 6:00 A.M. flight out of La Guardia, and Brody had taken a picture of April while she was texting furiously on her cell phone. On the flight, he looked at the picture and showed it to his wife.

Astutely, Midori said, "She seems to be going through an identity crisis."

Brody didn't think of the implications of that until he was sitting next to the young beauty alone.

"What does cocaine do to you?" April asked, and then followed that with an even more loaded question: "Can you die from doing it only once?"

Brody told her what dancing with Ms. White was all about. But her second question was the brainteaser.

Is she really talking about coke? Or is it a metaphor for something else? She framed it like a question from a critical thinking class: "If you could do something wrong, giving into temptation, something that brings joy to your flesh, but there was a chance you could die from doing it, would you?"

Tranquil but puzzled, Brody thought of the half-dozen ways he could answer April's question.

They discussed the subject philosophically rather than matter-of-factly. Somewhere in the conversation, they began to dovetail seamlessly. Not only did Brody have the answer to every question April put forth, but it was *the* answer. It was a master class in the art of living on the edge.

April knew Brody was married. However, she was being seduced by his unique ability to think microscopically but speak telescopically.

Imagine having the world's sexiest girl in a pool, sharing your cigar with you and sipping cognac from your glass.

Out of the black, she asked, "Did you know that Darby believed in the Trinity?"

She was bizarrely referring to John Nelson Darby. According to Brody, Darby was a part of the debate about who was the most seminal

British Biblical scholar of the nineteenth century. Saying that he believed in the Trinity, as April put it, was equal to saying that George Washington was the first president of the United States.

Without a doubt, that was the worst ice-breaker to start an adulterous affair.

It ruined the mood.

So Brody reached for his pool bag, pulled out a pen and a piece of paper, and wrote the following poem:

FERRIS WHEEL SEX APPEAL
UP AND DOWN FALSE AND REAL
STAR-CROSSED DOOMED DEALS
ELEMENTARY POETRY
CLANDESTINE MEMORIES
WHIMSICAL SINCERITY
CYNICAL IMAGERY
ELECTRICAL CIRCUITRY
SEEDS, SUN, FRUIT, AND TREE
PERFUME LIBERTY
DARK SOIL NEXT TO ME
GREECE, SPAIN, ITALY
SUNBURNT SPOILED LEAVES
WANDERLUST PHOTOGRAPHY
HONEY REVERIES
STARS TOUCH EVERGREEN
PHILANTHROPY HAPPENINGS
ACERBIC NOTIONS INGÉNUE
BEAUTIFUL OBVIOUS
ECLECTIC LAVISHNESS
BRAZILIAN MADNESS
WE ARE FALLING IN LOVE

He handed it to her, watched her read it, and added the finishing touch to his *fait accompli* by proclaiming, "You are *the* dirty rainbow."

At last, the stage was set. April from Wyoming had smashed the box labeled *Do Not Open!*

Everyone has a box they carry around with that ominous label. However, Brody's box was not even nailed down to begin with. It was held together with loose screws. April's box only existed in theory. What she was really asking of him was to help her build her own box. She wanted to understand what goes in and what to keep out. What she didn't fully grasp was that certain boxes are built in darkness. And where there was darkness, there was the absence of light.

Paige had told her that Brody was the master builder. When he took that photo of April at the airport, it caught the exact moment in time when she decided that, as soon as she landed, she would erase all the lines, all the invisible shackles of Wyoming.

Brody later told me, "There were stars in her pocket with eyes like rain, with a flower-shaped heart and a heart-shaped brain. We've all seen these types come and go, but here she was, trapped away from her oasis."

April was literally in Rio de Janeiro, but for the rest of that night she was in Rio de Brody. She would never be the same. And she made damn sure to carve her name on his tree.

2

Caveman Poetry

In Manhattan, there are multiple tiers of cliques and they tend to intermingle. However, it ultimately shakes out with the rich on top, poor on bottom. Below the bottom tier, there was a club with a group of misfits known as the 260 crew. They threw their parties on the Lower East Side at 260 Elizabeth Street.

Their leader was Don "Doberman" Tenenbaum.

His young parents left the Torah, TaNaKH, Talmud and Tradition behind for Tar, the least quality opium possible. Thus Don grew up watching his mother get hit. The heroin belt that his father used was the same one he beat Don with. The atmosphere was harsh: burnt spoons in sinks, blood-stained needles, used condoms, and twelve-inch knives. Dope fiends raising children who were learning to count with crack vials.

Everything out of his parents' mouth were lies. Life fabricated. Everyone Don looked up to went to the pen. His cousin taught him how to use a gun. Less than a year later, Don was his pallbearer. And the gun was called "Pesticide" because it was only drawn if people were "bugging out." Essentially, Don's mother left him in the streets as if she were littering. He thought toy stores were museums. And his therapist was a sawed-off shotgun whose barrel he spoke to every night. The only emotional outlet he had was shaking aerosol cans of paint and making art. His partner in vandalism, his glimmer twin of chaos, was Ken Rosenberg.

In 1908, during an anthropology class at Harvard entitled "Caveman Poetry," it was revealed that drawings found on walls in caverns outside Tripoli had depicted men holding court with women in various ways. During this class, a hypothesis was put forth that the cavemen treated these women with dignity and respect, because the women were always smiling.

In 1964, the *Caveman Poetry* exhibit was on display at the Met in New York. Claire Richards, a graduate student at Columbia University and a Southern Belle Baptist broke into the exhibit and changed all the smiles into frowns to suggest that, from the dawn of time, all women have been raped. To this day, no one has ever noticed.

Claire was an activist pacifist who was trying to match wits with Pablo Picasso, whom she rationalized "doesn't have the guts to do anything." Claire was a glorious blonde, standing five-nine and groomed to marry well. And she did. She married a reformed Jewish attorney—which is to say, Jewish on the High Holy days. On other days, he was a pepperoni pizza and cheeseburger attorney. His name was Barry Rosenberg.

On the day he married Claire (after her conversion to Judaism, of course), the entire building at 260 Elizabeth Street was deeded to them as a gift by Barry's parents.

At that point in time, the Lower East Side was known as the "Slum of Slums." It was a Sicilian neighborhood, replete with shops with guinea meats hanging from the ceiling. Barry cleverly used his office on the Upper East Side as his residence to enable their son, Ken, to enroll in a better school district, which landed him in P.S. 158. And that's where Ken met Don and sealed their relationship—the type of relationship that once it happens cannot be undone. This was identical to Lieutenant Leslie Groves's meeting J. Robert Oppenheimer on the Manhattan Project. Together, they were going to build THE BOMB.

Ken and Don were the classic dichotomy: The tale of two cities. The type of boxing matches that fight fans longed for. The clashing styles competing: Rich versus poor, book smart versus street smart, self-delusion versus the cold, hard truth, sick but healthy versus healthy but sick.

They met in fifth grade, in the Fall of '83, and were assigned to sit next to each other. Ken was charismatic. Don was alluring in that "What in God's name is wrong with this kid?" type of allure. Don rocked the same red jacket every day. Ken wore a different outfit each day of the week. But they both brought spray cans to school and tagged up the bathroom. They loved graffiti. Don signed off as Doby. Ken signed off as Wiz. Later on, this evolved into calling themselves Wiz260 and Doby260.

Graffiti was considered by many the coded messages of the drug-fueled wars, a sign of hopelessness during the crack epidemic in the Bronx and Spanish Harlem, and the defacing of valuable public and private property.

In 1983, all the trains were bombed both inside and out, and not a single person in authority considered these images works of art. No one understood the integrity of this art form, the reasoning behind it, or the kids who were authoring it. The gravity of the situation became so intense that by 1989, regardless of whether Gracie Mansion were taken over by a donkey or an elephant, the city had already budgeted the hiring of twelve thousand more police officers.

Manhattan's Upper East Side, a neighborhood known as the "squeaky wheel" due to its population of high-powered rich people, had a menace to society to deal with: 260. Unfortunately, these Dead End Kids were in a nasty graffiti battle with The Master Race; and in a predominantly Jewish neighborhood, that was considered a problem.

It had been long rumored that during the election campaign, both candidates held a secret meeting with current Mayor Ed Koch in a Church basement, where artists were referred to as "gang members" and targeted for arrest. A special covert task force, code-named T.O.B.A., was put together to deal with this job. To distinguish themselves, they had business cards made up with the name Theater Owners Booking

Association. This was allegedly David Dinkins's clever idea, because it was a homage to the only black vaudeville company in America.

However, it was also known as Tough On Black Asses.

Ironically, its first targets were two 18-year-old white Jewish kids. Lifelong troublemakers. Ken Rosenberg and Don Tenenbaum.

In addition to being a good cop, Captain Doug Doyle served the youth of the Upper East Side, mentoring kids with enjoyable experiences through flag football. With the mysterious identities of the vandals, Doug had to identify what he knew about whom. In other words, he had rat out his own kids.

Between June and October, eleven artists were murdered or found dead under quizzical circumstances. Finally, on November 7th, 1989, Dinkins was narrowly elected as Mayor.

Often heard as a rationale to the news of another dead graffiti artist: Pablo Picasso never tagged up the Two Line.

May, 2003

Ken Rosenberg had now been a popular artist for the last five years—the type that *Vanity Fair* does annual pieces on. He was invited to all the important social gatherings. In every photo, he had the look of a jockey on a winner. He was also a favorite of Roberta Smith and her husband Jerry Saltz. The premier critics of art. But word has been getting around that he had been in several irrational street fights. This brought abject publicity to his popular art gallery of graffiti.

Ken had it all, but his friends were watching it slip away as his mental condition deteriorated. Underneath his exotic exterior, he was a financially rich outcast with a need to paint that was never satisfied. He was showing all the signs of bipolar at best, and paranoid schizophrenia at worst.

Why was his mind going? If you asked his pathetic group of "yes" people (who, by the way, wouldn't last a day in the P.S. 158 playground), they would say he had hit an artistic void. But "does he have another set of masterworks within him?" asked the New York Times. Who cares?! Why was his mind falling apart? That's what those nearest and dearest to him asked, because they weren't buying any nonsense from the lackeys on his payroll who were devoid of insight into a cockroach, much less Ken Rosenberg.

It turned out that Ken was recently diagnosed professionally with a myriad of mental illnesses. A list literally too long to name here. But you name it, he's got it. He concealed it well because he took his meds (which is another list too long to name here) and had the money to have a personal nutritionist who had him on a strict macrobiotic raw vegan diet and all the accruements to keep him healthy and happy. But now he was unraveling at a rapid pace.

On a normal day, Ken sparkled with conviction and eccentricity. On an off day, he was mad, delusional, and psychotic. He often wondered why women stuck by him when he was driven into despair. He routinely put on Afro wigs, believing he was Otis Redding.

Unbeknownst to Ken, Don had been released from prison after serving twelve years.

Unbeknownst to Don, Ken had made a fortune replicating Don's artistic style from the days of their youth.

Pablo Picasso never fought in a war. He was a pacifist.

Picasso's revulsion with violence informed his most famous piece, *Guernica*. This piece is a condemnation of the first ever air assault, the Nazi bombing of Guernica, Spain.

The canvas is eleven by twenty-six feet, and depicts human and animal suffering, alongside the presumed destruction of the town itself, all in striking black and white. A reproduction of *Guernica*, which used to hang in the United Nations building, was covered up with a blue curtain when Colin Powell went to present evidence during the buildup to the Iraq War.

The real *Guernica* is now on display at the Met in New York, and Ken was in front of it, assembling a can of red spray paint to make sure people see the blood that Picasso was so deeply afraid to depict. Like mother, like son.

3

To Add Irony to Injury

June 14, 1989, Part One

Ken Rosenberg and Cyan Laurent, both 18-year-olds, were walking along what was left of Little Italy, deciding which restaurant to eat at. Cyan was wearing a Groucho Marx moustache and nose novelty glasses. He looked ridiculous, but he wasn't doing it for laughs. He was an artist—beyond hip.

The two of them walked the street as if they were mastering the waters of the disgusting East River. They were both wearing custom-made t-shirts tagged "260."

With his half-inch Marvy marker, Cyan crossed out the graffiti tag of "REGGIE" that was on a wall, showing major-league disrespect. After they stopped at each restaurant on the block to look at the specials in the windows, they finally decided to eat at Oggi's.

As Ken was pulling open the door, out walked Nicky Crowbar. Not one of the great philosophers of our time, but he was the thinker of *this* bunch. Cyan and Ken were excited to see him.

Cyan, who was French, but spoke some Italian, yelled, "Hey, Nicky Crowbar! My last night in New York. *Oggi in figura domani in sepoltura.* Which is to say, 'here today, gone tomorrow.'"

Cyan was leaving for Stanford in the morning because he was a freak in chemistry, and that was where you went on the west coast when you wanted to study such things. His first-class flight was at 11:00 A.M.

Ken handed Nicky a piece of paper.

"Charlie Parmesan's number's right there, bro," he said to Nicky. "Give him a call. He's been asking for you all day. He said, 'he'll hook you up solid'. But make sure he gives you the same shift as me."

Ken had been making a killing as a waiter at Vittorio's. Aside from Don, his other partner in crime (but the good kind, like chasing skirts and going to concerts) was Nicky Cracchiolo, nicknamed "Crowbar." In a street fight one time, Nicky punished a guy with a crowbar, and the name stuck.

Nicky looked at the paper, laughed nervously, and then crumbled it up in his hand.

Disappointed and shocked, Ken said, "Hey, whatcha do that for? I pulled some serious strings to make this happen."

Nicky was unsure of himself as he told Ken his plans, which he knew would trouble Ken's mind. With difficultly, he said, "Listen, uh, I'm not sure I'm staying."

"C'mon, dood," Ken replied. "Whatcha sayin'?"

"I'm goin' to Vermont. My mom had me enroll in—"

"You piece o' shit!" Ken interrupted. "You lousy piece o' shit!"

"Hey, wait a minute now. Just a sec."

Ken was exasperated, "After all we've planned? We finally get outta high school, and now you wanna go to college!?"

At the exact moment the word *college* escaped Ken's lips, he spotted Jack Track walking up the block. Jack had gone off to college the year before. To everyone's surprise, he returned, completely reinvented as a Frat Boy Jock from the University of North Carolina, all decked out in his UNC gear. Among this crowd of urbane, self-declared stylists, Jack might as well have been wearing a rented tux due back in nine hours.

"You wanna be like Jack there?" Ken said, pointing down the street. "Waiting another four years to start your life?"

"My mother wants me to try it out," said Nicky. "She said the change would do me good."

Ken hardlined it. "What do mothers know?" he snapped. "What do they *really* know? Change is good!? Is that the best she could come up with? All you'll do is move up the ladder each year with the rest of the tasteless inmates till you get released with a dumb looking hat. You know, you go into debt for that lousy hat. Besides, *you* only open the books when death is crouched at your door."

Nicky patronized Ken with a pat on the back.

Taking the crumbled piece of paper out of Nicky's hand and straightening it out, Ken said, "You're staying with me, working at Charlie's."

Nicky started slapboxing Jack, as teenagers ought to do. Then they cooled it and rested on a car. Nicky unwrapped manicotti out of tin foil and offered some to Jack before taking a bite himself.

Food was an important part of bonding with these guys.

"Yo!" Cyan called to Jack. "I heard this punk freshman, Walter from Dalton, broke your five-thousand-meter time."

"Get outta here!" Jack replied. "Who timed it?"

Cyan splashed metaphorically cold water on his face: "Hardcore Mordecai was there, man."

Jack knew the eyewitness of Hardcore Mordecai was as good as gold.

"The kid knocked a full second off it," Nicky said.

Humiliating Jack even more, he said, "And you know what that means, he is as fast as Lightning Harper."

That sent Jack into headlong arrogance: "All he did was beat a stopwatch. *Capeesh*, you Italian *fugazi*! It's not like he beat me!"

Metaphoric cold water dripped off Jack's face and broke out into allegorical sweat when Ken added: "Hardcore Mordecai told Walter you're gonna race him…. Tonight!"

Sounding defeated, Jack moaned, "Now, hell! Why'd he go and do something like that?"

"Hey," Nicky said to boost his confidence, "you're still the champ."

Grabbing hold of his beer belly, Jack said, "The *heavyweight* champ."

The boys laughed, as boys ought to do.

Cyan climbed up a parking signpost with a red Krylon aerosol can in his hand, and spray-painted his tag "PNB260" on the "no parking" sign. *PNB* was an abbreviation for *Post No Bills*, which was a city ordinance not to place any unsolicited advertisements on private or public property. His tag was designed to add irony to injury.

Ken tugged at his leg to get his attention.

Cyan jumped down.

Pulling a small box out of his pants pocket, Ken said, "Cyan, I got you a going-away present."

It was a box of oil pastels.

The guys watched Cyan as Ken reached into his wallet, scrambling for some loose silver.

"You know, Cyan," Ken said in a wishy-washy, pipe dreamy way, "one day I wanna be the first person to commission you to paint me something so I can have an original to hang on my wall. Consider this a down payment."

Cyan got a little too emotional. He was crying over a box of crayons.

Nicky was perplexed at this scene. He wasn't soulless. He got that it's the thought that counts, but to him it depended on who was counting.

Keeping it together, Cyan said through his tears, "These are the best, man. Thanks, bro. This is the finest present I've ever got. These are even better than Cray-Pas. Ah, geez, you must've vicked this from Pearl Paint."

At that moment, Orbit Wayne walked into the picture—an attractive girl wearing a tank top that showed off her unshaved armpits. Although the look was not appealing, our guys found it strangely absorbing. She recently found out that she had been accepted by Columbia University, but hadn't told anyone.

Cyan started shaking his blue Krylon aerosol can, which made a rattling noise.

"Hey," he called to Orbit, "you wanna wallpaper uptown?"

Orbit, who had a Mr. Bubbles bottle in her hand, blew a continuous stream of bubbles into Cyan's face, each of them popping off his Groucho glasses.

Everyone laughed except Cyan, although he did try.

"Hey," he said, turning to Nicky, "how about you?"

"I'd like to," Nicky said, "but I'm headed to Limelight to meet Hardcore Mordecai. Besides, I got a flight and can't risk getting booked!"

"I never get caught!" Cyan screamed.

When he heard the name Limelight, Jack did a double-take.

"Hold on!" he said. "You'se goin' to Limelight! That place's for posers. It was played out two years ago. They so desperate, they lettin' in Staten Island wiggers. I buried that place a long time ago."

"What's so wrong with nostalgia?" Nicky asked. "Some traditions relive the good times."

"You go over there and remember the good times," Jack said. "I'm off to Charlotte in the morning. So I'll be damned if I'm goin' into some sentimental time warp with Dom Perignon and a spoon up my nose."

In a flash of anger, the soulful kid from Manhattan who got turned into a jock at UNC may have made a fair point—the kind that keeps people thinking.

Jack started walking away.

Nicky looked at the others and did not understand what was the matter.

From his backpack, Cyan pulled out a vial of black ink to refill his marker.

"Why waste your God-given talent on graffiti?" Orbit asked.

"'Cause there isn't much danger in hanging art in museums."

"Maybe you should get into one first," Orbit cracked.

Orbit's words stung Cyan.

"Down with the museums!" he buzzed. "They lack energy and daring. They don't recognize graffiti as art, so I don't need them to validate my work."

Nicky caught up to Jack as he was about to get into a cab.

"What's wrong, Jack?" he asked. "What did I say? Let's hang."

Jack tried to cheer him up. "Nothing. My Dad got me doing him a favor…, baby-sitting some office buddy's brat."

"He stuck you with that? Doesn't he know it's our last night in the city?"

"You know my dad, Nicknick. He's all about rubbing backs. It's precisely why he set it up. It's the last night in the concrete jungle. You know what goes on here, come witching hour."

"Okay, but we'll see you later on, right? Because Dave got you in that race. You his horse!"

"Definitely. 'Round midnight."

"Yeah," said Nicky. "And, uh, because we all gotta do something together before Cyan and me leave."

Jack looked at him suspiciously.

"No kidding? You're going to college, too? What the hell's happening?"

"Vermont, maybe. I'm not sure what I'm doing, really. I'll tell you about it later."

While waving for a yellow cab that was flying down the street, Jack stated the obvious: "Ya know, if you're goin' up there, you're gonna have to get your driver's license. You can't be a passenger your whole life."

How ironic! Nicky thought. *He was getting into a cab as he said that. But we grew up in New York in the Seventies. We know where all the bodies are buried. We know all the hopes and dreams and fantasies. The hookups. The guys talkin' about the poker tournaments they almost won. The jobs they almost landed. The parents cracking in two. Some deep into affairs. Some deep into depression. It's an entire city of hurt people hurting people, but with style. And Hollywood went out of its way to tell us just how great the city really is.*

4

I'm Like a Circle, I Can't Keep Straight

Rio de Janeiro, Night Two

The house the Brentwoods rented for Paige's twenty-first birthday was state of the art design but located at the edge of a mountain rainforest. Its beauty was beyond comprehension, with a view of the South Atlantic that inspired people to get on their hands and knees.

The first morning was filled with Darius paying for all the girls to get surfing lessons. The day was filled with walking through local shops, and the night ended at an outdoor restaurant allegedly built from a crashed CIA plane. The table was crawling with ants, and the chicken dish that everyone ordered was walking around until the cook came out with a cleaver.

After having a nightcap, everyone went to bed exhausted. However, Brody and April were left gazing at the moon, completely energized. At last, they were once again alone under the stars, with the moon reflecting off an infinity lap pool filled with lizards.

"There are a million ways to draw a straight line," Brody said.

April giggled.

"I can only think of two," she said, as she stroked her finger across Brody's chest in one direction and then in the other.

Unimpressed by her attempt at sensuality, Brody stayed his course: "Certain grapes grow on certain vines."

April's arsenal didn't include phrases of sexual innuendo. For crying out loud, she was twenty from Wyoming. And Brody was from another dimension. So she did what all neophytes do: she once again stroked her finger across his chest and landed on his stomach.

"You need to lose weight, Brody."

And she was right. Not a fisherman by any stretch, Brody felt that he was losing her when the night was much too young. In his playbook, this was the time to grab her by the back of the neck and kiss her. But that could backfire.

Remain quiet and simply agree.

"April, do you have a nickname?"

"No, but you called me 'the dirty rainbow' last night, and I've been meaning to—"

Brody motioned her to be quiet.

"From here on out, you're Feline Daisy. You're a flower, grounded in sand, blowing back and forth. While you hear a Grecian chorus singing your sins, you feel the wind blowing in from the north. Now I must ask you a question: 'Have you ever seen a picture of your mother when she was young? Have you ever wondered when she ended and you begun?"

April was intrigued and definitely delighted she had a man speaking poetry to her. Or that's what she thought.

"Are you asking what my birthday is?"

Brody closed his eyes, slowly inhaled through his nose, and exhaled from his mouth two times. That technique allowed thirty percent more oxygen into his brain, letting him tap the base of his spine, where all the answers lie.

Then, staring into April's eyes, he said, "I say grow, Daisy. Grow. When will you get there? I don't know. Take the unusual way to go. But I say grow, grow, grow, Daisy, grow. Bets only pay when they win. Now, we're playing a difficult game, and you're holding your cards pretty tight. But we both know the moon only comes out at night—"

"Uh, Brody, we saw the moon this afternoon. What are you talking about?"

"Poetry, April. I was being poetic."

"But you were straightforward up until that point."

"May I continue without interruption?"

April giggled.

"Let's walk down to the beach and cast out our nets. That way, it will be hard to remember what I'm going to tell you later to forget."

Brody was urban and urbane. Not a farmer. He knew nothing about agriculture. His concept of food was calling a takeout place with some fancy name that had nothing to do with the animal that was sacrificed for it. Brody loved pizzas. He had no clue that they involved milking cows and growing tomatoes. To him, a pizza was just a "slice."

April grew up in Wyoming. By the time she was five, she was watching bold, wild, romping bison being lassoed by the neck. Those were true fierce beasts, stirring up dust clouds behind them. April watched those lassoes get ripped to shreds as easily as a Band-Aid comes off a boo-boo.

April had no problem walking down to the beach. They did it quietly so no one could hear.

When they got to the beach, Brody took a black ski mask from his pants and pulled it down over his face.

"This is how I walk into banks. Right before me and my crew give thanks. We walk up to the guy behind the counter, and say, 'Give us the ancient artifacts.' He says 'I got no cash.' I said 'You're not listening to the art of facts. I'm just making a harmless deposit because it's better to give than to receive, because why owe me?' And I want to open wine in Wyoming. And I need to spread you wide in Wyoming. And you know the reason why? We're not in Wyoming. And when I meet your dad, he's gonna scream to God, 'Why, homie!'"

After this oft-putting diatribe from a "confirmed Christian," April didn't have that ominous feeling that Dorothy had when she said, "Toto, I've a feeling we're not in Kansas anymore."

No. No. No. She was turned on. And I don't just mean that her panties were wet. I mean, she felt tranquilized, amused, free.

"For the first time in my life," she said, "I feel I'm in the right place, at the right time." Then she said impulsively, "I can feel you without touching."

There they were: she became him, and he became her. She had an unmistakable feeling that no bison would snap a Brody lasso.

But he couldn't shake the idea that April and Paige exhibited the worse kind of narrow-minded Christian traits. They hadn't made it their own. They didn't own it. It wasn't their identification. It was only something they grew up with, like TV.

April sized up Brody to be a game she could play—a mechanical bull that she wanted to see how long she could ride to win the prize.

5

The Things People Do, The Games People Play

October, 1982

There was a chill in the air during a weekday, when construction work was under way along York Avenue across from P.S. 158 to repave the street. A common occurrence in Manhattan. Each day at lunch, the hulking obese workers, mainly uneducated tough guys who lived out on Staten Island, would take their lunch pails and head to the benches at John Jay Park to sit and relax after back-crackin' their soul for a living.

In one moment, Don Tenenbaum turned himself into a living legend. From that day forward to the time of his arrest on September 10th, 1991, for robbery, Don would become known as Doberman, a.k.a. Doby260. He would be the foremost menace to an entire generation of 10-year-olds (and older) throughout every borough of New York City. Don became an existential terror at the heart of the 1980s' Upper East Side (the working-class part of 1st, 2nd & 3rd Avenues) when it was transitioning from tenement buildings of the Irish and German immigrants to moderate high-rise synagogues with doormen for Yuppies and Preppies.

During that time, the Upper East Side of Lexington, Park, Madison, and Fifth Avenues was filled with classic New York sophisticates. The graduates of Yale, Columbia, and Harvard. The Silver Spooners and The

Patrons of the Arts, who wandered aimlessly around the Guggenheim and dined frequently at expensive restaurants. However, Central Park was a full-blown nightmare and had been for years.

Right now, Don was jumping onto a tractor that had one function: to break up concrete that has been tarred over to repave the street. This was not a toy. Hell, this was more like a Yellow Tank. With the workers on their lunch break and everyone else at recess, Don (at 11 years old) hot-wired this Heavy Duty Machine and ran it up York Avenue.

People throw the word *surreal* around a lot. People like Brody embellish stories, but this was so surreal that everyone froze stiff. The type of stiffness you feel when a street fight is in the air; and the guy, right before he throws the first punch, announced which neighborhood he's from.

"I'm from 110th!"—Bam!

The vision of this machine wrecking the street, with a little kid at the helm, was that shocking.

Everybody knows a jokester. Man, in 6th grade in New York City, in the '80s, girls were already being peer-pressured into sex—by other girls. This was not some group of zombies. This was a schoolyard of 4th-, 5th-, and 6th-graders. You know, know-it-alls. All of them watched Don shatter not only the street but an entire construct of life. If you thought you were tough, you were being humbled. If you thought danger was hanging upside down on the jungle gym—that idea was dashed like a dumb ass hope. But what really shook the populous? What's the punishment for this crime? It's incomprehensible.

This had to be jail time! Maybe public execution. I mean, I was told Alexis Grey got suspended for dipping Jenny Taylor's hair into an inkwell! Nerdy Alan Werlurzer had to stay after school for an entire year because he told the teacher to "shut up!"

But what all of them, including my older brother Eugene saw was Don smiling from ear to ear as he wrecked havoc. What makes anyone, much less an 11-year-old kid, do such a thing? Political protest? I think not! Lost a game of "Truth or Dare"? Buggin'. As the construction workers finally figured out that something was amiss, they ran toward him. Don jumped off the industrial Caterpillar tractor, ran around the block, and cut school that day. He didn't return until two days later. My brother said, "It felt like an eternity." But for those two days, there was an imaginary statue being built before their eyes.

Don Tenenbaum—Doberman. A mad dog. Public school was nothing but a stifling misguided academic brainwash to make you think what "they" want you to think, including that "two plus two equals four." Almost everyone at P.S. 158 felt that way. The school (the best in the district) had nothing but crappy teachers. Too many kids in each class, and everyone's parents were divorced or in the process of divorcing. Teachers, my ass. Baby-sitters, dealing with kids lashing out, was more like it. But now all that was crushed into perspective. The Doberman stole a tractor and gave a new look to the street.

What's next?

Who can top that?

The Doberman became a living universal symbol of *Go to hell!* He was *the* rebel with *the* cause. The Do-Anything Kid! The whole event hung around the necks of everyone like a medal that you get for finishing a race. But it affected everyone differently. Or it was more like asking people how to interpret those black ink drawings.

"Tell me, what do you see?"

Of course, all the kids told their parents, who called the school for answers, because what parent could actually believe this insane story? They knew about the cliques and the bullies and the food fights in the cafeteria over a mama joke, but this was a kid stealing a crane and destroying a street.

The Principal had to make an announcement over the P.A. system during the second day of Don's absence: "Mister Donald Tenenbaum performed an irresponsible and illegal act that could have caused harm to himself and others. He has been sent to Juvenile Hall for the reminder of the year."

That's what she said, but this was what Ken Rosenberg heard: "The Doberman is your irresistible hero! Not to be trifled with. The kid who *didn't* miss the boat. The kid that took a chance. The kid who has no regrets, no worries, no fears. There is no bogeyman. He *is* the bogeyman. He's celebrating his victory in juvie. And he'll meet you at The Coin Operative."

The video arcade where socioeconomics are not in play, The Coin Operative was a pile of kids from 10 to 20, all jam-packed, playing video games. The arcade was a powder keg, a small glimpse into the jungle. People scoping each other out, making plans, talking shit, and, most of all, having fun. Whether it was a piece they drew that they were gonna bomb on a train, or a poem they were gonna scream in the park, it all happened at the arcade on 78th and 2nd.

June, 1983

School was out. The Summer solstice was officially here, so the time was right for fighting, dancing, and—you fill in the blanks. Between November '82 and June '83, Ken was busy getting good grades and tagging up trains and aluminum gates with "Wiz260."

All throughout that time, he would see a variety of murals or other works of art or tags. They were everywhere on everything. And nothing thrilled him more than to see the tag "Doby."

One night, after noticing a freshly sprayed tag, Ken ran around the block yelling, "Donnie! Donnie!" And it worked! Don Tenenbaum reunited with Kenny.

"Don. How's it been, man? How's it been?"

Ken was startled into awareness that Don had become perception meeting reality, mixed with unexpected aggression.

"Why you taggin', sucka? What's your life like, Rosenberg? I need answers because I own this block. Where's your tag at? 'Cause when I see it, I'm gonna cross it."

Ken tried to interrupt, but Don was high on coke. Radiantly high.

"My tag's not about makin' friends," seethed Don. "It's about makin' ends. It lets people know where I can be found. So people will see your tag and maybe think you sellin'. And that means they ain't buyin' from me. So if that cash ain't comin' in, and you the reason, then I'm breakin' your chin. Then your mother gonna press assault charges, and they gonna send me to juvie for six months. And then, the first day out, I'm gonna break it again. This is what I do."

"You sell drugs?" Ken asked. "What kind?"

"That's the least I do, Ken. And you don't know what this is about. You don't know nothin'. P.S. 158? Who respect that? You don't even know the Genovese are on 76th, right up the block. You just actin' out. You try to stop their rise. They see to it that your whole family dies. And I get paid to push what they pay me to push. And I'll push an envelope under a door or I'll push a guido onto the floor and stomp his ass out. It's not what you buy, Kenny. It's what you sell! So, quit taggin'. Quit braggin'. Quit while you have a head."

Ken responded quickly: "I wanna run with you. Let me join up. Two heads better than one."

Never one to contemplate a single thought, Don said, "Sure."

But Don's modus operandi always developed later. It was an instinct. He loved being solo, but Kenny could be an unwitting fall guy.

6

About to Get Blacked on

June 14, 1989, Part Two

From 59th all the way up to 84th, Madison Avenue was the city's longest stretch of luxurious shops, crammed one after the other with the biggest names in fashion. During the day, on this exclusive avenue of international couture, fat wallet people strolled along, piercing the windows with their lustful eyes with their hands on their platinum cards.

But now it's eerily quiet, and Jack Track was watching the stores roll by. When the cab arrived at the destination, he got out and walked into a corner bodega on Lexington, where he bought a pack of gum. As he was paying at the counter, a guy and a girl behind him grabbed his attention.

"Jack Track!"

When Jack turned around, he was excited to see some good-for-the-soul old friends.

"Jack, you're lookin' great!" the guy said unconvincingly.

But they both knew better.

Grabbing his waist, Jack announced, "Yup. The famous freshman thirty pounds."

"I thought it was the freshman *fifteen*," the girl said.

"What they don't tell you," Jack retorted, "is its fifteen every semester."

Jack had forgotten the guy's name, but was too embarrassed to ask.

"We were just talking about you," the guy said. "You heard that Walter from Dalton destroyed your record?"

"Blah, blah, blah," Jack said dismissively. "He didn't beat me."

The guy, whose name was on the tip of Jack's tongue, said, "I'm so glad we bumped into you. Because now I know who to bet on."

Jack nervously unwrapped a piece of gum.

"You know about the race?" he asked.

The guy whose name Jack could not remember for the life of him, but recalled that he definitely banged his sister, said, "Everyone knows. Three in the morning in the park. See ya there…, Chubsy Wubsy."

Somewhere along the Number 2 Train, Cyan Laurent, still sporting his Groucho Marx glasses, stepped out of the car and quickly scribbled his tag of "PNB260" on the wall with his marker. Then he casually walked across the neighborhood, looking for fresh spaces to tag.

When a garbage truck stopped at the corner, two sanitation workers loaded trash into the back of the truck, which instantly ground the stuff up. As the truck rolled away, Cyan spotted a storefront with its metal gate locked down. After shaking his Krylon aerosol cans, he began to paint a large outline with precise control. Then he filled it in with red.

Because of the LSD he was on, Cyan thought he was painting inside an impressive art gallery that was being prepared for an opening.

Almost immediately, the gate was covered with one stunning piece of work after another. It was clear that Cyan was precociously gifted. After fifteen minutes, he was pulled out of his trance by the voice of an older man, which snapped him back to the reality of being just another punk graffiti artist wearing Groucho Marx glasses.

"Excuse me. Good evening. How are you?" said a man in his early sixties.

As Cyan turned to him, the man could see the confused look on the face of the boy with the Groucho Marx glasses.

"This is a good look for you," the man said. "Your paintings are wonderful. It's a shame they're on a metal gate. Do you know what I would have paid for these if they were on a canvas?"

Cyan thought, *I'm hallucinating.* "No," he said. "Whatcha gonna pay?"

"I paid ten grand for something similar to these."

Cyan was skeptical.

"Then, I'll want fifteen thousand," he said.

"Although I'm a great patron of the arts," the man countered, "fifteen thousand is a bit steep."

Cyan laid down the smack: "If you want it, you'll pay. The rich always pay for culture, rationalization and enlightenment."

Since this was not his first whorehouse, the man made his move: "I'm Eric Daniels. I can assure you that I'm enlightened. Have you ever heard of me?"

Cyan shook his head. Bad timing to be naïve.

The great Eric Daniels, who coined the phrase about New York, *It's not who you are, it's who you ain't,* replied with tenderness, "Forgive me an ounce of vanity when I tell you that I own the biggest personal collection of underground art on the East Coast. I really love what you've done here."

"Thanks, pal, but I'm not seein' what you're seein'. It didn't come out the way I envisioned it. Look, I'm sorry, I don't know who you are. I'm not into the SOHO-Chelsea thing. I don't got the clout."

Knowing talent when he saw it (and a hefty commission), Eric spoke with boldness: "I can give you that clout. You could be part of my stable of daring artists. You don't have to do uncommissioned works anymore."

Cyan was hypnotized by that sentiment.

"Perhaps we can work something out," Eric said, pulling something out of his vest pocket. "Here's my card."

Cyan studied the picture of two men dressed in leather, kissing.

Cyan put the card in his pocket.

"And here's *my* card!" he said, as he punched Eric in the jaw, knocked him to the ground, and ran off.

Cyan was putting the finishing touches on yet another piece. Unlike the last voice he heard, this one was aggressive. Oppressive.

"Yo! Whatchoo writin', funny boy?"

"What's it to ya?"

Cyan was just another white kid about to get blacked on. He was now standing face to face with a kid on the streets known as Shotgun Sugar. A classic B-Boy. A one-man carnival. Oh, by the way, he stood six-foot-seven and weighed 315 pounds.

"I saw you going over Reggie," Shotgun Sugar spat. "Don't play me, motherfucka. You be PNB two sixty."

Always proud to be PNB260, Cyan was now lying through what may be left of his teeth: "Nah. You got the wrong dood. My tag is Nunya…, as in nunya fuckin' business."

Shotgun Sugar slapped Cyan's Groucho glasses off his face. Cyan bent down to pick them up.

"No, you that punk, PNB. I spotted you, punkass. Goin' over everyone like you gettin' over. Reggie's gonna put a hurt on you. You think you're king, buffin' up people's shit?"

Since Cyan was high on LSD, he reckoned that he had nothing to lose and proceeded to dig his own grave.

"Let me guess, liver lips. I bet fourth grade was your senior year. Fuck you and Reggie! *Va fa 'n culo!*" Which was Sicilian-American slang for "Go fuck an ass!" Although Shotgun didn't know that.

Cyan must have thought he was nine-feet-eight with no regard for his own life, because then he said, "First of all, who you think you scaring? You hit a guy with glasses on! That's an international sign of full bitch! You ain't no killer. I'll punk your shit. I don't *say* mean shit. I *do* mean shit, because I mean *this*. This is what I'm about. Word to my mother, I bet all the money in my pocket I'll drop your ashy, black, gorilla-self with one punch!"

Without hesitation, Shotgun Sugar knocked Cyan flat on his ass with an open hand. Bitched-slapped! Then POW! Four fresh knuckle prints on the side of Cyan's face, which made him fall on his back, completely stiff. His head felt as if the world were moving. He started gasping for air and then passed out. Cyan's brand new beloved pastels fell out of his bag.

Shotgun Sugar took them for himself.

"Thanks," he said. "I can't wait till Reggie stomps you out. You a sad ass wigger. So today, my friend, you became a *nigger* 'cause you blacked out.

260 had grown into a small army of 318 teenagers, all hell-bent on wreaking as much havoc as they could. There's an old maxim, "When you got nothing, you got nothing to lose." The 260 maxim was, "We got nothin', you got somethin'. So we gonna take it." There's an older maxim from the Mafia: "Don't ever talk about the Mafia." 260's maxim was, "Talk about 260."

Those ideals were best embodied in Don Tenenbaum, a.k.a. Doby260. He was unquestionably the undisputed leader of this ultraviolent gang, which also had several talented graffiti artists among them—mainly Cyan Laurent, a.k.a. PNB260, and Ken Rosenberg, a.k.a. Wiz260. There's no data to tell us how many of these kids came from broken homes, were stuck in poverty, got addicted to drugs, et cetera. They all came together because Don Tenenbaum was *that* much of a charismatic leader. We do know that there were a few members who were "protected" from going to jail. They were the kids who were so rich that they could get (that is, steal) money from their parents, who had so much that they wouldn't notice they were bailing out their kids' friends.

Jack Track, for one, could not get into deep trouble. His dad was the CEO for a pharmaceutical company. Ken Rosenberg had to be protected because his dad was an attorney, and his place at 260 Elizabeth was the gang's headquarters. Nicky Crowbar had to be protected because his aunt owned an Italian restaurant on Lexington where everyone took their dates. The top fifty members of 260 got complimentary meals there. But Nicky's aunt didn't like being taken advantage of.

"I'm running a restaurant here, NickNick, not a soup kitchen for the Dead-End Kids."

The 260 members, who were from all over the city, came in all shapes and sizes. But the most conniving member was Ken Rosenberg. He was the opposite of magnanimous. And he always had heavy bread on him that he would put in the till at 260 Elizabeth. Everyone presumed that he was getting a hefty allowance from his ma and pa, or that he had an in with some drug dealers.

In reality, his days went like this: He would do bicep curls, working out hard until he was covered in sweat. Then he would start breathing heavily, and his muscles would tense up. His face would go into agony as he finished the final set. Then he would grab a towel to wipe the sweat off his face. Seems innocuous enough to me, but Cyan found out that he was doing this in front of gay men in his boxer briefs.

Ken's major client was Duffy Jensen, a 53-year-old divorcé, who lived on 83rd and Amsterdam and had his own advertising firm.

Duffy would beg, "Oh, please! One more set. You know how I like it when your face gets grotesque."

"Sorry, Jensen. Total muscle failure. I'm toast. I got to get running."

Duffy flung a few hundred-dollar bills on the floor, like the arrogant ass he was.

"Here's your money, young child."

Although his blood was boiling, Ken responded politely, in the-customer's-always-right kind of way, "From now on, Mister Jensen, could you refrain from jerking off when I'm working out? It annoys me."

Duffy flipped through his pop culture rolodex that everyone in Manhattan must possess, and hissed with venom, "Whatever, Lolita. If you don't like it, I can get someone else for cheaper."

Ken came out of the building freshly showered and looking sharp. Waiting for him was Cyan, who looked, as usual, like he had recently gotten his ass kicked. Ken was so used to that scene that he didn't even bother to ask about it.

"Listen, Ken," Cyan said, "you sure you're not gay? Working out in your underwear in front of a gay guy? That's noticeably homo."

"It's called making that cheddar."

"Ya gotta draw the line somewhere. I understand, money's everything. But doing gay shit?!?"

"Three hundred an hour to work out," Ken said, showing Cyan a wad of cash. "You gotta be gay *not* to do it."

"But what about your dignity?"

"It's doing perfectly fine," Ken said triumphantly. "You got twenty minutes? 'Cause I gotta take care of something across the street."

7

The Closet Christian Meets
Mr. Hyper-Empathetic

Labor Day, '98

Of the innumerable ways that Brody can be identified, he was studious, cerebral, erudite, academic, and bookish. I met him on Labor Day after being dragged by a girlfriend to his small avant-garde apartment in the West Village. She told me that this guy who was in his early thirties taught the Bible "like a rock star." For the novelty of it and the sake of continuing to have sex with her, I went. I've done lesser things for stranger reasons.

The only thing rock star about Brody was the length of his hair. And he wore boots with women's jeans that flared. It all looked natural on him. It wasn't a costume. It was authentic, but the crowd in the apartment was straight from central casting looking for oddball New York types. The collection of people paled in comparison to Brody's sheer zeal for the subject matter. This was his Bible fellowship. And he was in love with it and presumably himself.

I've always battled with the premise about the importance of what's being said, as opposed to how it's being said in direct relation to who's saying it. In other words, what's more important: the teaching or the teacher?

Brody was paying $2,200 a month for a three-room apartment in the West Village. It didn't have your generic framed photos or posters on the walls. There was nothing that was a dead giveaway about what music he listened to, or what movies he liked. Instead, he had small wooden framed boxes with messages in them—notes, numbers, essays, clippings, poems, and fortunes from cookies. It was more of laboratory than a living space. Every square inch of the walls had a saying or a clipping from a magazine. He had them aligned in chronological order. Every date from the birth of Buddha to the death of his favorite aunt was clear to see.

Brody started speaking in the staccato rhythm of a machine gun.

"The birth of Jesus, his life, his baptism, his unjust crucifixion, his burial, his resurrection, and his ascension are literally interrelated to the moment you find yourself here. Every single moment of every single day has led us here."

That last sentence was the first of many bold statements that I came to realize Brody stood by and would die for.

"There's not a corner of this Earth that was not affected by these monumental moments in the history of mankind. You may not have read the ideas laid out in *The Communist Manifesto*, published on February 21st, 1848, written by a twenty-nine-year-old Karl Marx and a twenty-seven-year-old Friedrich Engels, but your life was most certainly affected by those ideas. That minor example of information would be considered a moment of translucence. This is where fractions of light…, or in this case, information…, crossed your mind in a superficial manner, but not the detailed images. The risk in not comprehending detailed images is that you cannot see what exactly is happening or taking place."

It did not intimidate me that Brody was more pinball machine than logical bouncing ball. The fact that my girlfriend was not sleeping with him, even though I could tell he was a wicked flirt and she was transfixed by his sex appeal, was surprising. For me, talking about Jesus was innocuous, but once he threw in *The Communist Manifesto*, I was hooked.

He spoke rapidly but clearly:

"For instance, it's recognized around the world by every denomination of Christendom that Jesus walked on water. In the annals of literature, both fiction and nonfiction, Jesus walking on water could be considered the most famous documentation in recorded history. To believe Jesus walked on water, to acknowledge that as a reality, to casually read the record as it's written, is a moment of translucence."

Brody took a dramatic pause or became distracted by thought—with him, I could never tell the difference.

"And to make it even more impossible, Jesus walked on a freshwater lake that was being ravaged by a serious storm! But why did Jesus walk on water? How did he do it? When did he do it? Where did he do it? Who witnessed that remarkable event? Is there a bigger purpose beyond him miraculously walking on water than just knowing he performed that miracle?"

Brody had two speeds: lightning fast and faster than lightning fast. As he spoke with candor and joy, we felt we were being sprayed with bullets.

He shouted, "The pursuit to answer these questions is greater than the influential and quintessential American maxim 'the pursuit of happiness.' This is the living adventure of supernatural living."

Inspired words fell out of his mouth.

"God's Word is the never-ending spring of love, wisdom, mercy, forgiveness, beauty, health, and abundance. To take God's metaphorical hand and walk through his sphere places you on a journey that is beyond description. Each word, like a single note played by a single instrument in a glorious orchestra, has its greater purpose. However, on the whole, they make up the words that the Holy spirit teaches."

I was captivated by the sense that what I was hearing was important, and meant for *me*. A rant usually has some sort of negative suggestion buried in it. Preachers come off as Southern professionals fleecing people of their money. Brody spoke rapid fire, seemingly unrehearsed, as if he were a faucet for God.

"When Joseph, the rich man from Arimathaea, boldly asked Pilate for the mutilated body of Jesus, those words at that time in history did not have spiritual authority. But once they were put in the Gospels, they acquired incredible significance. And unlike the books and arcane laws of man, there are no revisions, no contradictions, and no caveats. God got it right—the first time. The astute observation that it is difficult to see things that are not there becomes moot when you have record upon record of the disciples seeing Jesus performing miracle after miracle. And yet, on four occasions, Jesus had to turn to them and specifically ask with incredulity, 'Oh, ye of little of faith?' I will slowly but surely put you alongside Jesus in a chronological order of events and perhaps give you a greater understanding in the moments that you exhibit little faith."

There was a profound sense of regret pouring over my soul. Followed by relief. I was ashamed that I had blindly pigeon-holed anyone and everything Christian. I had no idea that *this* was a slice of Christianity. Brody made complete sense to me. Forget little faith. I had *no* faith. I didn't even care for Baal Shem Tov and now I wanted to know why. Apparently, I had come to the right place.

However, the overwhelming sensation of being loved was penetrating my soul. I felt it all around me. It was in the floorboards and the walls, which were painted a cheap canary yellow, but love was coming from them.

I couldn't tell whether I was going up or preparing for a letdown. Or was I being hurled into deep space, never to return? Brody continued without comprehension or consideration of what was going through my mind.

"Jesus gave us insight into how he was able to live the life he did."

Brody looked around the room, making eye contact with each of us as if to let everyone in on the great secret on the printed page.

"John chapter five, verse nineteen. Now Jesus answered and said to them, 'Truly, truly I say to you, the Son is not able to do anything by his own will, but what he sees the Father do, that he does. For those things that the Father does, these also the Son does likewise.'"

Brody closed the book.

"And who said there's no such thing as a time machine? Now, here we go directly into the past, to have the eyes of our understanding enlightened, that we may see the untapped power of God's Word that's right in front of us."

Brody motioned that he had closed the book prematurely and opened it up again, flipping through its pages. A softer, breaking voice spoke.

"To put it lightly, Jesus' life is the most extraordinary one ever lived. After I poured through the four Gospels, which are the only manuscripts known to man concerning his ministry on Earth, here is the brilliant conclusion: 'And there are also many other things which Jesus did, the which, if they should be written every one, I suppose that even the world itself could not contain the books that should be written. Amen.'"

Much is said, and rightfully so, about Christian behavior and ethics. I've seen Brody do and say things that run counter to the Christian life. Somehow he gets away with it. Maybe I don't know him as well as I thought. The story of Brazil unfolds against him, but in the end he triumphs. Every time he escapes, he gives his God credit for lighting the path. It helps that his wife, Midori, is most likely an angel. But why bother getting into trouble in the first place? Midori is half-Japanese and half-French. Her name means green—the color between blue and yellow.

Maybe *I'm* Christian—a closet Christian. I believe in Jesus but won't admit it, certainly not publicly. When I first approached Brody concerning putting his teachings in a book, his response was organized rather than puzzling, his usual style.

"Once I'm done with the teachings," he announced, "you can do what you want with them. But if you write down anything about me personally, please go easy, man."

Brody was the warmest man I've ever been around. He never wore a fragrance, but always smelled nice. Yet, I've met people who told me he's an absolute sociopath, "possessed and dangerous." Which was not strange to understand. He looked and acted crazy. And there are two types of people in Manhattan: those who are crazy, and those who *act* crazy. A nuanced difference.

★

After that first evening, I spent the next four months faithfully attending his Bible fellowship. I soon came to the conclusion that he was empathetic. I'd even say hyper-empathetic (a phrase not found in the American Psychological Association's *Diagnostic and Statistical Manual of Mental Disorders* because I coined it myself).

Brody once remarked, "When people get caught with their hand in the cookie jar, they say, 'This is not what it looks like.' But I don't play those games. I just ask if you want a cookie."

Brody would rather die than cover up. He's *exactly* what he looks like. But don't get it twisted. This was not a man shamelessly living life backwards for the sake of living backwards. This was a man who seemingly was not like us. A stranger. A resident belonging to another world. He doesn't need to throw dust in the eyes of the beholder who comes upon his bad scenes, because he knows you have your bad scenes, too.

Brody never seemed in place and was aware of it. If he wasn't, folks made him aware of it. He was not welcomed most of the time. Love him, hate him, you couldn't ignore him. Ignore him, he got pissed. Where he was infectious, he could also be frustrated and oppressed. He would speak to whomever, whenever, without rhyme or reason. So if you felt that he was telling you something intimate from his heart, a secret per se, you later found out that everyone else knew the same story, but their versions were slightly different—perhaps better.

I remember one night at a Bible fellowship, when he blew the roof off the place with a sermon. Eventually, after everyone else left, I picked his brain about what he had taught. He was coming down from the high of performing. After all, it *was* a performance. But as he was dusting himself off, he said to me, "No matter what could've been or should've been for our lives, it pales in comparison to what will come."

At that moment, I realized that Brody was equal parts hopeful and cryptic. He truly believed in a place where everything *will* be alright. He needed to get through all the muckety-muck of *this* life to better understand the *next* one.

Brody once told me, "I'm a circle. I can't keep straight."

To write the story of my life with Brody, I couldn't tell it in a linear way. The reader would miss the point of his zigzag lifestyle. There's something riveting about a guy who actually believes there are a million ways to draw a straight line.

Brody spoke in seductive tones, as if he were being electrocuted. He also spoke in the same elegance as a mother coaxing a fever from her infant. He was all over the place. But that was his style.

His actions were bizarre and so utterly original that I got into the habit of writing some of the better-known events down. Brody was lovable because he genuinely cared about other people's well-being. What made his compassion unique was that he always seemed to be worse off than anyone else. Regardless, there was a great calm to him. Something soothing. He said the right thing, at the right time, to the right person, the right way. Then it all imploded into some hilarious ill-advised outbursts.

Brody turned red when he was calm, and looked relaxed when he was excited. His eruptions did not follow the same logic as his thoughts, but were presented with the opposite purpose. I've never seen anything like him.

I once heard a story about him throwing a glass on the floor, which shattered into pieces, with a nasty slice cutting into a girl's cheek. When she saw her own blood, the girl trembled and fainted. Brody casually walked over, said *something* in her ear, and the wound disappeared. His ability to do everything wrong was balanced by his ability to do everything right.

However, his appetite for life was so vast that at times his rights seemed wrong, and his wrongs seemed right. He was not the best at what he did. He was the *only one* who did what he did.

Someone told me, "If you ask Brody for the time, he'll tell you the history of clocks…, and you won't know if he's lying." Brody would take that as a compliment.

In the corner of one room, there was a basketball-sized sphere made from aluminum foil. I was curious about everything in the room, but especially the ball.

"Brody, what's with the ball of Reynolds Wrap?"

As usual, Brody replied in esoteric terms: "That's the American flag."

I would have expected any answer, but that one didn't make sense, especially since he had an actual well-worn flag hanging on his wall in the other room.

"Then, what's the flag in the other room?"

"I don't know. I thought it was a lovely design."

This episode was early on in my four-month attendance at his Bible fellowship. I can't remember precisely when. But Brody could because he documented everything. We met twice a week, and I didn't miss one teaching for four months. But this was my first experience with him by myself. I had come over to ask him questions about death and what he knew about shamayim better known as heaven. So many members of my family had died during my life—aunts, uncles, and grandparents—that I had heard over the years that they were looking after me. I never knew what to make of that. No one ever visited me after dying. That was the purpose of my visit that day: I wanted to know what the Bible said about such phenomena. But any plan with Brody, I quickly learned, was not to be counted on being direct. It was always roundabout. You could count on him *not* to stick to a plan.

"Brody, explain what you mean about the ball being our flag?"

"I wouldn't say our flag, because it's not my flag at all. It's the Americans' flag. I guess I'm American. Actually, I'm clearly American. I was born in America, but the flag doesn't represent my experience."

"Explain the aluminum," I said.

Brody walked over to the ball and threw it up to the ceiling.

"Simple. Aluminum has thirteen protons in its nucleus. And thirteen is seen thirteen times on the back of a dollar bill. And, of course, the whole country's organization was founded on the unanimous Declaration of the thirteen colonies of the United States of America."

As Brody tossed the sphere up, I realized that I'd gone down a conspiracy theory portal. What really spooked me was that Brody conveyed that message with such vigor that every possible question I could think of, he already had the answer for. Although he was not teaching the Bible, he obviously had another strike zone.

I've since lost contact with the girl. I think she's married and lives in Arizona. That doesn't matter. What does matter is that that incident occurred many years ago. Since then, Brody has grown in faith, but I haven't. Yet, my faith in him is paramount. I believe *he* believes. I know he takes his belief deadly seriously. And he genuinely loves me even though I took advantage of him.

8

Ghost in the Machine

Arthur Brown inherited a wide-open field of 177 acres in Missouri in 1964 then founded a college that would teach the good book. With the help of naïve flower children in their early twenties, he built the campus from the ground up. The twenty-somethings were let loose to conjure up their own customized Jesus and spread the good news about the ultimate hippie. The acreage had the most humbling of beginnings because Arthur, his father, and his grandfather were all farmers of fruits and vegetables. They grew everything, in season and organically, selling the produce to local grocery stores. By 1971, it became a rehash of the Woodstock Festival from a few years prior. Simply replace Hendrix with Jesus.

Born in 1905 in Missouri, Brown was still a production of colonial America, although it was rapidly developing into industrial America. Farmers were still profoundly important, even sixty years after the gold spell was cast on the country and the world. In colonial America, every family raised its own food, made its own clothing, cleared its own land, and even constructed and furnished its own home. It was totally self-sufficient.

By the summer of 1932, Brown was a 27-year-old preacher and determined to build a legacy beyond his own lifetime. Anyone can profess Christianity. And seemingly anyone does. However, the people who learned from Arthur Brown exalted studying the Bible above living it. A spiritual treadmill. Brown's teachings on several subjects were revolutionary only to the naïve. Furthermore, all of his published works were blatantly plagiarized from nineteenth-century British scholars. Although there's an extensively researched biography on the man, no one can pinpoint the time and place when he got his hands on a copy of *How to Enjoy the Bible* by E. W. Bullinger. Brown's detractors pointed out to his congregation multiple times that his book was really a layman's version of Bullinger's collected works. But no one within his flock seemed to care. As a preacher, Brown was beyond reproach.

What drew so many people to Brown was his passion for the Gospels and his belief that their words were not only true but *very* true. This made for an infectious flock of like-minded people.

Brown's magnum opus was *The Seven Secrets to Abundant Living*, published in 1963, right as the hybrid seeds of several moving parts were blossoming: the coming of age of the Baby-Boomers; the American Prosperity Movement; the British Invasion; Color TV; and the assassination of John F. Kennedy which would explode into the Vietnamese War and the draft.

There wasn't an accredited academic institution on Earth that had ever acknowledged Brown as *the* man or *the* teacher for God. That was Brown's own assessment. There wasn't a seminary on Earth that has acknowledged his work in any field concerning Biblical study as pioneering or revolutionary. Again, that was Brown's own assessment.

There is a grand difference between the theological teachers of the Bible (especially of the New Testament) before and after the life of P. T. Barnum. Simply put, the only thing Brown ever did that was entirely original was barely hide his influences by taking credit for others' peer-reviewed theological studies.

Bullinger had peer-reviewed properly cited works that were formally published, and Brown then ripped them like a Xerox copier. Am I supposed to believe that was the sum of his life? That he was a wholesale kleptomaniac? Be careful what you slice of it, because we're all sinners.

Did Miles Davis invent the trumpet?

Did Ray Kroc invent the hamburger?

However, their contributions were transcendent. Not even Germany can take credit for the idea of invading a country! How much of life is stood on the shoulders of giants? How much of life is made on the broken backs of others?

To access Brown's version of "abundant living," you had to *literally* buy into his premise that "what the mind can conceive and believe, it can achieve."

In the American lexicon, the term *a more abundant life* was coined by Franklin Delano Roosevelt on December 6th, 1933, when he said, "If I were asked to state the great objective which Church and State are both demanding for the sake of every man and woman and child in this country, I would say that that great objective is 'a more abundant life.'"

FDR's spiritual advisor was none other than Napoleon Hill, who can be considered one of the founding fathers of "positive thinking." Hill first gained attention with his book *The Law of Success*, published in 1928. It was followed in 1930 by *The Magic Ladder to Success*, and then, in 1937, by the absurdly titled *Think and Grow Rich*. All three books were bestsellers during the Great Depression.

All of Hill's books became blueprints for the Modern Christian Church because of the changing tide of parishioners tired of the message of hellfire and brimstone. For what it's worth, Hill openly worshipped "devil spirits," making no bones about it. Brown's copies of Hill's books were well thumbed through. Astonishingly, his *Seven Secrets to Abundant Living* had chapters of Hill's work plagiarized word for word in his own "Christian" book. Ouch! Tough pill to swallow.

Brody accepted Jesus as his Lord and Savior on September 27th, 1991. Three years later, he met Darius Brentwood at his apartment in Manhattan, where the magnate was holding a Biblical Study class that was framed after Brown's, *The Seven Secrets to Abundant Living.* However, Brown died on August 20th, 1980. After that, in a phenomenon that Brody could never shake, Brown became his personal *Geist in der Maschine*: An esoteric figurehead of a long forgotten ministry that couldn't rest in peace. Everywhere Brody went and publicly taught he met "defenders of Brown's faith." And they were mainly faithless but still gravitated towards something that was no longer there.

Shockingly, Brown was "resurrected" from the dead by his limo driver, Greg Martingeer, who claimed to have been the only person at Brown's deathbed. The only trouble is that when Martingeer read Brown's last will and testament to the "teacher's" entire congregation, the legal documents showed that Brown had left his 60-million-dollar-a-year empire to Martingeer a year after Brown died!

Then, in another turn of mind-numbing events that many couldn't see coming from a mile away, Martingeer self-published a non-peer-reviewed book, entitled *Living the Secret Dynamically*. And guess what? It doesn't have a single footnote to Brown or Bullinger. Clearly, Martingeer was passing off the book as his own, and had the gall to inform readers that they needed permission to reprint his work.

I know of this trivial, absolutely meaningless stuff because Brody told me all about it throughout one of his deep soul-searching sessions.

It just so happens that Brody met his wife, Midori—his soulmate—at a presentation of *Living the Secret Dynamically*. Her father, who was a minister, died six months before Brody met her. He was a naïve twenty-something that had been taught at that Arthur Brown's pseudo-college. As I mentioned earlier, Midori was half-Japanese and half-French thus making Brown a *Fantôme dans la machine* to Brody.

Midori was a mix of Provençal design and ratatouille lunches, with Japanese silk kimono belts and sashimi dinners. This fusion happened when Midori's *père*, a French baker living in Japan who taught English as a second language, met Saku, her *hahaoya*. The couple got married at the base of Mount Fuji as they watched the sunrise. Later, they had their only child, Midori. According to their own legend, they made love on a patch of moss that was so lush they thought it must have been the day they conceived their daughter, and so they named her Midori ("green")—which was technically impossible.

The real story was that Midori's dad made a mean black truffle omelette for lunch, her mother made sushi, and they made love in a kitchen. Her dad had forsaken his passion to have his own bakery to enter the field of ministry by becoming a door-to-door evangelist, selling the wares of Arthur Brown and his books on how to prosper.

Brody once told me that after the first time he slept with Midori, he consulted the *Oxford English Dictionary* to get all sorts of meanings about greenness. Then he went a step further by separating the color into blue and yellow. Next, he broke out all the etymological ideas of the words from French and English.

"Why in the world would you do such a thing?" I asked.

"Because," he said, "when I was bangin' her, I glowed. I figured it had something to do with her name."

Simply put, to every other person on this planet—dead and yet to be born—the reason why he was glowing is that he was lying with a woman who was half-Japanese and half-French, with big juicy breasts, a flat stomach, and long lashes on her gorgeous face. Her name could have been Mudbath, and he would *still* have glowed. Although, as I've said on numerous occasions, Brody doesn't operate in this or any other dimension.

9

Coconut Cocktails and Real Estate

Rio de Janeiro, Day Three

During the day, the whole group went to a Monarch butterfly–hatching exhibit. Brody couldn't help laughing at the irony as he watched a life cycle right before his eyes—a perfect metaphor for a couple who was not meant to be.

Brody speculated that the point of entry was through April's eyes. He told me it came to him in a flourish.

Later that day at the beach, she waltzed out of the South Atlantic with a glow, then hydrated herself with aloe and ginger.

Opening a coconut in front of him, she asked, "Can I get you something?"

He thought to himself, *A sense of security..., the warm blanket kind.*

She was offering a drink beneath a blinding sun, on top of burning sand, dripping wet, wearing a black bikini that accentuated her freckled skin. Even the most professional gentleman has a few lines for an occasion like this. There's a few ways every guy knows how to play this. But Brody was only a visitor to our planet.

"Can I get you something?" she repeated, scooping the ripe meat out of the coconut.

"This is known as endosperm, ya know," she said.

Brody took a piece of the coconut and gestured for her to put it in *her* mouth.

"Yes, you *can* get something for me," he said. "You can restore me, liberate me, saturate me with adoration. It's some sensation feeling you without touching."

One can safely assume that whenever April stood in front of a mirror naked, she had no complaints. It's even safer to say that no one else did, either. She may have even thought to herself, *I can have anyone I want.*

But all that confidence came crashing down because nothing prepared her for the rhythmic love letter, spoken aloud.

In Wyoming, things were pretty straightforward. But in addition to time zones, April crossed lines. And that was good enough for her. Brody, however, crisscrossed wires.

As she sensuously chewed the coconut meat, she never took her eyes off him.

"I'll place your name on the deed," he said. "Wrap the key in seaweed. A minute will feel like a day, swinging on a hammock, hand on your thigh, flying a kite, under a crescent moon, soft, sooth, the healing wound."

Back in her tacky pink bedroom in Wyoming, the following articles from *Cosmopolitan* were sitting on her nightstand. They all speculated on the same variant theme: cluelessness about carnality.

WHAT MEN WANT.
IS HE CHEATING ON YOU?
HOW YOU KNOW IT'S LOVE.
WHAT HE'S REALLY SAYING.
THE DIFFERENCE BETWEEN MEN AND BOYS.

I love women. They keep it simple. However, Brody thought they were God's greatest creation. If he ever wrote a book about women, he would call it, *Women Are from Mars, Men Are from Who Cares!*

Brody had already put two and two together. If April really was a virgin, it was in having a glass of water blended with coconut meat.

If endosperm had been in season (and it was), it's a most powerful aphrodisiac.

He practically chanted, but only loud enough for her to hear, "I think you would let me. I need you to let me. I hope that you let me. I wish that you let me. I must insist that you let me. I would pay you to let me. I would cry if you let me."

That was Brody's version of "I like you."

When she heard his plea, her mind was bent backwards.

Brody had a kill stroke, and was about to unleash it. Lowering his voice, he added a twang to it.

"Tonight, I'm going to ravish you."

April was no dummy. She probably didn't know what ravish meant, but her grasp of how he said it made her think her greatest fantasy.

He marched on, like a soldier in the snow, never looking back. Glancing at his wrist, which didn't have a watch on it, he said, "At the witching hour of two in the morning, leave your door open and go into the shower. I'll come in. I'll gently put you up against the wall, turn you around, and consummate our bond."

Weighing in at one hundred and eight pounds, hailing from Wyoming, with piercing blue eyes and shapely thighs, the out-of-sight neophyte, April Graves!

And in this corner, weighing fourteen million pounds, is the undefeated elephant from beyond the dark matter of the universe, Desire!

Brody would never have actually stepped into a ring to fight a girl. That would have been pathetic—a game for losers. But rigging the fight? That was right up his alley!

Brody once told me, "I absolutely, positively never open my mouth unless I'm absolutely, positively right."

Brody had taken a calculated risk with his proposition. He must have thought he was right.

Charm was right up there with love potions, Cupid, and all that other hocus-pocus nonsense to make people feel the desire to be wanted.

But Brody was more charming than charm itself. And he knew it.

He could say anything and get away with it. Why? Because he said it with charm and could wrap you in it.

The sun had dried April off. Knowing she looked better wet, she invited Brody out to sea. They had to walk fast because the sand was as hot as lava. Once she was safe in the ocean, April felt she could finally speak, but Brody wouldn't let her. The sonovabitch hardly let anyone speak.

"You know," he said, "when I say gently, I actually mean vigorously. The only thing I would do gently to you is take out a razor blade, cut your inner thigh, and suck your blood."

He heard April's breath leave her body.

"I would do it where no one could see."

She dived under water, came up, and brushed back her hair, which had recently been cut short. Her smile was as bright as it was wide, illuminating her face.

"Brody, you're married."

"To the world's greatest woman."

"Then, why are you saying this?"

"I feel it. You know what? Forget all the sex talk. I don't want to leave here without knowing you're going to be in my life for the rest of it. I want to share life with you. Now, you may not believe me, but you're the face of Christianity. You're modern-day Christianity. The hope of Christ's return is so real in your heart. But more than that, you can reach out to an audience that only *you* can reach. I sure hope you're thankful for everything you inherited. You're something else!"

No one had ever spoken about Christianity *that* way to April. Not even her own father. And definitely not her pastor. One can only imagine the profound effect that statement had on her. Like when a doctor tells you that you only have six months to live. The gravity of what Brody had said was irreversible.

April was meditating on those words when Brody amplified his mixed message.

"I want to be inside you."

He smiled *the* smile.

With Brody, everything would always be alright—although

everything detoured to hell along the way. He was a natural leader—in leading people astray.

April was frozen. Frozen stiff.

At that moment, Paige charged into the water. Unfortunately for Brody and April, the flip side to Paige's effervescence was her vicious attitude, which inspired her to stir up shitstorms whenever things didn't go her way. Watching from the sand, she had determined that Brody was hers, and she was Brody's. Even her own mother knew that Paige was to darkness as a moth is to flames.

Paige was twelve years old, going on thirty, going on eighteen, when she and Brody became friends. She was a classic New York kid. And Brody was the classic washed-up, never-was has-been that the city continually produced on a minute-by-minute basis. Even as a survivor of every elitist pompous system that New York had made up, Brody was still chewed up and spit out.

Paige was now turning 21, but had already been used like a whore dozens of times. She was the worst-case scenario of a spoiled rich girl, with problems that only massive shopping sprees could solve. She had no tact. Brody always said she was loose with the truth.

A girl who used to *be* the party was now busting up parties.

"For the entire goddamn trip," Brody told me, "she was acting like a cop."

Rio De Janeiro, Night Three

Brody's wife Midori's great discipline was she listened with intention. She was a great listener. Darius, on the other hand, like Brody, was a talker. He spoke as if he was giving lectures. As a commercial real estate magnate, Darius was comfortable with talking about the salary per capita every twenty blocks in all of the boroughs. Not necessarily enticing content but Midori's ability to engage and listen was at a high level since she had to banter with Brody her entire adult life.

Midori was an expert flirt and since this trip was all-expenses-paid for by Darius she felt her contribution was to let an older distinguished gentleman think his pie-chart conversion ratio talk was the bee's knees.

With her great ears, came the ability to hear multiple voices and parse out what was being said in another conversation while pretending to be transfixed on the one she was having. In other words, Midori was half-Japanese, half-French and full spy-girl.

Midori was super-confident. Because of her Christian background, she believed any and all infidelities to be as something *he* would have to personally deal with justifying to His Maker. She knew that was a losing proposition for Brody. She was far more concerned about protecting Brody's mental health, which wavers on any given day.

Midori was not a potter. She was never looking to mold Brody. She fell in love with him for who he *was*. Do not be mistaken, though. She had a leash and a whip but the lease was long and the whip only came out when she felt he was devolving. She never had a problem with any of his platonic relationships. To many, Midori's nickname was "the friend burglar" because all the women in Brody's life, love *her* way more than him. She was a fierce *shugo tenshi*.

To Midori, April was just another girl who was caught up in some fantastic tale that Brody weaved like a nomadic slave girl making baskets to hold the Master's wife's trinkets. When she was bending her ear to hear Brody speak, she tuned it out because she just heard him repeating several of his famous fables. Besides, she never had caught him with another woman and we know this because Brody was still alive.

If there was a miscalculation on Midori's part it was underestimating that old saying, "the only thing better than pussy is new pussy."

Once again, everyone headed to bed in their assigned rooms, leaving April and Brody alone to forge their against-all-odds relationship—ironically sitting on a day bed.

"Wanna cut school today?" Brody said.

"Now, what's that supposed to mean?"

"I'm asking, can you tell the difference between a Port wine stain and a strawberry spot?"

"I suppose I could by smelling it."

Brody caressed her hair.

"Oh, I don't know, April. What can I say? Sometimes dumb things are smart. What is the future truly, except for one moment from now?"

"Why don't you say what you mean?" she exclaimed.

And right there, Brody paused, closing his eyes, inhaling through his nose, and exhaling through his mouth three times. Then he put April's hand on his heart.

"Let's travel across Europe mostly on foot, 'cause I read that the rain in Paris tastes like real rain."

He opened his eyes as she said, "Sounds like a plan."

"Then we can head to Africa," he said, "and swing on date palms, 'cause I heard that touching a cheetah instantly makes you calm."

April put on her imaginary boxing gloves to summon up the courage to say, "Brody, what do you want?"

"You walk around like you've never been beaten. Like you never lose. You slither."

Just as Brody had done a moment before, April paused, closing her eyes, inhaling through her nose, and exhaling through her mouth three times. Then she took Brody's hand and put it on her heart a.k.a. her left breast.

"What do you feel, Brody?" she purred,

Brody was overwhelmed with the sensation of being on a sinking boat. His mind was racing as he remembered that he couldn't swim.

The feeling of being extremely hot as he jumped into a cool pool was not there. He felt as if he were in a pool hall, putting all his money down on his ability to make an impossible trick shot. She had left him with no choice but to lie:

"April, I feel that if I taught you how to make wild boar lasagna, it would somehow be better than how my own mother made it. I feel like you will always be cool, but never cold. Always warm. I feel like—"

"That's enough for now," she said. "I'm tired." And slinked out of the room.

How could she *not* have been tired? Even the stamina of youth is tested when you go from Wyoming to New York to Brazil and spend three days and nights in constant movement in serious heat. And, my God, the space between the lines that they had drawn was vanishing.

Was April his lover? They hadn't even kissed. They had been merely holding hands, gazing into each other's eyes.

Brody was intimately aware of his state of mind and the duality that was seesawing between his ears. As he looked at Orion's Belt, he ingested another lithium pill. He was up to 2,500 milligrams a day, and it was *not* producing any effect. Unbeknownst to anyone but Midori, he was now in various hyper-manic states almost constantly.

As a child, Brody never had a straight answer to the question, "What do you want to do with your life?" Too many things held his interest. He was addicted to learning. It would keep him up at nights. Ironically, he was a massive failure in school, a ninth-grade dropout.

Orion's Belt is made up of three prominent stars. Looking up at the vast array, he audibly asked God Almighty, "What do you want me to do?"

He asked the question with finality. In other words, he was not going to ask anymore. In addition to his own Bible fellowship, he had been attending a Biblical study class in Manhattan for the last fourteen years, and was loyal to it and the other people who attended. However, the class had grown increasingly cryptic and cold. The light that had been there was not everlasting. It was the light that comes from a candle—consistent but disappearing. And he had no authority to change it. Oh, he had tried. Lord knows, he had tried. But of the countless ways one can be identified, he had been looked upon as charmingly odd rather than supernaturally significant.

The night finally came to a close as he crept into bed beside Midori and proceeded to write a love letter to April, carefully crafting each word to destroy every possible wall in her mind. Sadly, he knew his strategy would work, for he had written this type of letter before. He was inspired. April was transforming into his muse. He actually wrote the letter on parchment paper that he carried around, knowing that she would never get one like this again. He felt that he was writing with his own blood. All he needed was the moment to show it to her:

SOUL LIKE AN OCEAN WHERE THE MOTION IS PURE.
BIOLUMINESCENCE IN A CHEMICAL CORE.

YOU'RE A DEWDROP RAINBOW IN THE SPIDERWEBS OF DAWN.
PEAKING THROUGH A WINDOWPANE OF WHATEVER COUNTRY YOU
ARE ON.
WINGS ON YOUR SHOULDER AND WITH A MOUTH MADE OF PEARLS.
DANCING ON THE VAPORS AT THE EDGE OF THE WORLD.
I'VE SEEN YOU SIPPING ON COOL SHADOWS
FROM YOUR GLIMMERING GLASS.
ALL I WANT TO DO IS WHISPER MY SECRETS AS THE DAYS SHIMMER PAST.
YOU'RE A CHERRY BOMB, APRIL GRAVES.
AND I AM APRIL'S FOOL.

10

This Country Worships an Aluminum Dick

Mid-September, 1998

Don Tenenbaum had been locked up for the last seven years and had five to go. His life was over, ruined, destroyed, and many thought he wouldn't last five more.

I was in a self-proclaimed Bible fellowship with some of the best-looking Puerto Rican girls you could ever lay eyes on. So I wasn't leaving. Praise Jesus! I didn't care much about the Bible. I definitely didn't relate to God. I related to girls. Mainly, the good-looking ones with the curvy bodies. But when the Jesus-loving crowd left, Brody loved hanging out with me and chatting up weird stuff.

"The Monument to George Washington," he began, "is an obelisk. It rises up and tapers into a pyramid shape at the top. In other words, it is soup-to-nuts Egyptian, rather than being associated with America…, or ancient Israel, for that matter. Now, I've got a question? Why does our country, an enlightened one, take its design from the ancient Egyptians, who enslaved our Hebrew brethren? Haven't we been taught that this is a Christian country? Yet, we find a subversive salute to the Egyptians right in our capital."

And his rants never ended. They always sounded so hypnotic, as if he were rapping to a beat.

"When one looks into the sky," he harangued, "one should see the following at any given point: a collection of birds, the blue sky, clouds, and the sun, moon, and stars above. It's that simplicity that allows anyone anywhere to look up and beyond their own selves. Certainly, you're looking at things that are not man-made. Whether you believe in God or not, everyone's going to agree that what I listed off is not the design of a human mind."

As I went into his kitchenette to get myself a drink, Brody kept rambling.

"The Hebrews' awareness of birds may be partly due to the fact that they lived closer to nature than we ever will, trapped in Tar Beach as we are. They were actually dependent on birds for food. They must've felt the same envy that we feel when we see birds flying through the sky. But there's another aspect to the Hebrews' perception of flying creatures. From the surrounding Mesopotamia cultures, they learned stories about birds that possessed supernatural powers, and they saw some people actually bowing before bird idols. But the Hebrews didn't follow their neighbors down the blind alley of animal worship. No way, José! They believed in the one Lord who created all living things. With this firm ground beneath their feet, they looked around them and saw birds not as gods with power to act in unpredictable ways, but as creatures fashioned by the same Lord who controls the ordered harmony of the universe and who made man."

Who cares about stuff like that?

As I opened a can of Pepsi, Brody screamed as if he wanted to be heard by everyone in the West Village: "Now, if the design of the Washington Monument were not an overt tip of the hat, the pièce de résistance was the completion. Congress produced the largest single piece of cast aluminum to place on the tip. It served two purposes. Practically, it was a lightning rod. But as a spiritual symbol, it was a message of rebellion to God and His Word."

Every time spent with Brody could be housed into one of three categories. The first was a crash course in Biblical studies. He would say something, then whip out a nearby Bible to literally show you where it was written. The second was a hysterical history class. The third was a walk through the catacombs of his mind. You never knew which one you were getting until it was too late.

When Brody stopped to catch his breath, I excused myself to get some vanilla ice cream at a local spot I know, which makes it fresh. I hoped, while I was gone, he would forget what he was talking about.

I'm a practical fellow, so when I walked into the store, I already knew what I was going to buy, because I didn't want to spend any more time than I had to. I've never been to any type of store with Brody, but there's no way he ever shopped with a list. Buying ice cream would probably take him three hours. It hurts my brain to think how *he* would behave in a grocery store.

After making a pit stop to pick up some wine, I came back to find Brody with an easel and a large piece of paper on it, which was littered with notes. I hoped that this was some old work that he was dusting off. No such luck. It turned out that this was fresh material, ready made for me. I opened the ice cream.

At the top of the paper, Brody had written the number 13.

"Okay," he said, opening a Bible, "let me show you this. Here. Genesis, chapter fourteen, verse four. This is the first time the number thirteen appears. Let me read it to you: 'Twelve years they served Chedorlaomer, and in the *thirteenth* year they rebelled.'"

Distracted by the fact that I had bought three pints of vanilla ice cream, Brody huffed and puffed for me to pay attention:

"Now, any time a word or number makes its debut appearance in Scriptures, that is what defines it. Thus, thirteen represents rebellion. Whoever designed the Washington Monument understood that passage. They understood how aluminum represented that rebellion. They understood that after the thirteen colonies rebelled against the King and Queen, it took them thirteen years to establish the country as victorious."

He took a spoon and stuck it into one of the pints.

"Living in New York," he continued, "you get an unpatriotic sense. You know, like America's a big bad slobbering dog, screwing things up for everyone else. And, no doubt, she's made some mistakes. But right around the time that Hitler was first publicly announced as the *Führer* of the Nazi Party, on July 29th, 1921, America had its first Miss America Pageant!" Brody let out a howl of a laugh. "If that doesn't tell you the difference in ideals, what will?"

Between bites, I said, "Brody, may I ask you a question?"

"Shoot!"

"It's pretty well known that we've always had the best intentions of all the superpowers. In fact, that *this* country is the light of the world tells us this world is a cesspool. So I don't consider what you said insightful. It's common knowledge. But what disturbs me is you relate Hitler to Miss America. And what's even scarier is I know you know the date, name, and places, too."

"Oh, of course! Sixteen-year-old Margaret Gorman, on September 7th, 1921, in Atlantic City. And Shitler was thirty-two years old."

"That's what I'm saying. How do you even remember this stuff?"

"First, I don't. I write it all down. So somewhere around this place is the information. Second, there's absolutely, positively, now that I think about it, no supernatural significance to the fact that their ages were a multiple of the number eight. What I was saying is America loves girls, and Germany, at the time, loved a psycho."

"Brody! Is anything nothing to you? Or is everything something?"

"Look here, Mister Ice Cream Man, I was explaining how this country worships an aluminum dick, instead of Almighty God, before *you*, not I, interrupted the program with your inquiry."

"I got that, but answer the question, 'Why do you think everything is connected? There's no connection to be made between a girl in Jersey and Hitler in 1921!"

That insulted Brody.

"Oh, no way, man! It's *all* connected, interrelated, governed by choice, regardless of circumstances, not predestined, and we inhale the consequences or reap the rewards of those decisions."

Since I already had the numbers to all the Spanish girls from Brody's Bible fellowship, I decided I could press my luck here.

"But it's not that complicated," I said. "I bet you don't even know your neighbor!"

"I don't. Fair point. Astute. Sometimes people right next to each other are worlds apart."

I decided I had had enough. I'm naïve. I can't confirm that what he's saying is true. It *sounds* true.

I make my way for the door.

"Hey, brother, before you go, the periodic table is entirely dogmatic. It's not a belief system. It came to Dmitri Mendeleev in a dream. On the chart, aluminum is number thirteen."

Oh, boy!

Brody always closed his "teachings" with this phrase: "You ain't seen nothin' yet!"

Before I met Brody, I was living in a safe, mundane world, where things just happened. Now everything was manufactured by the Great Pen in the Sky. And Brody may be the Author of Confusion or the Bearer of Light. I don't know which. I just want to go home and eat ice cream.

However, I gotta get back to Ken and the morning he decided he was gonna rearrange Picasso's priceless work because, that morning, Don walked into his gallery.

And it crushed Ken's soul to see him, because Ken never visited Don in prison.

And for all intents and purposes, Don was now visiting Ken in his.

11

Artists Are Now an Endangered Species

May, 2003

Real simple logic. There are Major League baseball players, and within that already exclusive group of guys that get paid to play a game, are guys better than the rest—the elite of the elite. But anyone, at any skill level, can get a group of friends, head out to the streets or the park, and have fun playing the same exact game, with the same exact rules.

This logic also applies to people who can draw and paint. Anyone can draw. Anyone can paint. And there are subdivisions of styles of drawings and techniques. Plus there are schools that teach variants of each style.

Comic Books? Art! Mona Lisa? Art! Everyone knows this game of catch. Anyhow, graffiti was always vandalism, and it's still vandalism. Much like a dance with a stripper was once twenty bucks, and it's still twenty bucks. Some things don't change. Everything else is a moving target.

Ken Rosenberg was a vandal who could actually draw. So well that he got accepted to LaGuardia High School of Music and Art, and learned fine art. Ken had that elite talent, that Hall of Fame swing talent. The kid could flat out draw. He was gifted from above and then honed his gift. He got lucky. Then he got smart.

One thing led to another.

He started showing in galleries and museums, and even selling pieces. Then he was invited to a visual art movement group—a hundred artists down in a loft in SoHo.

He stood around, thinking to himself, *Not one of these pretentious assholes could bomb a wall, or a train, or even a fire hydrant!*

And that thought reframed his entire life. But that was in the summer of 1989, and Cyan Laurent was the one who actually got him into that party. But from that party, he got his gallery.

Don "Doberman" Tenenbaum had not seen the outside since '91. There he was, standing in an art gallery called Endangered Species, looking at an array of black-and-white photos, oil paintings, large canvas stuff, and self-portraits. The works. Each piece had a small bio under it with a price tag.

Don thought to himself, *You gotta be kidding. Four fuckin' grand!?*

But he also thought to himself, *This is some bad ass art. The work is great, the ideas are greater, the execution unblemished.*

He was in the gallery with a few sexy girls, and didn't even notice an even sexier one behind the counter with a cash register painted by Peter Max. Everything in this place was art.

Then he noticed a section of tiles from a subway with his tag "Doby260."

I'll be damned if that isn't my first tag from 125th street.

He approached the small bio next to it, which read: "An Authentic Tag, by Doby, circa 1989."

As Don was about to figure out how much this was going for, he saw the price tag: "Not for Sale."

Then he got a whiff of Drakkar Noir, a scent not found in Riker's or Sing-Sing, which immediately told him that Ken Rosenberg, good old "Jewboy," must be standing right behind him. Old Wiz260 himself.

What a rush!

Don restrained himself from turning around. He was flooded with memories. The Great Deluge. Twelve years of what could have been. That's what everyone on the outside thinks. But on the inside, it's twelve years of—.

It's too painful to finish that thought, so let's work around it.

High school cliques hurt your feelings because you weren't cool enough to be accepted? Wait till you see a group of unrestrained guys, high on who knows what, and you can't go to a different high school. You'll be sitting in their homeroom with no chance to avoid them. Oh, you'll be in their clique, because there *are* no cliques. It's only inches. It's unseen lines you cannot cross. It's a prison within a maze within a game, where every decision you make is most likely a life-or-death one. Is it life or a version of death? Either way, every school sucks. Every group of guys suck and you are forced to do whatever.

On the outside, there's the illusion of choice. Coke or Pepsi or maybe a craft root beer.

On the inside, no more illusions, only choices—many of which, if not all, are made for you. Even when you say, "Fuck it, I'm gonna have to stomp this fucking douchebag Mexican out because he promised me two cartons, but only dealt me one." Is that really a choice? It's more like a domino effect. It's a big, fat, sick game of Russian Roulette. All day. Every day. But Ken was choosing to wear Drakkar Noir. Now that's a choice.

He actually said, "It's been working for me since 1989. Might as well keep doing it."

Don thought to himself, *He must've become superstitious.*

Then he turned around, looked at Ken, and said, "You ain't seen nothin' yet!"

The moment Don said that, he practically collapsed into Ken's arms, crying like a fool.

Overjoyed and crying as well, Ken said, "You got that right, Doberman! You got that right!"

With his neck stiffening up on him, he stuttered all the way through his apology for not even once sending Don a note, making a call, or anything—let alone visiting him in prison.

Don was just as nervous, almost uncontrollably shaking his head as he accepted the apology, letting Ken know that everything was alright.

"It's okay, my brother. It's okay. I'm here. Gimme five. I'm still alive!"

Almost simultaneously, Ken said, "When did you get out? How did you find me?"

"Take me to a restaurant, bro. Chinese. Japanese. Italian. Colombian. I don't care. I've literally been eating shit forever. Don't ask me about the yard. I just wanna know why I'm seeing so many people on the street here talking to themselves."

Don stepped out of the time machine he went into back in '91. Damn! Does he even know what Starbucks is?

This reunion was twelve years in the making. And from all his previous experiences with Don, Ken was pretty sure the Doberman would be pent up and ready to release his fury. The rage was deep inside.

For crying out loud, he was in a cage. He should have burned the gallery down and broken every piece in the place.

Although the gallery was heavily insured, Ken felt that was the fate he deserved. He had nothing to do with Don's imprisonment. But he was around when everything went down. He ducked out the right door.

God Almighty, what has Don gone through? The Doberman's docile! He's been institutionalized. What's he gonna do to get himself back in?

As they got on the C Train, Don said, "The city's much taller now. No fuckin' way are there eight million people. Must be more like eleven. I can feel the energy, Ken. I can taste everyone's vibes."

Ken took Don to a macrobiotic restaurant.

"This is living food, Donnie. It will light you up from the inside."

Don responded as if he were sedated: "I was thinking a burger, man. Greasy spoon. Coffee. You heard my mom died?"

Ken shook his head sympathetically.

"I got an uncle I'm gonna stay with in Sunnyside. He's got hookers lined up for me. Cuban cigars. I got second thoughts about it actually."

"Donnie, stay with me," Ken said. "I've done great, my man."

Not surprised to hear that, Don said, "They got grapevines growin' in the pen. I heard things about you. Not much, but, you know, that you 'made it.' Whatever that means nowadays."

Ken paused to reflect. "Don, I'm a multi-millionaire—"

As was his custom, Don interrupted: "Let me take a stab at it. You got problems that money can't solve."

"How'd you know that?"

"Because you always had! I figured nothing truly changes, man. We were who we were. We are who we are. I was who they said I was. We knew what we did was wrong. The only thing right was the paint. That's it. Everything else, it's all a façade. One big exquisite façade."

12

Eve Came from Adam's Boner

Late September, 1998

When Brody invited me to a home in Westport, Connecticut, he rented a BMW convertible so we could get there in style. I had to drive, because he was born and raised in Manhattan, and had never been behind a steering wheel.

He was going to teach the Bible to ridiculously rich white kids. A well-behaved lot. Properly reared by Latin nannies. The type that never know what anything costs, since they never have to talk about money because their daddies have so much of it. Somewhere along the line, they were taught that "the love of money is the root of all evil," but they have no idea that the *lack* of money causes just as many problems.

These kids were the children of parents who had learned everything they knew about their particular brand of Christianity from Brody's personal *fantasma en la maquina*, Arthur Brown.

The trip up from the concrete jungle's noise, pollution, and energy to the suburbs' mountain air, rivers, and enchanting foliage was a ride into Shangri-Anglo-Saxon. And this set the tone for what lay ahead as we drove up a milelong cobblestone driveway to a mansion that must have been recently featured in *Town & Country*.

The whole place smelled of pumpkin pie, cinnamon, and freshly printed money. As soon as we walked in the front door, a butler handed us hot towels that smelled of lavender. I guess that's what you do when you have a swollen 401k, a 529, and offshore accounts.

To put this in perspective, when one thinks of Jesus, even on a superficial level, he is known as a spiritual guru. In other words, he is not Attila the Hun or Genghis Khan or Alexander the Great. He is a peace-loving hippie.

But Arthur Brown taught his flock that the Gospels (you know, the books that say the Jews, in concert with the Romans, unjustly tortured Jesus to death) fill a book with "Mountaintop Checkbook Verses"!

And his naïve followers actually fell for that concept because (a) that the Bible is a blank check to a loaded fortune sounds reasonable, and (b) they believed everything Arthur Brown said—not necessarily what the Bible actually said. These pathetic parents didn't study the Bible. They memorized what Arthur Brown told them to.

When we got there for the kids, the parents were there, too. Except no parent actually previewed what Brody was going to teach. They just implicitly trusted him because he was certified by Darius Brentwood to be a "whisperer to troubled kids." Darius was a latter-day E. F. Hutton type. When he spoke, people listened because he had all the right credentials. An undergraduate from Harvard with a master's degree from M.I.T., he owned a large swath of real estate in Queens.

Brody's words of advice for Darius and Lesley's daughter, Paige, apparently had a measurable effect on her. So the Brentwoods figured, "Hey, if this guy Brody can help Paige enjoy a personal relationship with God and the Bible, that logically means it should work with *all* the kids."

Paige was there that day. But before I continue about her, let me tell you about the time Brody invited me to take pictures of pigeons' feet. That was a week after I reunited with him at Mang's. His theory was concise. A pigeon's feet are mainly mangled, for a variety of reasons. Mostly because they land in wet tar and rip their toes trying to get out. You can hardly find an uninjured pair. Anyhow, he was obsessed with finding one pigeon with perfect feet.

I hadn't see Brody since New Year's Eve in 1998, and, as I said before, I only spent four remarkable months with him back then. But in those few months, my life changed many times over.

Now, on this park bench, he told me, completely unprovoked, "Describing Paige Brentwood is like describing the Big Bang. Her light and speed and spectacle are so preternaturally pleasurable that they had to explode. There was nothing more paradoxical to be around. Paige is the best tasting wine, ten years before she was supposed to be."

To me, Paige was another non-descript teenager at the event. I don't remember meeting her. All I remember was what Brody taught. Let me paint this picture correctly. The room was filled with baby-boomin' WASP parents to spoiled kids, who were convinced that they somehow were *not* baby-boomin' WASP kids. I didn't know who was having the bigger identity crisis—the parents or the kids?

I suppose there were fifteen kids in attendance between the ages of 11 and 16. An already confusing time…, even for rich kids.

Brody asked the parents if he could videotape each kid while he interviewed them about their life. The parents agreed. He asked each kid different questions, but the one question he asked of all of them was, "Have you ever seen a miracle?"

They all said no.

Brody's plan was to show them the video the following year to see how they had grown in their understanding of themselves.

After the interviews, everyone gathered in the massive living room, which the owners of the house called their "solarium."

Why are they calling it that? Brody thought, since the room was as dark as pitch because the curtains were drawn shut. And for some reason, the question put him in a mean mood.

In his usual provocative way, Brody spoke in seductive tones as he told the kids, "I would like to talk about Adam and Eve and the first time they had sex."

As for me, I was already fully indoctrinated into BrodySpeak and was a card-carrying member of BrodyWorld. But I saw the famous "evil eye" being flung at Paige's parents.

"Adam," Brody began, "was a virgin, as was Eve. They lost their virginity to each other *after* they were unified in marriage. During the marriage vows, they agreed that only death would part them. Adam had an uncircumcised penis, and Eve had a fully intact hymen in her vagina. The erect penis burst through the foreskin, causing blood to spill, which forced the hymen to break, which also caused blood to flow. This was a blood covenant."

All the while that Brody was speaking, he was doing the classic hand gesture of finger-in-the-hole sign language.

"In ancient cultures," he continued, "blood was not to be trifled with. Now it's treated like red water, but life is in the blood."

Now, some of the kids were laughing, and some of the parents were gasping. But everyone felt awkward. And there is something in this world known as "the fear of public speaking"—a problem that Brody clearly did not have.

However, this fear must have taken over the whole room, because no one stopped Brody. Not even to raise a hand to say, "Excuse me, I have a question." Or to do anything to change the subject.

Needless to say, that might have been considered bad taste in such a crowd. I mean, it was obvious that none of those parents had touched that subject with their kids.

But smiling ear to ear in the corner was Paige Brentwood. It was like Brody was her own personal stink bomb. And he was stinking up the joint with all his talk about the penis not having a bone and why he thought "the correct translation of *rib* should have been *penis*."

Yes, he said this to young kids in front of their parents. According to Brody's sources, Eve was taken from Adam's dick, not his rib.

I'll never forget that day, especially the part about life being in the blood. That concept hit me hard, and I have never truly recovered from it. It apparently smashed the funny bone of Paige and a few other girls in the room, because by then they had already popped their cherry to some average dorks. And they were feeling a mix of guilt and pleasure.

If Brody were a drink, he would've been called Guilty Pleasure. That's what he is.

These were wealthy WASPs, all nonconfrontational, so eventually Brody's "teaching" never came to an end. According to Brody, when he saw big, fat question marks hanging over the faces of the parents, he knew it was time to shift gears. The problem was that he had no Plan B.

Brody took a deep breath. He gave too much to think about and digest. He overdid it. Nevertheless, he continued!

"We call ourselves Christians," he said, "and demand that we not conform to this world, but everything…, and I'm talkin' *everything* in this day and age…, is a lie. A goddamned lie. In every single language, *September, October, November,* and *December* mean "seven," "eight," "nine," and "ten." But on our calendar, in this self-proclaimed Christian nation, we designate them as months nine, ten, eleven, and twelve. We moved them out of the way to make room for July and August— months dedicated to Julius Cæsar and Augustus Cæsar. Both men were completely at odds with the will of the Father. I can tell you right now, we are not in the month of October, there is no way this is a Sunday, and this couldn't possibly be the year 1998. It's all lies. And you go to school to hear that George Washington was the first president, but there are other books with even more compelling evidence that Washington was the sixth president. Monday, Tuesday, Wednesday, Thursday, Friday, and Sunday are all fallen angels with gentile names. January, February, March, April, and May. Same thing. False gods. Fallen angels. If you stared at the moon for months on end, it's obvious that there isn't a twenty-eight, twenty-nine, or thirty-one day cycle. It is twelve months of thirty days. Geometrically, it's a full circle. Because twelve times thirty is three hundred and sixty. So I say, search! Research! Do! Redo! Let yourself grow. And grow big. Seek and you will find, but remember that those who find it are few, and maybe even fewer than that. God Bless!"

Brody still has the videotapes and watches them on occasion, but has never been invited back.

13

Lament for Thomas Maybell

Valentine's Day, 1984

Every year on Valentine's Day since '81, someone came into The Coin Operative, trying to take out the high score on PAC-MAN by an unknown player named ACE. But the record stood untouched.

Valentine's Day was when Don Tenenbaum was going to take his annual stab at the record. He had been practicing at it for years as his meditation and medication. For the last two years, beneath the name ACE was DBY, which everyone knew was Don.

The arcade became a major hangout for the growing crew known as 260 and other teenage gangs. Each public school in the neighborhood knew which kids were at the spot, because they saw their grades slip, and bad news travels fast among parents who are losing money to frivolous nonsense. The street itself became a dump for vandalizing buildings. The atmosphere was pure sex, drugs, and hardcore violence.

Around 7:00 P.M., two young punks strutted in. These kids, Joey Styles and Dick Henry, were walking time bombs and always had been. They weren't there to play. They were pushing people off the games, turning people around, looking for a particular kid. They were basically doing an interrogation. They never found who they were looking for, but they settled on cracking someone's head. And that someone was a beautiful kid with a beautiful soul named Tommy Maybell. He was playing *Missile Command*, next to Don, who was gunning for the PAC-MAN record.

The fight took less than a minute, but according to everyone there, time stood still. It happened so fast, you couldn't even stop it if you tried. While Joey Styles was bashing in Tommy's head with a baseball bat, Dick Henry was making loud threats for everyone to turn away.

There was paralytic fear everywhere.

The dood who ran the business and sold the tokens was a giant—a six-foot-four, 250-pound Greek myth monster with a heart of gold. While teenage girls were screaming at him to call the cops, he barricaded himself in his office.

That's the spirit of fear, the spirit of murder. If you're not trained in this stuff, it doesn't matter how big you are or think you are. The invisible powers of darkness will drag you down.

Tommy was dead.

As the cops were trying to put things together about the assailants, Don never took his eye off PAC-MAN. That's Don's world in a fortune cookie. Murder two feet away?

What the fuck! I gotta break this record.

Maybe Don was apathetic. He could have smashed Dick and Joey with his bare hands. After all, he was The Doberman.

Don was thirteen at the time. Did he know what complicit means? Most people who would ever walk a mile in Don's sneakers would never have made it to 14. Maybell was a senior in high school.

Don was living a low-hanging-fruit life, which meant beating the unfathomable heights of the highest score on PAC-MAN. And you had to get the score on Valentine's Day, because thems the rules of the streets. That's when there would be a witness to make sure there was no jimmy rigging.

Don never took his eyes off the game. Even when a cop asked him to stop playing so he could talk, Don paid no attention. A cardinal sin. The cop unplugged the PAC-MAN. Don was nowhere near the record, but he was in a serious zone.

"Who gave you that right?" Don said.

"The city," said the cop.

"Who gave the city the right?"

"The state."

"Who gave the state?"

"The federal government."

"Who gave the feds?"

"Do you really expect a civil law lesson? Because I'll smash your head right here and pin it on the scumbag who did this one. Easy peazy lemon squeezy."

"You don't have the gun to protect me, but to protect yourself. You nothin' but a fuckin' pig."

The cop dragged Don by the hair, threw him into his car, took his I.D., and wrote down all the info.

"Now you on my shit list," said the cop. "This here is a list of people I shit on. Get the hell outta the car, dipshit!"

Maybell had been a popular kid. He never caused Mayhem but he was the bassist in a hardcore band called Mayhem. Within two nights, he had two hundred friends armed to the teeth, some literally with grenades, canvassing every neighborhood to find the killers. Revenge is a mother. This whole damn world is nothing but unresolved beefs. All two hundred kids made a pact. These were preppies from Dalton, Baldwin, and York.

"If we find them," they said, "we kill them. We don't tell the cops."

What a maelstrom. Dick and Joey had committed a mistaken identity murder. Wrong place. Wrong time. But that's all it takes for two hundred well-to-do's to think they can play the game of the seriously demented. A good movie or song can get you amped, but these were rich preppie kids, and Maybell was beyond a tragedy. You're only supposed to get what's coming to you! But Don laughed at that concept. What did he have coming to *him?* Death, jail, maybe worse.

After Joey Styles was arrested, he was thrown into Riker's to await trial. While he was there, he was raped multiple times, stabbed several times, and watched kids commit suicide every day. Hurt people hurt people. Just another day at Riker's. The punk-ass preppie kids acted as if they were from the Slum of Slums. You wanna know the distance between the Summer home hammock in the Hamptons and strapping up with a shotgun? Stretch out your arm. That's how close we all are to turning on that switch.

For years afterward, the members of 260 would plug in a tabletop version of PAC-MAN and play it for hours in memory of Tommy Maybell. After Don went to prison, that tradition continued. The members would get drunk and chant, "Rest in peace, Tommy. Come home soon, Donnie." Then they would get fired up, hit the streets, and let out their tectonic plate shifting anger. A human tsunami. Hurt people hurt people. 260 just mugs you…and on Valentine's Day, they break your heart.

14

There Are No Masseuses in Prison

May, 2003

Whatever political side of the fence you fall on about crime and punishment, there are punishments that don't fit the crimes. And that isn't the worst of it—there is no rehabilitation in prison. That is a fact.

For the first six years, Don shared a cell with a drunk driver who had killed a father and son. Don was serving twelve years for Robbery in the Third Degree in a Class D nonviolent felony. A rich white kid would have gotten probation, but Don, a kid who practically raised himself, defended himself and did it poorly. In a moment of frustration, he told the judge to "suck a mean dick," when he was offered to have his charges dropped if he ratted out some key members of the Genovese family. Don wasn't like that, so he went to jail for a much longer time than the crime demanded.

The drunk driver who killed two people got out in six years. Don mentioned (while he was staying in Ken's 8,400-square-foot loft, getting a massage by a supermodel) that if the death penalty were in effect for getting caught with alcohol in your blood, driving drunk would disappear.

"If you knew," he said, "that you would be immediately executed for getting caught driving drunk, then you would know you were literally committing suicide, and wouldn't dare do it. It's so peculiar that the drunks survive, and the sober ones get killed. So what's the reward for getting drunk behind the wheel? You survive with blood on your hands. Being sober on the road gets you killed."

Now, of course, Ken was gonna let Don rant, rave, blow off steam, chill, smoke a joint, and do whatever else he had to do to unwind and accept his not being incarnated anymore.

But surprisingly, Ken thought the idea of getting the death penalty for drunk driving had merit.

Even more surprisingly, the supermodel massage therapist decided that *now* would be the time to disagree with Don and provoke him as if he hadn't thought his position through critically.

"The death penalty," she said, "is inhumane and cruel."

As if Don hadn't been locked up in a chaos cage, with all the time in the world to think this through.

Right then, Ken realized that he hadn't introduced Don to the supermodel as "Fresh-Out-of-Prison Don Tenenbaum"! Instead, he had innocently asked his personal masseuse if she could work on his friend, and she presumed that the friend was another idiot Upper East Side rich prep douche.

As soon as the words were out of the masseuse's mouth, Don abruptly jumped off the table, looking around obsessively, as if he were assessing a yard fight.

Please God no! Ken thought. *He didn't destroy the gallery. Now he's gonna bury the loft!*

And the loft was much more important to Ken.

The first thing Don did was smash the speakers that had been playing Eastern music—the kind you hear at a crystal store in Santa Monica.

The supermodel bolted out the door when Don yelled, "I'm right, ya know. And I've never had a massage, but I can tell you right now you suck at it. Absolutely suck at it!"

At that point, Ken said the one thing you never say to a guy in a rage: "Relax, Donnie, relax."

Don leaned in to Ken with belated pain and grief: "You've been slurrin' drunken stories, tellin' me what you thunk about me in my prime time and my glory, but I don't wanna know. This loft, your gallery, is nothin', but your heart's in some technological cube! Your bullshit success is rooted in misguided rage. You tell me I was livin' a life that you say is legendary, but all you are is a copycat. And let's place emphasis on *cop* in that *copy*. Because all you did was climb the ladder. You sing my praises that I wrestled with the weather, and the weather won, but you insisted that the wind cheated. You sound like a total fraud. You got it all, and act like you got nothin'. Inside made me stone. And I guess, there were some miraculous things we did back when they called me 'Doberman, the do-anything kid, the uncrowned king.' I remember them callin' us a mirror match, but now I'm here to give you seven years of bad luck. I adored your minor tribute to me at your shop, but to you it's the incarnation of an odd celebration of the good ol' days. All you want people to know is you is hard, and you know a guy who's locked up in the slammer. I bet you told people you visited me. You *never* fuckin' visited. What fuckboy choices are you making on the daily? Should I go to the Guggenheim, or visit Don in Sing Sing? Now I'm out. So smell that rotten flower for a few weeks while I'm in town. You ain't special. The thirty-eight is special."

Out of nowhere, Don pulled out a .38 special, pointed it at Ken's face, and said, "You wanna relive history or make it?"

Ken crapped his pants twice over. And that was after he was suffering a panic attack because this grief bomb was being dropped in his impeccably curated loft, which screamed, "SUCK-FUCKING-CESS!"

"If you say, 'relive history,'" Don said, "I'll kill you and put you out of your misery. If you say, 'make history,' then let's go tag up the Two Line, 'cause Pablo Picasso never had the heart."

"I got an even better idea!" Ken said, "but first let me change my pants."

15

In Memory of Fischel Lebowitz

November 1, 1998

I met Brody along First Avenue at 83rd Street for the New York City Marathon on the morning of the first Sunday in the month. His pops lived in a two-room apartment overlooking the marathon route. When Brody was growing up, he and his dad would throw half-oranges out the window to the runners. Brody invited me over for this tradition. I thought it was going be a Bible fellowship type of thing, but it was only him.

When I walked in, Brody closed his eyes, slowly inhaled through his nose, and exhaled from his mouth two times.

I quickly turned on my tape recorder as he said, "Verbs denote actions. You want something because the desire is there to possess or do something. You need it because you feel it's essential, and you have to do something about it…. *Seduction*. You attract someone to a belief or course of action that's advisable or foolhardy…. *Production*. That is, you make or manufacture something from components or raw materials. You make or form something as part of a physical, biological, or chemical process…. *Destruction*. You put an end to something's existence. Could be someone or something by damaging or attacking it. You completely ruin or spoil their day, maybe even their life, emotionally, physically, or spiritually…. Then there is *giving*. Where you freely transfer the possession of something to someone."

Brody paused as he watched the last of the runners. Before that, we spent the morning watching the elite athletes run by with the helicopters, motorcycles, TV crews, and even the flamboyant mayor in his car. And the crowds were big. Cheering them on. Then, about thirty minutes later, came the masses of joggers. An endless sea of competitors and personal besters, pushing themselves to their limits. Predetermined genetic limits, based on how much they put in or how long they had been training. After three hours, we were left with the rest. Those who couldn't run, but were lightly jogging. Their cramping kicked in. The lack of conditioning and stamina exposed them. Finally came the older folks, who were trying to beat cancer or were cancer survivors, who had promised themselves to run the marathon as a reward. People without legs in wheelchairs, and people on crutches. Only their few friends were there to cheer them on. The sound of the clapping was bittersweet.

When that crowd walked by, Brody prayed aloud for them and their journey. Where did he get the depth of soul to do such a thing? I was touched by it. Where's the mayor now? Where are the cameras? Where are the crowds? Then he again closed his eyes, slowly inhaled through his nose, and exhaled from his mouth three times.

I quickly checked my tape recorder as he said, "Sometimes I'm strong. I'm talkin' that I have the quality or state of being strong…, physically powerful…, emotionally powerful…, mental qualities necessary to deal with events that are difficult or stressful. To withstand great force. It comes and goes."

He walked away from the window and lay down on a couch that had to be at least fifty-eight years old. I saw mountains of dust come up from it. Brody closed his eyes, slowly inhaled through his nose, and exhaled from his mouth three times.

I flipped the tape in my recorder as he said, "All my friends are losers, secondhand abusers. That's what they all say. Things will never make out. Things will never shake out. Nothing will be written on our graves. There's more to us than that, like there's more to a purr than a cat. And when and where the ball will roll, I'll bet good money to know.

But what they don't know is what they can't see. How our friendship grows and continues to be. In a world full of crooked squares, it hurts to be round, but they don't sing the songs underneath the underground. Today was harder than others, like well-worn lovers. You hope it won't spin uncontrolled. There's a peace and calming. It's so alarming because you never know when it will go. The world will find a place for you before you're old enough to know what to do. And if that place is hell, you better get moving till you find that well. But what they don't know is what they can't see. How our friendship grows and continues to be. In a world full of cold blank stares, it hurts to be a clown, but they don't sing the songs underneath the underground."

Once Brody finished saying all this, which I presumed was a poem he had written, he cried inconsolably. I remember asking if he wanted a coffee. What an asinine question! Brody was pouring out deep tears.

"Brody, what's the matter?" I said. "What happened? What was all that about?"

He wiped away his tears, and said, "Today is the tenth anniversary of the murder of my girlfriend. She was killed in a drug deal gone bad. They…tied her to a couch…, hammered her skull, and set her on fire."

Brody looked at me with a look that I will never ever forget.

He said, "She was essentially cremated. I was waiting for her in the park, and thought she had stiffed me."

Brody took a breath, inhaling through his nose and exhaling out his mouth three times.

Then he said, "I've been in street fights, maybe four or five. The hardest thing I had to learn was the day Vanessa died. The first time I tasted her sugar on my tongue, I knew right then and there my life had begun. Now I've woken up and not seen the sun. 'Cause I ain't the heavyweight champion. She always hooked me up with milk and honey. Even though she had little of her own. Back then, I had been confusing love with money. And I've got none to give or to loan."

By December 26th, 1988, the record for homicides in a single year in New York City was broken. Vanessa was one of the 1,842 people straight-murdered in New York. The surge of violence was widely attributed to the rise of a new form of coke called crack. She was only sixteen and four months pregnant with their daughter, named Hannah. They hadn't told anyone until the autopsy revealed it. There was no use burying the bodies, since they were charred.

Vanessa's sister threw the ashes into the East River.

16

You Go from Doing What You Can to Doing What You Must

June 14, 1989, Part Three

Helen Spitzer was sitting on a red velvet Chantilly loveseat when Ken glanced over at her tanned legs. When she bent over for her drink that she had put on the floor, he peered down her blouse and saw a blue lace bustier.

Helen was fifty-three years old, never married, and a sophisticated socialite of the Upper East Side by way of owning a premiere dog salon. Ken had met her at a party, where they casually hit it off, but things advanced quickly when she found out he was a "pet" of Duffy Jensen. Bad news travels fast; bizarre services travel faster.

"What are your plans, Rosenberg?" she said.

"There's a big race around the reservoir tonight."

She couldn't believe he didn't understand the *actual* question.

"No, Ken, I meant with your life. You can't go around exercising in front of men your *whole life*."

"What's the expiration date," Ken shot back, "on sleeping with older women?"

Helen threw him a disapproving look.

"Sorry, Helen. I don't have *any* aspirations."

"But you're so smart, Rosenberg. Don't let your brains go to waste. I know a few people who could get you into Boston University. You don't want to end up poor, Rosenberg."

Duffy Jensen had already put Ken in a nasty mood about the gulf between rich and poor.

"Go to Boston U.," Helen continued, "and you'll make connections. One thing leads to another, and you'll have real money. The F.U. kind."

"What's that?"

"Fuck-you money. Like when your car's stolen, and you don't bother calling the cops or the insurance company. You go buy a new one."

Ken couldn't believe that he had just slept with her. For a moment, he had forgotten that he was a male escort, paid to blow his load. Since he had had girlfriends, he knew what a true-blue relationship was.

"What's wrong with being poor?" he said. "I see how you look at blacks."

"Stop right there! I'm no racist!"

"I meant the opposite, Hellpot! You love chocolate!"

Helen raised her right hand in a fist.

"Yeah, black is beautiful!" she said. "Power to the people…, honky!"

"I'm not talking about politics. Women like you sometimes lust for other things besides what money can buy. Something with real value."

He grabbed his crotch.

"Big black, baby! All of it!"

Caught off-guard, Helen said, "Ken, behave yourself. You're a circumcised Jew!"

"You wanna be let loose in the ghetto, Helen. You wanna be Helen of Troy Avenue. You wanna wear an Afro wig. Say, 'Right on!'"

Not knowing whether to escalate the debate or just play along because she was still horny, Helen said, "Right on!"

"Did you know, Helen, that I was the first Jew to win the school spelling bee? I won it with *inoculation*: i-n-o-c-u-l-a-t-i-o-n. *Inoculation!*"

"That's my point, Ken. You could be a man of prominence if you went to Boston U."

"I know that. But does it matter that I know it? Because we've somehow manufactured the finest city in the world, and yet you still can't come out and say you love black men…. You've got no idea what I'm talking about, do you?"

"Actually, I don't. You're right…. Now, this is not a professional diagnosis, but I think you're depressed."

She turned off the lights and watched him stare into space in the shadows. Then she came up behind him, and said, "This time, I want to be gagged, so I can scream with all my might."

Jack Track arrived at the remarkable five-floor townhouse between Madison and Fifth—an 18,000-square-footer spread across twenty rooms, with a wine cellar bigger than ninety-nine percent of the apartments in the city.

He pushed a number and waited for the buzzer. When it rang, he passed through the entrance to a nine-step staircase, which placed him in the first-floor reception area. There he was greeted by 43-year-old Archibald Gershovitz, who had just returned from an hour on his handball court in the basement.

In his UNC sweatshirt, Jack looked completely out of place. But going right into his version of aristocrat mode, he said, "Mister Gershovitz, how are you?"

A wise gentleman, Mr. Gershovitz said, "Now that you're here, I feel fine. C'mon in." He put his arm around Jack. "You're a real lifesaver, boy. The nanny's attending a funeral in Haiti, and I hate leaving Alexis alone. I avoid it at all costs. Anyhow, your dad tells me you're on the fast track. What have you been majoring in?"

As if on a job interview, Jack said, "Economics. And I minor in American history."

Mr. Gershovitz, a man who salivated over books on war, said, "Does that include the Civil War?"

"Yes, sir."

Mr. Gershovitz beamed as he put on his tie.

"God, if we only had time to sit down and talk. Can't beat it. Great stuff. I'll tell you what. You finish in four years, come back with a degree in finance, and you'll have a job waiting for you at my bank. You can count on it."

"I really appreciate that, sir. Thank you very much."

"Great. I'm going to need a guy in my firm who can help me debate that the Civil War was not about freeing the slaves. It was just a cover for federal oversight!"

Mr. Gershovitz called out, "Alexis! Come downstairs! Jack's here."

While they waited for Alexis, Jack looked around the reception area, admiring its glory. No expense for design had been spared.

Mr. Gershovitz went into his stump speech about a daughter he probably hadn't had a real talk with in over a year: "She's a sweetheart. Usually crashes out around ten-thirty. At best, you may find yourself talking with her about boy bands and dolls. At worst, you may be playing with them."

At that moment, in pranced Alexis Gershovitz, a homely, immature 15-year-old, wearing a pair of boxer shorts, a tank top, and sunglasses, with a lollipop stick hanging out of her mouth. When she first laid eyes on Jack, she lifted her sunglasses and winked.

Jack waved hello, then paid strict attention to Mr. Gershovitz as he outlined his itinerary: "Okay, I left money for take-out on the dining room table, and you have my pager number. I'll be back around midnight."

Mr. Gershovitz let himself out.

"So," Alexis said, "ever seen a porno flick?"

"How old are you?" Jack said.

She responded in purring cat mode, "Old enough to be seduced."

"You ain't even old enough to see G movies!"

She responded with confidence: "I'm fifteen and I can tell you like me. And I don't need to see G movies. I'm a G. An O.G. of Fifth Ave."

Jack was put way off by that remark. As if he had been punched in the back of his head.

Scanning each corner of the room for cameras, he said, "C'mon! Stop! Get outta here!"

"I live here."

Jack changed the subject: "What's your favorite color?"

"Let's not start the night off with your best pickup lines."

Hot damn! Who is this crazy minx?

Reaching into her boxer shorts, she pulled out two cigarettes.

"Where were you keeping those?!" Jack asked.

He was sure she would have some booby trap answer, but she plainly asked, "Ya want one?"

Alexis lit both.

"No, thank you. Does your Dad know you smoke?"

"I'd rather ask for his forgiveness than his permission."

Jack realized he now had to parse every word he was about to say.

When Alexis handed him one of the lit cigarettes, he again declined, so she smoked both of them.

"What school is that?" she asked, pointing to his sweatshirt. "Is it an Ivy League school?"

"No."

"That's too bad."

"How so?"

"My dad said that the only colleges worth going to are in the Ivy League. I'm going to Princeton."

"You know that Princeton's in Jersey, don't'cha?"

Alexis, an O.G. from Fifth Avenue, found that impossible to believe.

"No, it's not. My dad's not gonna send me to a college in Jersey."

"I got news for you, honey. All Ivy schools are built on top of toxic waste dumps. Princeton's only ten minutes from Trenton. Ever been there? But who cares, you're years away!"

"From what?"

"From college," Jack said, dodging bullets.

"I thought you meant sex."

Jack's right eye started twitching.

"You're fifteen!"

"Well, when did *you* first have sex?"

When Jack ignored the question with a disapproving glance, Alexis threw out an insult.

"Of course!" she taunted. "You're a virgin!"

"Okay, if you really have to know, I was sixteen! Just before my sixteenth birthday! Okay? Kill this conversation right now."

"So funny you say right now, 'cause I was thinking about hooking up with my doorman across the street right now."

Jack wheezed with suppressed laughter.

"When I turn eighteen," she said, "I'm gonna go to the mountains and take E."

Jack was now confused in a dozen different ways. This picture was not making any sense.

"Alright already!" he said. "Enough with the demented stories. Go play with your Barbie dolls."

"I can't. I blew them up with an M-80. It was a massacre.... You know, last year I was depressed, so my dad put me on Bioxin. It made me have weird dreams about my sister."

Jack was starting to get depressed that his dad had put him up to this babysitting favor.

"I read my horoscope today," she said enthusiastically.

"You know what my sign is?" said Brody. "Stop! ...Just stop, will ya? You don't believe in that stuff, do you?"

"Just the dirty ones."

Realizing that he was slowly losing this battle of wits, Jack said, "Alright, what did your horoscope say?"

"There will be extraordinarily powerful..., um.... Hold on, I'm trying to remember. It'll come to me. Oh, yes, powerful feelings arising and, uh, try to remain calm..., because the person you're with will want to do something chaotic."

This got Jack's attention, because he didn't want powerful feelings arising between him and a 15-year-old, especially of the extraordinary kind.

"You're making this up."

"I have a photogenic memory," she said.

"You mean photo*graphic*."

"Whatever.... It went on to say, 'Agreements will be dissolving.'"

Playing along, Jack said, "And what did you make of that? Because it seems to me maybe *you're* the chaotic one."

"That's right. Now take off your pants!"

Jack was being beaten at the game of life by a 15-year-old.

"Uhh…maybe you have homework I can help you with?"

"Take off your pants!"

"No!"

"I said, YES!"

"How about fucking NO!"

"Yes, please?"

Jack thought, *Use reverse psychology.*

"I'll absolutely take off my pants!"

Alexis didn't see that coming.

"I was just kidding."

Although Jack had gotten the desired effect, his judgment was clouded.

"Exactly! That's what I thought! Watch your step, Princess! Watch your step!"

When Alexis pulled out a condom, Jack was disturbed. Quickly sticking out her tongue, she said, "It's for my boyfriend."

"Hey," Jack said confidently, "this is madness."

"But you did it at sixteen!"

"What the hell?" said Jack. "I give you personal information, and you use it against me!"

This was going to be a long night for Jack.

17

The Tin and Copper Man Finds the Gold

Mid-November, 1998

Standing in the middle of his kitchen, Brody showed me how the best egg-and-cheese sandwich is made. For him, this was a form of rocket science. He used a preheated skillet with a butter mixture whose recipe could not be revealed while he was alive, but the instructions were in his will.

I turned on my tape recorder, which I now kept handy to record all his sermons. I didn't realize until it was too late that the tape had run out, so I said, "Brody, wait! Let me flip the cassette, so we can start over. I gotta get this down."

Brody never had a problem with me taping anything. But when he started from scratch, I noticed that he was telling the story a bit differently, and brought that to his attention.

"Brody, before I flipped the tape, you said to preheat the skillet for precisely twelve minutes. Now you just said eight."

With his bearings just a bit off, he said, "Oh, yeah. It must be this heat. Look, man, it don't matter. The secret to the taste is in my hand."

Then he flashed a knife, which I didn't even know he had and cut the sandwich in half. At first, I thought it was just a regular breadknife, but later I realized it was a switchblade.

Brody closed his eyes, slowly inhaled through his nose, exhaled from his mouth three times, and said, "Over on 50 West 86th Street, on Friday the 13th, August 1971, a black man was carrying an air conditioner, when the access to the walk-up was blocked by two men shooting up heroin. When he asked them to move, a scuffle broke out. One of the men pulled out this switchblade and stabbed the black man directly in the heart. I got this switchblade from a labeled box of evidence back in 1986 that I found outside a police station. I just up and left with it. They must have been moving stuff that day."

I thought to myself, *This is gross. I would've been better not knowing. Or is this another one of Brody's hyperbolic tales?*

Brody put the knife into a wooden block in the shape of a fat Buddha. Then he gave me the sandwich. After I took a bite, I couldn't believe how something so unoriginal could taste so good.

"What's the real recipe for this?" I asked. "There's no way this is just egg and cheese and some fancy shmancy butter. I also get the feeling that knife story is a sham."

Brody adopted a philosophical tone as he said, "It's made with devotion. Plus the right utensils and cleaning up as you go."

"What about the Buddha knife holder? Isn't it an infraction of Buddhist dogma to have the knife go into his belly?"

Brody closed his eyes, slowly inhaled through his nose, and exhaled from his mouth four times, and said, "On the corner of 105th and Riverside, there's a Buddhist church. Outside, in front, there's a fifteen-foot-tall bronze statue of Shinran Shonin, that survived the bombing of Hiroshima. The dedication was made on September 11th, 1955. It was a call for world peace. I was there one afternoon after I taught some Bible class, and that's where I found the crumpled instructions for how to make this sandwich."

"Brody, you could open a restaurant that only made this sandwich, and it would be packed forever."

Brody gave me that look you get from your mother when you make the same mistake twice.

"Do I come off like a guy who wants to make sandwiches all day? With all due respect to those who do…, and don't get it twisted, my man, because we all know that *with all due respect* means with *no* respect, I'm not above the crap wages and time spent making sandwiches for a living. I'm just saying, I'm on this Earth to find divine recipes and occasionally make them. And I'm happy with that! And you should be, too."

Then he kissed me on the forehead and went into a zone, as if the heavy breathing transported him, and he rattled off the following speech without pausing:

"The lowest point of the Dow Jones during the Great Depression landed on July 8th, 1932. The land of opportunity had become the land of despair. The American people were questioning every principle on which the nation was based: democracy, capitalism, and individual thought. In the Summer of '32, Hollywood's most bankable star was a German Shepherd named Rin Tin Tin. The state of Nevada, controlled by a powerful crime family out of New York, had legalized gambling. Hitler was gaining momentum after eleven years of being the head of the Nazi Party. Mussolini had just celebrated the eleventh anniversary of the National Fascist Party. Stalin had completed his tenth year as head of the Communist Party of the Soviet Union. Japan, plagued by bloody internal wars, while simultaneously conquering Manchuria, Mongolia, and the whole of China, hastily replaced its recently assassinated prime minister with Saito Makoto, who immediately had Japan resign from the League of Nations."

As usual, I had no idea whether or not what Brody was saying was true. It sounded good.

"Vaudeville," he continued, "which had been a unique form of American entertainment for the past fifty years, felt the death knell as *Variety* magazine, founded in New York City to cover the Vaudevillian lifestyle, moved its offices to Los Angeles to report on movies and movie stars. An Australian named Harry Bridges became the leading figure in America's twentieth-century labor movement by organizing the longshoremen on the West Coast. In a few weeks time, the Summer Olympics were rolling into L.A. That turned out to be the first Olympics *not* visited by a sitting U.S. President, because Herbert Hoover decided that his presence was needed in D.C. to fix the economy. Only twenty-four of Brazil's sixty-nine-member Olympic team competed, because

Brazil was so poor from the Depression that the only way they could get the team to L.A. was to put them on a barge with twenty-five tons of coffee to sell to ports along the way."

"C'mon," I said, laughing. "That *can't* be true."

"It's *absolutely* true," Brody said with a shrug. "But the story gets even better. The Brazilians only managed to sell twenty-four dollars worth of coffee, but the United States had a one-dollar head tax per person for everyone entering the country. So, their absolute last hope of getting the whole team ashore rested on the Brazilian consul in San Francisco. That poor sap sent out a courier with a check written out in *cruzeiros* for the equivalent of forty-five bucks, to cover the other forty-five guys. But by the time the courier arrived in L.A., the *cruzeiro* had been devalued, so the check was only worth seventeen bucks. And to make matters worse, the check bounced! With mass uncertainty permeating every aspect of human life, birds could still be seen flying majestically above, defying gravity as usual. Droves of immigrants from around the globe continued to descend on the home of the brave and land of the free. And if you're brave enough, *everything's* for free."

I have this tape in my possession and listen to it on occasion, but what caught my attention that day were his last words: "Home of the brave and land of the free. And if you're brave enough, *everything's* for free."

On the tape, I said to Brody, "I've seen that phrase tagged up on the last car of the 6 Train. I saw it every day on my way to college, and it was signed Wiz260."

Brody flashed a smile as he said, "I told Wiz to write it!"

I couldn't believe my ears.

"You know Wiz260?! My brother Eugene went to school with Wiz and Cyan. I'm writing a book about 260. *You* were in 260?!"

Brody acted as if he were taking the witness stand: "There's not a single scrap of evidence that 260 even existed. It's all been scrubbed. Your book is gonna read like a fairytale! Who cares about a street gang? Half the members are dead, the other half in prison. Then a few of us are making what you will outta life.... Eugene? That means your brother is El Grande?"

"Yeah!"

"You're Eugene Solomon's little bro, Benji?"

"That's right!"

"That's crazy! He used to talk about you. What a turn on the river! You let El Grande know you go to a Bible fellowship?"

"Sure! I've been trying to get him to come with me. Could you imagine if he showed up?"

"Oh, Lord, that would be a trip! I'll tell you what…. Just invite him over for pizza. Let him know you hang with Hammer260. He'll flip. We played wiffle ball, and I had the unhittable curve that everyone called 'the hammer.' Once I had two strikes on ya, I dropped the hammer. Lots of legit beefs were settled on the Great Lawn, playing wiffle ball."

"I can't believe you were in 260!"

"Oh, it gets better. Our fearless follower through the darkness was Don Tenenbaum. He's the guy that got me into the Bible after he got locked up! I still visit him every month. If you're writing a book about 260, you only need to become pen pals with Doby. He's 260. He *was* 260. He'll forever *be* 260. He's in Sing-Sing now."

Brody scrambled through a pile of papers, pulled out an envelope, and handed it to me.

"Here's his address at the prison," he said.

"Brody, you're older than my brother, right?"

"I think about four years. I was in twelfth grade when I first got wind of 260, because I used to rock hard at an arcade called The Coin Operative with my best friend, Tommy Maybell. He was a light, and he got killed there. Lots of folks thought 260 did it. Early rumors were that Doby260 had his hand in it. But that wasn't the case, and from there we just gelled. So, look, you can't be writing this or taping it. I'm serious. This part is off the record."

I turned off my recorder and put it in my bag.

"I was the point man for the Kleenex. I knew the supplier. Doby and 260 were handed bricks and brought back the cash. I used to run guns as well. It was wild times. They all looked up to me. Only because I was older and hung out with girls. But me and Doby clicked. I was never a big fan of Wiz or Cyan. They were reckless rich-kid jerks to me. There was Jack Track, you know about him?"

"No. Just bits and pieces. I only know his name."

"Okay, well here's a story for your book. Consider it my one and only contribution."

"Oh, c'mon now! I've been researching you guys for months! Let me interview you about 260."

Brody got a bit surly.

"You're showing me the characteristics of a taker. I'm here giving out…. Goddamn! I haven't even begun to tell you one story, and you're already pressuring me for more. That's a taker. I don't hang with takers. So let's start from scratch. Let me give you the one story I want to share about 260."

I pulled the tape recorder back out and inserted a blank Maxwell-XL cassette.

"Nike, the shoe company, is essentially built off the feet of Steve Prefontaine. He was killed in a car crash on May 30th, 1975, at the age of twenty-four. That cat was a winner. At one time or another, he held every track record between two thousand and ten thousand meters. I'm telling you, he was nationally recognized as *the* man. He already had a monster career as a runner back in high school and college. In 1972, while he was training for the Munich Olympics, he was smashing the records for the five thousand meters. And on July 9th, 1972, he set the American record for the five-thousand-meter race, but came in third during the Olympics. It just so happens that the track around the Central Park Reservoir is also five thousand meters, and in 1988 a guy named "Lightning" Shawn Harper consistently smashed Prefontaine's record. But he was never validated. Some people even wrote about it to *The Guinness Book of World Records*, but they never answered. Perception, reality, facts, and figures. The numbers don't lie? Please! That's all they do is lie, because Pre doesn't have *the* record. He has *a* record at a particular course in Oregon. Validation, masturbation. Freedom of speech."

"But, Brody, this is classic soapbox lecture. The best of the best find themselves at the Olympics. Did Jack ever try to train for the Olympics?"

Pissed off, Brody said, "I'm the Keeper of the Korny. The Custodian of the Senseless. The Olympics have disrespected the aboriginal power of the natural world. There's no organic balance. It's simply what the Olympics say is the law of the land. There's only one universal system of records. One massive, interconnected, multinational authority of the streets! The streets are the international system of who's who and what's what. The streets tell you why is why, which is which, where is where, and what happened to whom when. That's the natural way information is kept! That's the gargantuan makeup of life through information. And that's the truth that sets you free. It's agreeable with the Almighty Creator. Anyhow, Jack Track was supposed to race Shawn, but Shawn was killed by the cops. The actual record is held by "Lightning" Harper. The Olympics started out noble, but they devolved into proxy wars without violence. Five hundred pounds are five hundred pounds, and five thousand meters are five thousand meters. There are guys in lockup who have shattered all sorts of lifting records, but I think you get the point. What matters is what the streets say."

"Brody, I don't follow what you're implying. Jack could've simply gotten to the Olympics if he wanted to."

"What part of what I said didn't you understand? Shawn Harper has the record. Forget about what the Olympics say."

I shut off the recorder and Brody said, "The statue of Shinran is made of bronze but bronze is a combination of copper and tin. Copper is twenty-nine on the periodic table and tin is fifty. Together that makes seventy-nine. You know what's seventy-nine on the periodic table? Gold! Olympic gold! You see I find the divine recipes and I also find the gold!"

18

It's Not What You Buy, It's What You Sell

May, 2003

Don Tenenbaum walked past several closed doors on the third floor at Doctor's Hospital, stopping at one marked DEPARTMENT OF PSYCHIATRY, DR. EDMUND ROSE.

He entered.

Ken's great idea was to get Don to pretend that he was a private investigator, so he could cop information about an old member of 260: Brody Shaw.

A secretary in the waiting room was sipping coffee as she read a paperback novel at her desk.

"Hello," Don said, flashing a badge. "I'm Don Tenenbaum, P.I. I have a ten-thirty appointment with Doctor Rose."

The secretary pointed toward an open door.

Don walked into the room, which was covered with every possible framed degree and photos of grandchildren.

Dr. Rose, quite remarkably, was ninety years old. On his desk, there was a bottle of gin and several packs of cigarettes. When Don walked in, he stood up carefully.

"Hello, doctor," Don said. "It's nice to meet you. You needn't get up."

"I needn't do lots of things," the doctor replied, "but I do them anyway. Nice to meet you."

He walked over to his patient couch and lay down, as he said, rather quietly, "Don't mind me, young fellow. I know this is for the patients, but it's rather comfy."

"I haven't heard *young fellow* in years."

"You look quite young to me."

"Doc, I'm thirty-six, with all the essential worries. What I'm trying to say is, there's more years behind me than in front. Trust me."

"Good grief! With that mentality, I would have only seconds left."

Glancing at his watch, giving it a startled look, Dr. Rose grabbed his chest and pretended to die.

Don panicked.

"Oh, my God! Doctor Rose!"

The old doctor sneaked a peek at him through his left eye as Don ran for the door. But Dr. Rose, no longer able to contain himself, erupted into laughter.

"What kind of sick joke was that, doctor?"

"I must agree. It was a terrible thing to do. But I figured that a private investigator like you would like a little drama. You know..., a red herring. Something to distract you. To put you at ease while the other hand pulled off the trick."

"Let's keep the drama on the stage. Okay, doc?"

"Oh, my boy, but all the drama is on the page."

"I did a bid in Sing Sing," Don said, a bit peeved. "And you're starting to remind me of a guy that was in for life, who dispensed wisdom that only comes from above when you're locked in a cell twenty-three hours a day."

Dr. Rose had seen it all.

"You know, Don, I have the essential fears as well. Are you afraid that when you fart, you may break your hip?"

Don shook his head.

"Well, then, you have something to look forward to."

In his best P.I. voice, Don said, "I'm under the impression that you've accepted a large sum of cash from my client to divulge secrets about another client of yours. That is ethically unsound and illegal. But I'm under the impression you agreed to those terms when I walked into this room. I need you to answer every question I ask about your patient, Brody Shaw."

Dr. Rose sat up on the couch. Don sat down on a chair and took out a pen and a small notepad.

"Brody Shaw," said the doctor, "was the most brilliant case I ever had. He was a schizophrenic, totally withdrawn from reality. Suffered from hallucinations, delusions, and frequent blackouts. He filled the blank spaces of his memory, by storing up fabrications that he believed were facts."

"How long has he been that way?"

"For the last ten years or so. No one can be certain."

"What was so brilliant about him?"

"He practically cured himself."

"How?"

"By reading books."

Don wondered if Ken were pulling a joke on him, but he decided to play along.

"What does that mean, doc?"

Dr. Rose walked over to his desk and pulled out a file.

"Brody Shaw was under my care for three years as a fully realized schizophrenic. We had him institutionalized for three of those years, during which every CAT scan showed that his frontal lobe was damaged. That was probably brought on by his addiction to cocaine as a teenager."

"You're saying cocaine is bad for your brain? I thought it was just bad for the heart and the septum."

Dr. Rose stared at Don as if he were a dummy, then continued.

"One day, he was no longer showing any disturbances. It's as if they just disappeared. When I asked him what had changed in his life, he said he had read *The Great Gatsby*."

"And you believed him?"

"It wouldn't matter if he had read the ingredients for Coca-Cola. What mattered was that he was no longer plagued by schizophrenia. Nevertheless, we watched over him intensely for twelve more weeks."

"Then what?"

"We had to let him go. His CAT scans showed minor improvements."

Don was turning into an actual investigator: "So what do you do with your other crazies? Tell them to read the classics?"

Dr. Rose whispered, as if he were being taped: "I'll admit to you that, yes, we did try that, but nothing consequential ever happened. Brody cured himself. Every time he felt himself sliding into abstract behavior, he promptly sat in a corner and read that book."

"And you signed him off as healed?"

Dr. Rose got serious.

"Brody Shaw, who was completely tutored in the perversities of an insane asylum, decided to do something in an intuitive manner. No psychiatrist would prescribe reading to cure anything, let alone a deteriorating mental disorder. But Brody did it himself. And it worked. The other doctors and I were entirely cynical about the matter. They wanted Brody to go about his treatment the 'proven way.' However, in this case, the 'proven way' meant electro-shock therapy."

"What you're saying is that you had a potential madman on the loose, and it's only by the mercy of God that he hasn't killed himself…, or worse, killed someone else?"

Dr. Rose got even more serious.

"Doing what your gut tells you to do is hardly related to one's general maturity or competence!"

"But isn't reading a book to make himself feel better an admission that he was still sick?"

Dr. Rose spoke with more authority now, as if he had been banging his head on the wall for years.

"It's an admission that he was trying to get better. Simply put, it's as if someone with cancer reads a book, and the disease goes into remission. Do I grab the book and tell him how silly he is because what he's done defies our logic?"

"When was the last time you saw him, doc? Doesn't he come in for checkups?"

Dr. Rose flipped through a journal.

"I haven't seen him in quite some time. Perhaps five, six years."

"What happens if he doesn't read *The Great Gatsby*?"

"I think what you're asking is, What happens if he's not medicated properly?"

"No. I'm specifically asking, What if he can't get his hands on a copy of the book?"

Dr. Rose was irritated that Don had missed the point.

"In that case, most definitely he will start killing people and eating them!"

"Wait! My client didn't pay you to make jokes. He must know everything about this man, because Brody's an important person to my client. What can we expect of him?"

"The same thing, I suppose, that you can expect from yourself."

Don was pissed.

"Doctor! Enough with the whimsical approach! I appreciate that you're old enough to dole out wisdom, but we're talking here about a man who my client can no longer trust. But he also can't reconcile himself to the idea that Brody is dangerous."

"By definition, he's still a schizophrenic. But he's found peace in books. I don't have all the answers. That's the wisdom talking. But he's probably like the rest of us. He needs tender love and care. That's the alcohol talking…. You said your client is afraid of him. That means you know where Brody is."

"At all times. Why?"

"When I first met Brody Shaw, he came to me as a compulsive gambler."

"Doc, my client just recently saw him bet a hundred bucks on a cockroach race. By the way, I'm told he didn't even have the hundred. He expected my client to pay for the loss."

"Well that's just it. He isn't a compulsive gambler."

"My client said he saw it."

"Your client saw a confidence game."

"Now, how would *you* know that?"

Rose went through his files once again.

"Because, one day he came in here all sweaty and told me that he owed the mob twenty-five grand. Then he started waving a gun at me, saying he was going to get killed and needed to protect himself. I told him if he gave me the gun, I would help him out. So he did. But it was all part of a con. He told me the gun used to belong to Orson Welles."

Don's eyes went wide.

"My client bought Orson Welles's gun! It's his! Where is it?"

Dr. Rose pulled the gun out of his desk drawer and handed it to Don. Then he sat down, stunned.

"My god! You're saying that Brody Shaw stole your client's gun? I went to his bookie and told him he couldn't threaten my patient. I wouldn't allow it. So the bookie showed me that Brody only owed him six hundred bucks. Not twenty-five thousand!"

"Okay, doc. So did you just pay his bill right there and walk away? And, like, book it to his insurance?"

Dr. Rose was stupefied.

"No. The bookie told me about something called the tell."

"Excuse me, doc. Why didn't you just pay the six hundred? You already took the gun from Brody's hand. You found out, instead of twenty-five grand, he actually owed six hundred fuckin' bucks. Why didn't you just pay the bookie the six hundred?"

"Because Brody had me in some kind of rabbit hole. I'm old and, as you said, I like drama."

"Wait a sec, doc. That makes no sense. So what happened with the tell?"

"They got me in a room with a card game going on, and I'm supposed to tell the bookie when the other guy was giving away his bluff. I was supposed to nod to the bookie and…. Look, I'll admit it. I was dumb. I should've just paid the six hundred and left."

"So what happened?"

"One thing led to—" Then, too embarrassed to finish the phrase, Dr. Rose said, "I ended up writing a check for six thousand dollars."

Don screamed in disbelief, "How did you get so badly conned?!?"

"When a con is done right," Rose admitted, "you can get the entire world to believe anything."

"So, Brody turned you into a mark, you lost six grand and you want it back from him?"

"Actually, Brody conned me so bad, I lost two hundred and fifty grand."

Don was in shock.

"How in the world did he do that?"

By now, Dr. Rose was in tears.

"He didn't. His con crew did it. He had me believing his mother was dying. He had me going to a hospital room to talk with some old lady who I thought was his mother. It was elaborate. Only a sick, sick mind could think it up."

"But you knew he was a schizo!"

Dr. Rose whined, "I should've just paid the six hundred! I know. It burns my ass. And this is where it gets worse. He took that two hundred and fifty and dumped it into some bogus charity."

"How do you know he did that?"

"I don't. But shortly after the check cleared—"

"Wait a sec, doc. Who did you write the check out to?"

"Mr. Woo. He had me write the check out to some mystic healer, who he said could cure his mother of cancer."

Dr. Rose was crying as he looked at all the photos of his grandkids.

"I want him dead," he said.

"Thanks for your time, Doctor Rose. I can assure you I'm not a part of a confidence game. Thank you for returning the gun. But hasn't it occurred to you, a man just pretended to be crazy, to be sent away to a crazy house, and then plotted all along to rob you?"

Dr. Rose was pissed off as he pointed to all his degrees on the wall.

"You think this was a shell game, and I picked the wrong cup? Brody Shaw, if..., and I'm placing an immense emphasis on the word *if*..., if he lied to do it, then he's some sort of stuntman. Because he was administered doses of synthetic drugs that would have turned any normal person *into* the crazy one they were *pretending* to be. He's a delusional paranoid who cured himself by reading *The Great Gatsby*."

"Look," Don said, "my client doesn't want this man dead. But when the time is right, and I conclude this investigation, I'll find out what happened to your money. And you can press charges, if you can prove this really happened. But the reason I know where he can be found is he has been teaching a Bible fellowship for teenagers in Central Park since 1992. And to make this story odder, Brody just told my client yesterday that he would return the gun to him today. But he had no idea this meeting with you was taking place."

"Of *course*, he knew the date," Dr. Rose said, "because he's one big fat con man who happens to be suffering from paranoid delusions. He's tapped into a part of the brain that no other human on Earth ever has. He's not brilliant. Einstein was brilliant. Brody's ultra-brilliant! If Einstein ever met Brody, Albert would walk out of the room in embarrassment, that's how smart Brody is. Einstein had a theory about a space-time continuum. Brody *is* that space-time continuum. I want him dead. Not because of the money. I want him dead because he won't let me examine him and find out how in the world he does what he does."

"So it's completely out of the realm of possibility that you were just plainly conned to an extent that you've never experienced? And you want to see it as a case study, rather than a clever robbery?"

"Have you ever met Brody Shaw?"

"Yes, a long time ago."

"And what was your impression?"

"I thought, this guy knows how to rob banks without ever getting caught. Didn't think he was special. Come to think of it, the only special thing about him was he was honest."

"So you're essentially admitting that it would be hard for him to lie."

"I said he was honest. That doesn't mean he doesn't lie. Doctor Rose, it has been my pleasure, and your secret is safe with me and my client. By the way, you never realized Brody Shaw's initials were B.S."

19

A Dream Without Love in It
Is a Dream About War

Rio de Janeiro, Night Four

The next night, everyone was either in or by the pool, having cocktails. The day was filled with adventure, so they were all left with blowing off steam, knowing that there were several more days like this to follow.

Darius owned the day. It was under his complete control. And you couldn't lodge a complaint, because he effortlessly led the group from breakfast to lunch to dinner to every single thing in-between.

According to Brody, "He was walking in spirit. It was as if he had rehearsed the trip, although he had never been to Brazil."

Darius didn't speak Portuguese, but navigated everyone and everything to perfection. The trip was the most loving example of leadership Brody had ever experienced. And Darius relished the role of leader, delighted that he was so locked in with God's will for this once-in-a-lifetime trip.

"If I had asked Darius to bring down Orion's Belt for me," Brody told me one time, "I believe, at the very least, he would've tried."

Darius was the caretaker and caregiver. At the end of the exhausting trip, Brody wrote a lovely thank-you letter to him and Lesley, and had everyone else sign it.

If Darius owned the day, Brody rented the night. Mischief,

deception, coded sensuality, and open portals into souls were all on his menu—and all aimed right at April.

For the last three nights, Paige was up to her old self, the lower self, the burnt-out druggie self, the been-in-and-out-of-douchebag-relationships self.

Brody was floating in the pool with a drink in his hand. He was tranquil until Paige brought him to the other end of the pool and whispered in his ear, "I told April we slept together."

"You did?!"

"Yes."

"When?"

"Oh…, I don't know. I don't remember."

"I meant, when did you tell her we slept together? Because we haven't!"

"Uhh, sort of."

"What are you talking about?"

"Remember…, when—"

"You gotta be kidding me. We *never* slept together! You're a champion among harlot. A real carnivore. I've never been your lover. I never slept with you! Are you joking? You've never been my mistress!"

"I told her."

"When?"

"At school in Wyoming. Actually, I don't think I told her. I think I told someone else who told her, and I basically sort of confirmed it to her on the flight down."

"Paige!"

At that point, the stakes got higher, because Paige had some sort of instinct about how Brody lived. In her mind, she played her cards as follows: If I'm not going to have sex with him, she isn't, either! So I'll plant a story that Brody and I had sex, which will make him look like a married scumbag.

Now that thinking would have worked if April hadn't been going through a serious identity crisis brought on by this getaway.

But the situation then became a bit more complicated, since right before Paige pulled Brody over to speak, he had given April his bombshell love letter. The one that was custom-made to detonate her soul. The one to make her fall in love with a married man.

Paige was smart, but sometimes she was easily distracted by her own bitterness. Where she thought she had put a landmine in Brody's path, she had indirectly accelerated the photosynthesis of sexual deviancy.

As Brody watched April reading the letter on the other side of the pool, he could see a huge metaphorical cloud over her head, filled with exclamation points. That the letter had not been drowned in the pool was a good sign. That April was now laughing and sipping wine was even better.

Brody was completely hypnotized by her supermodel figure, which was increasingly weakening his self-control. April literally looked like a movie star, moved like a cat and was now caressing her hair, dipping her toes in the pool so Brody could see right up her jean skirt.

When she finished reading the letter, April motioned for Brody to come over.

"You slept with Paige?"

He thought about the best way to answer her. He had never placed money on any bet he knew he couldn't win, but did take calculated risks.

If he said no, that would put everyone in "he said/she said" machinery, making trust impossible. So he went with Paige's lie.

"Yes, I slept with her. But when did she tell you?"

Brody let her think about that. Either way, this trip had now changed course.

"Don't hold it against me, April." said Brody

April was looking off somewhere, seeing something. Her eyes said that she was coming to some conclusion.

Brody had just told a newly minted 20-year-old girl that he had had an adulterous affair with her best friend. In his bizarre way of thinking, he had no choice but to reinforce the lie.

To his amazement…it worked!

April somehow weighed the pathetic behavior of a married man having sex with another woman against having the experience herself.

And not having had it was so potent that her judgment went into the ether.

"At that moment," Brody told me at Mang's, "I knew she had left her judgment behind in Wyoming…, assuming she had any to begin with."

During the course of Brody and April's conversation, Brody navigated many of April's thoughts that she held in secret. When she lied to him, he immediately knew it.

"I'm a virgin," she said.

Technically, she could be, he thought. *Maybe no one's ever gone all the way inside of her.*

But the words they were speaking to each other, about each other, were going well beneath the skin.

As a striking blow to finally begin their affair, he said, "I've fallen in love with you, and there's nothing, not a single thing, you can do about my feelings."

"Wanna bet," April said cunningly, "Brody, I'm tired. I'm going to bed. You can't follow me, but I want you to."

As he watched her walk away, he was tired from the day, the heat, and the emotional upheaval. He was upset.

They never touched that night. They didn't have to. They certainly never kissed. But they were at peace. They were together.

Brody was no stranger to temptation. Only those literally born yesterday are. As he watched April leave, he noticed that she was taking a slower step each time, until she stopped and turned around.

"Brody, my mind is racing with thoughts about you and us. I know you won't follow me, but I need you to."

Brody motioned with his finger for her to come back. And he said quietly, so that not even a worm could hear, "Responsibility is *your* ability to respond to whatever situation unfolds. Accountability is *your* ability to account for your actions, no matter what they are. Stability, however, is *not* your ability to be stable. We do not control the ground we walk on. It's just there. And we're just here. Alone. Together. Connected."

April was frustrated. "I don't understand you, Brody. Not ever. But I want to. I want to *be* with you."

Brody motioned to the room Midori was in, then he motioned to the sky, and sighed deeply.

"We can dream about all sorts of passionate things," he said, "but I don't know what you're made of. Can we be *tied?* Can we be true? I can wake Midori tomorrow and say, 'I want to stay here with April forever.' But can you see us staying in this whatever place? Can you feel us crashing through a wall?"

April spoke as if she were proclaiming from her own constitution, "You're what I've dreamt of my whole life. And it's a cruel cosmic joke that you're married, and older, and need to lose serious weight. There's no space anymore, Brody. I've poured myself in. We made love in a dream. I lost my virginity to you."

Brody wanted to interrupt that line so badly, but he was a sucker for poetry. And, as I said before, he called her "poetry in motion."

"What do you say to that, Brody? What do you see in me?"

Brody closed his eyes, slowly inhaled through his nose, and exhaled from his mouth four times.

"I see a rose stuck in a mire," he said. "And you're on your own. I hear you like thunder across the sky. I'm blinded by your beauty. I feel like a shoestring is holding us together. I feel like we can outdance them all. I see you're free, with no invisible shackles. You're mine and I'm yours."

"I know," April whispered. "And I'm afraid."

Brody motioned again toward Midori's room. "Afraid of what? The needle going in? Or the needle coming out?"

"Stop with the metaphors, Brody! What are you saying? I love how you talk. It's so cool. But right now I need straight answers, please."

"The needle goes in," Brody said, "you inject the venom, and the damage has begun. Some people vomit when it hits their blood, and some feel like it's kissing God, because there's no longer void in your heart where love should be living, but it's all right there. I'm metaphorical heroin to you, and you've never done it. But it's staring you in the face. Just like this has happened to every person the moment before they open the dragon's lair. How did they get that close to the door in the first place? They knew someone who injected the venom, and kissed God. And that someone for you is Paige. She didn't puke."

"Okay, Brody, I've caught your wave, but why be afraid of the needle coming out?"

"The needle coming out is worse, because you know what you injected was temporary. And you don't have another hit. The high will go away, and now it's just a matter of how hard you'll crash. Because you *will* come down, April. I'll be inside you, we'll be one, and we will orgasm. Then Midori's been betrayed, and my bond with her has been slashed. Then one of us will feel like we were kissing God, and the other will vomit."

Intrigued, April said, "But what if I don't come down?"

"I can't see the future, Feline Daisy."

"I bet you have an idea."

"Does it involve a backless dress?" Brody said.

"I think you have it all written out upstairs…, the next one hundred moves."

"Your Honor, she's leading the witness!"

"And I bet you'll give me your strategy tomorrow."

"You know me too well for someone who's just met me."

"So, I'm right!"

"About what? That I like you? Obvious. That I've fallen in lust with you? Double-check! We've gone past Go. Now we're playing. Are we gonna buy the property we landed on? Do we even know *what* we landed on?"

"Tell me step one," she said. "I promise I'll sleep like a baby."

"Step one: Wait a year. I need a full year."

"A full year to decide?"

Brody was astonished by her naïvete.

"No, silly. A year to untangle the bright blue ball of rubber bands known as my life. I gotta leave New York and Midori."

"Have I told you, I've always wanted to go to California?"

"I've been there," Brody said, "and it's pure wanderlust."

April returned the favor: "Sounds like the place for us. Every time you talk, I see your breath and out comes gold dust. So, that's it then. California's our destiny."

Brody got serious: "The needle goes in, and we've only got one shot. You're a stunning beauty trapped in Rio, inhaling pure glorious lithium because below us there's a salt mine. I can taste it. Which, by the way, is third on the periodic table and God made the seas on the third day. He only knows if the Brazilians are putting cocaine in the peaches around here! Have you had the tangerines they leave in the basket every morning? May God be worshipped for creating the tangerine alone! It's delicious. I know you'll taste much better, but I only bet when I know I'm gonna win. That's my training, sweetheart. I gotta keep it basic. Step one: Wait a year."

April got up, lifting her dress a peak to show her naked body, and said, "You better have step two by tomorrow morning. Or else!"

Quasi-stunned, Brody said, "Or else what?"

"Or else you'll find this radiantly sane, young woman tying you to a tree with honey slathered all over your fat body. And I'll be laughing as the bugs and animals eat you alive."

"I believe you." Brody said.

The night finally came to a close with Brody creeping into Midori's bed—*after* penning another love letter to April!

Was he was willing to lose this extraordinary woman beside him? That was painful to think about, but it had to be thought.

A dream without love in it is a dream about war.

20

They Tore Sigmund Freud Down, Too

Late November, 1998

Dr. Albert Ellis had long since been considered one of the originators of the cognitive revolutionary paradigm shift in psychotherapy. As of 1982, he was considered second only to Carl Rogers and above Sigmund Freud as the most significant psychotherapist in the world. A remarkable accomplishment. He was a noted workaholic, who turned his brownstone on the East Side into the Albert Ellis Institute.

Every Friday night, if you allowed him to do your psychoanalysis in front of his students or an audience, you would put your name on a list and for the measly price of five dollars, if you got picked, he would "heal" your problems. You would also get a cassette tape of your "session" with the Great Dr. Albert Ellis.

Brody found out about him through Ken Rosenberg, because Ken's therapist had bought a few paintings from Ken and told him to check out Dr. Ellis. You know how it goes in New York. One thing leads to another into some sort of vague embroidery that only makes sense looking back on it years later, maybe hours later.

So Ken invited Brody to go see what all the fuss was about.

There was Brody Shaw, a dropout from ninth grade, who still hadn't gotten his G.E.D., watching the pomp and circumstance of a public therapy session. It just so happened that two hundred students were visiting that day.

Ken put himself on Ellis's waiting list because he was afraid of flying. No big deal but Ken was headed out to Los Angeles for a mega art show that would put him into another financial stratosphere.

At that point in time, Dr. Ellis was far away from his prime. He was slowly dying and deaf in his right ear. So whatever question you asked him in his deaf ear, a pudgy British woman screamed it into his left ear, creating a comedy of errors.

"I'm afraid of airplanes," Ken said.

When the woman repeated it, Dr. Ellis asked, "You're afraid of *ear plants*?"

That type of nonsense went on, with all the participants lined up to hear a singular reason why they were phobic and how Ellis's solution could heal them.

As Brody was listening to Ellis and reading his brochures, Ken got his answer on how to conquer his fear.

"What's the worst thing that can happen to you on the plane?" Ellis asked. "It crashes and you die! So, don't be afraid of the plane or the heights, but be afraid of death. However, once you're dead..., you won't care anyway."

That was literally this legendary man's answer.

Ken never went back but Brody went on occasion.

One time Brody invited me. Now, either the American Board of Professional Psychology was a dumb idea to begin with, or their wheels fell off because Brody realized Dr. Ellis's answers were never thoughtful.

The time he brought me, Dr. Ellis was on a roll. He was just "healing" people without much of an explanation.

When a woman told Dr. Ellis that her father disapproved of the man she was about to marry, he answered "Has it ever occurred to you that your father is crazy? Marry the man!"

The crowd laughed, but Brody snapped. When the laughing died down, Brody bolted up from his chair.

Knowing there was no chance that Ellis would hear what he was about to say, Brody said in a full-bodied voice so all of his students could hear: "Doctor Ellis, you pathetic old fool! You're not her father! You've never even met either man. But you diagnosed the father as crazy for telling his *own* daughter, who you *just* met, that the man she was going to marry, who you *never* met, is the man for her! Your soul is dead inside. My analysis for you…, *your* parents didn't love you, so you say all parents are crazy and stupid. You are the *nabal*, the ones who have shamelessly crossed the Torah. A self-hating Jew who has denied Moshe and the prophets. The man who proposed to this woman is *not* destined to be her husband, and her *father* knows best. You're interfering in the primal forces of love and life, doctor. You gave her permission to launch headlong into a marriage unblessed by her own father. This institute of yours may have helped some. I'll give you that. But you've built yourself a charade, and this place will fall. When you die, I would be deeply afraid of your ultimate outcome, if I were you. Repent and apologize to that man's daughter!"

That was Brody at his least charming.

That was Brody the psycho.

During this whole rant, Dr. Ellis was escorted out by his nurses, and the evening came to an abrupt end.

As Brody was pushed out by security, he saw something that startled him into an awareness that he had not felt in a long time.

In the hallway, sitting on an A-frame easel, there was a picture of Josephine Carmella, an Italian girl he had gone to elementary school with. One day, during 4th grade, while her entire family was parked in a car, she realized that she had forgotten some bag for the trip and went back upstairs to get it. As she entered her apartment she heard an explosion. Then, when she rushed downstairs, she found the car completely totaled. Her entire family, her mother, father, and brother, were dead in a car bombing over some mob stuff her dad had been involved with. Brody had witnessed the whole thing.

His hyper-empathetic heart exploded for her, pulsating two hundred beats per minute. "I'll be damned!" he muttered. "Josephine Carmella fell for this con man!" She had gone on to become Dr. Ellis's leading disciple and held the top position in family counseling at his institute.

He let out his howl of a laugh.

Then, pointing to the picture, he asked the security guy, "Is she here now?"

But the man just kept him moving toward the door.

Back out on the street, I asked Brody, "If you saw her, what were you gonna say?"

"Shit!" he said. "How would *I* know? ...I might have said, 'This guy makes the local junkie sound like a genius.'"

"But, Brody, how did you even *know* those things you said? I mean, that was some awful slanderous stuff."

"Listen, Benji, I read four of his books, and immediately realized this guy was cuckoo. This is a man who got famous for getting over his fear of women by asking over a hundred of them at the Botanical Gardens for a date, and they all rejected him. It took him a month, but he finally got over his fear of rejection. I understand the premise. That's just how the cookie crumbles. Right now, if you and I were to go up to the Botanical Gardens, we would be bangin' the first girls we kick it to. So Ellis had fear, but he didn't have game. I think that's because he's gay. He probably would've cleaned up if he asked guys, but he did that in 1932. Back then, if you stepped to a man, and he wasn't gay, you would've been stomped on the spot, and the cops would have told your attacker, 'Have a beer on us.' Everyone knows that. So, in my estimation, Ellis didn't conquer his fear. He confirmed that he was gay. That's a different ballgame. You see, I can go to any point on this Earth, and tell any girl I see, 'I know you want me. You won't be the *first*, but you can be the *next*!'"

That's when I realized that Brody was haunted by anyone who's been validated. This time it was Doctor Ellis in the role of Arthur Brown as the *fantasma nella macchina*. Although Brody was appreciated, he wasn't validated with any degrees—and that was *not* enough for him. He wanted to tell everybody how hard he worked to be able to do what he did, but he was begging for recognition. And he might never get it.

21

So Much to Love, So Much to Fight for

May, 2003

While Don and Ken were walking the museum mile, they made plans. Big plans. Completely unattainable plans. Like a discussion of how they would spend their lotto winnings without buying a ticket.

"Wow," Don said, "there's no more graffiti on the walls anymore. I only saw adverts on the train. It was like being in a commercial."

"Everything's changed," Ken responded. "One half of the city is trying to lose weight, the other half is starving…for attention. It's not New York anymore. It's not the Bronx Zoo. It's a private exclusive island for the rich. One half is trying to bend into Hindu shapes, and the other is bent out of shape. One half is positive affirmation, and the other half is positively affirming wrong conclusions."

Soaking in the scenery as he reflected, Don said, "Well, I'm not gonna sharpen my blade anymore. I can hurt them in different ways. No matter what this place looks like, there's so much to love. There's so much to fight for. And I've got no idea what my next move will be."

Surprised by this, Ken said, "Whatcha talkin' 'bout? I'm told ya hear things on the inside."

With a touch of sarcasm, Don replied, "Oh, sure, Ken. If you had dropped by even once, I would've told you all the hot scores. But mainly

I heard torment. Smelled fear. Then I got used to the stench. But I did hear something, and I'll be damned if it didn't remind me of our old friend, Brody Shaw."

"Brother, I know where he is. He sits at Mang's for hours, reading and putting together some Bible study shit."

"Then, let's go. I need to talk to him."

Inside Mang's were pictures of famous people who had eaten there. Brody loved to stare at those photos while his subconscious worked to make sense of his racing thoughts.

When Don and Ken walked in, Brody stood up to give Don a bear hug.

"When was the last time you two saw each other?" Ken asked.

"I don't know," Brody said casually. "Maybe two months ago."

Ken's mouth dropped.

"You guys saw each other in *prison?*" he asked.

"Of course!" Brody said. "You kidding me? Don could've turned my ass in to get a reduced sentence. I owe him my life. The least I could do was visit."

"How come no one told *me?*" Ken said.

"Because," Brody said bluntly, "you were too busy reframing your life, and you're self-absorbed. I don't know. Don't care. It's in the past."

Don nodded in agreement.

"Don," Brody said, "you got that let's get in trouble look. I like it!"

Squinting his eyes, Ken said, "I got that look, too. We're gonna make history."

Brody was not impressed, "Let Don do the talking."

"I heard somethin' about buried treasure here in the city," Don said, "And when I heard it, I said Brody Shaw would know if this is true. It's known as Cleopatra's Needle. If it's true, I know a crew that could help us take it down."

Between bites, Brody quickly rattled off, "The Mitsrayim obelisk. Erected at Central Park on February 22nd, 1881, right near the Metro Museum. There's lots of moving parts to the story, but underneath, the thing has some serious junk in it. Just gotta do it at night. But before we go into the details, can we all appreciate *this?*"

Brody pointed to a picture of a black-and-white photo of a gorgeous blonde.

"This picture of her in Saint Tropez," he said, "fills me with hope that one day we'll be on its beaches drinking champagne. I'll tell her about the book I read on the flight. And God created woman, and she loved man. He created the ocean so we could enjoy the sand. And even though this picture is fifty years old, God bless Brigitte Bardot."

Ken turned to Don. "I want to discuss my plan to give Picasso his overdue. You're talking buried treasure, he's mindlessly rattling off dates, and now we get to hear a poem about some old bitch. Not to mention, based on my Orson Welles gun, we know he took Doctor Edmund Rose for a quarter of a mil!"

Brody was mad, like a hurricane at sea, but he was nowhere near endangering these poor souls on land. He paid no attention to Ken or Don, instead pointing to another photo.

"The sun from Renaissance Rome," he said, "rose one more time, shining on a girl in poverty. Dressed up in white, she swayed through everything, knowing how to make her deals. The Earth was flat, and the sun revolved around it. Lighting was God's wrath till Franklin flew his kite. And there are things in Heaven that we can't comprehend. God bless Sophia Loren!"

Speaking now directly to Brody, Ken said, "The gig's up. We know you're a con artist extraordinaire."

"Oh, that's rich!" Brody said. "Coming from a guy selling ad-hoc paintings to the elite for millions. Let's not worry about what I did to get the cash, or what I did *with* the cash."

He pointed to another photo: "I see you sitting there, surrounded by your cats, reading verses on isolation and happiness. Now that you're thirty-five, things can't get better…, if, and only if, you're caught by a butterfly hunter. I love your understated whimsical ways. I pray to God you'll ask me to stay. And the Lord knows I'll be back the very next day. God bless Faye Dunaway."

Ken slammed the table, which drew everyone's attention.

"Brody," he shouted, "stop the game playing. You think you're the only crazy one here? I got wind from old Reverend Sarah that you were rockin' a twenty-year-old in Rio. That's beyond the pale, even for 260."

"I see you forgot some of our exploits," retorted Don.

"Hey," said Ken, "he's married to Midori and has grey hair!"

Getting more upset, Brody pointed to another picture. "Offbeat therapies with three wives who had sung. The cancer spread up and down his steel-caged lungs.

He was only fifty, but would last forever. The king of cool, like Mustangs and leather. And there are verses that heal you right away. There are verses that illuminate the next day. And his favorite verse was John three sixteen. God bless you Steve McQueen."

Mildly frustrated, Don said, "Brody, is that your way of saying yes? We'll take down Cleopatra's Needle and destroy a Picasso because that motherfucker never had the heart."

Brody said with a smile, "If that's your way of asking, then I'm all yours!"

They shook hands.

Then Brody said to Ken, "Hey, douche, you'll notice my ring is still on my finger. Midori's still my wife."

"Yeah, but you got nine other fingers," Ken said.

Brody always hated getting beaten, especially by a clever punch like that. Unable to resist getting in the last word, he said, "Yes, but those are my trigger fingers."

Then, closing his Bible and periodic table, he said, "Boys, Joseph was seventeen years old when he brought that nasty report to his brothers. Seventeen is the atomic number of chlorine, a natural element that purifies water. So his brothers threw Joseph into a dry well. Before that, the flood both started and ended on the seventeenth day of the month. His father, Jacob, spent the last seventeen years of his life in Egypt. The process of being baptized, means you need to immerse yourself in water for purification. Joseph's brothers had to cross two rivers to get to Egypt where they would repent. I find those facts wonderful, like the fingerprints of the Almighty. But, on occasion, I do like writing poems about women, and I also like robbing banks. And if you got a problem, Ken, with me doing *what* with twenty-year-olds, take it up with Midori."

"I don't take girls up," Ken said. "I take them *down*."

They all high-fived on that, and left the restaurant, ready to take back the city.

✳

Brody spotted a man in a custom-made suit. "Guys!" he said. "That's Gail Wynand!"

"Who?" said Ken and Don.

"He's from the book, *The Fountainhead!*"

Don was disappointed. "Brody," he said, "the gig's up. Is some insurance company watching you? You don't need to *play* the psycho. We *know* you're nuts!"

"No! I'm telling you, it's Gail Wynand."

"Brody, don't you have any Xanax?" Ken asked.

"I need a Xanax," Brody exclaimed, "because I saw someone from a book?"

"Now I'm thinking more of a leash!" Ken shot back.

"Brody, it's just a kid," Don said, trying to cool down the situation.

"Wanna bet?" Brody said, extending his pinky finger.

"You haven't got the guts to ruin the pinky bet on this, do you?" Don said, extending his own pinky finger.

"I can't believe we're enabling this," Ken said.

"Damn you, Rosenberg!" Brody snapped. "Give me your pinky!"

"No way!" said Ken. "This could be one of your stupid cons. Let me just ask the kid for his I.D."

"No!" Brody protested. "That kid's about to steal a book. That lady coming this way. He's gonna steal the book from *her*."

Just then the kid snatched the book from the woman and ran off.

"Holy shit!" Ken said. "Let's get him!"

"No!" Brody said, holding Ken back. "We can't interfere in such matters. I'm not squirming out of the bet, man. It's not a co-winka-dink. In the book, Gail steals a volume of Herbert Spencer from a lady."

"This is a con," Don said. "Another con." Ever since finding out about Brody's long confidence game with Dr. Rose, both Don and Ken became weary of whom they are dealing with.

They stayed where they were as two cops across the street came by to see what was going on.

Before the cops got to the woman, Brody dragged Ken and Don up to her.

"Excuse me," Brody said. " Sorry to see that your delightful afternoon has been ruined. But could you kindly tell us what book that boy just stole?"

"He stole my volume of Herbert Spencer," the woman said.

Ken screamed at the top of his lungs, "You definitely *paid* her to say that! I get it now. This is what you're doing with the doc's money. Turning everything into a vaudeville show."

Don said to one of the cops, who had just walked up, "My god, Brody! This cop shield is authentic. Are you buying uniforms now on the black market?"

The real cop was confused.

"Guys," Brody said, "I'm not messin' around. This is a real cop."

"Sure, Brody," Ken said, pointing to the officer's holster. "Then, this must be a real gun."

When Ken reached for the gun, the cop slammed him to ground, and his partner drew his own gun.

"Freeze!" he yelled.

Don was laughing, still thinking this was a prank.

"Goddamn it!" Brody said. "That *was* Gail!"

Brody, Don, and Ken were all squirming in the back of a squad car.

"I can't deal with this!" Ken fumed. "We're together for ten minutes, for the first time in twelve years, and we're all arrested!"

"Brody," Don said, "this is gonna fuck my parole."

"Don," Ken said, "I got lawyers, man. Money and lawyers. We'll be fine. This time you won't be representing yourself!"

In full hurricane mode, Brody screamed, "Why would you guys think I would devalue a pinky bet? I told you, I only bet when I know I'm gonna win. That's a 260 code!" Then, giving Ken the evil eye, he added, "This is what money does to people. It makes them forget what life is about."

"What book is happening now, smarty pants?" Don said.

"The one that Benjamin Solomon wrote about me, but it never got published."

22

How to Propose on the First Date

Early December, 1998

Brody's Bible fellowship was mobbed. Be boppin' he hoppin'. People were jazzed to hear what this guy had to say about the world and God's living word.

"I didn't prepare anything tonight," Brody began, "so it would be foolish for me to start opening the Bible randomly. When I look across this room, I see faces. I don't see the invisible soul and spirit trapped inside your decaying bodies. I see what you want me to see. So tonight I want to propose a simple exercise that you will start sometime this week. I want everyone here to become a member of your Public Library. You go in there and pick a book that has a cover you love. Then you get a book on a subject you absolutely know you'll hate. Go with your blind prejudices. Finally, pick a biography of someone you know nothing about. *Capeesh*?"

The crowd nodded.

"Here's what this is gonna teach you. It's gonna make you think critically. The first book will test your perception. What you thought something looked like. Was it what it appeared to be? For the second book, I want you to write down how many pages you got into it before you realized you *truly* have no interest in the subject.a For the third book, I want you to read all the way through and tell me how much of yourself you saw in the person, even though it was someone you didn't know from Adam."

Generally speaking, the crowd liked the idea, and I went along with it myself.

The following week, when we all came back with notes in hand, Brody said, "Okay, what did you learn? What happened? I wanna know!"

And we all went through our own process and explained how the exercise was meaningful to us and how we saw the value in what we learned.

"The trees of New York," Brody said. "The handsome trees that live in the three-feet-by-two-feet hole in the world's worst dirt. It's not even real dirt. They grow out of concrete. On a single tree, we tilt down from the crown and all its branches to the trunk, and further down to the taproots and lateral roots, which are seldom exposed. All as strong as concrete, defying all reason. It's something to marvel at. We're New Yorkers. We're powerful. We're just like these trees."

"Yeah, Brody," I said, "but what's this got to do with the book exercise you gave us?"

"Books are made from trees, aren't they?"

Brody let a silence pass through the room. Then he said, "I'm glad you all had fun. Now it's time for us to get down to some Bible. Let's start with why the King James version of the story of Cain and Abel is complete hogwash. Because of horrible mistranslations from the Hebrew to the English, the King James translators let an unrepentant Cain get away with murder."

After his fascinating lecture on how Cain did *not* get away with killing Abel, Brody had me tag along to a private screening of *Hemingway in the Moonlight*. The word on the street was that it was going to be all the rage, and he knew someone who got him tickets.

The screening was held on the thirty-fifth floor of 666 Fifth Avenue. All throughout the floor, sunlight filtered in through sheer curtains drawn over the windows. The walls were decorated with original abstract paintings and sculptures strategically lit by ornate chrome lamps placed to highlight the best features of the art. The taste was exquisite, but far too eclectic for any one individual. The pieces had to be owned by a conglomerate.

When we first got there, Brody spotted a wooden tablet that celebrated King Semti's festivals in the Second Dynasty of ancient Egypt. Every museum in the world would have wanted that piece. Brody immediately recognized it as a form of sun worship. In his busy mind, he started connecting dots by accessing the endless amount of trivial information he had picked up as the Keeper of the Corny. The Custodian of the Senseless.

"Why is this piece here?" Brody asked. "There's no Ivy League–educated curator who could get his silky hands on a piece this important. Something this precious only travels through an elite crowd, always on loan, never owned, and the price is dear."

Just then, a tall, thin, silver-haired man appeared, pushing open double-doors that led to the private theatre that was actually an atrium with a large projection screen. After he gestured for us to follow him, we walked over a luxurious marble floor through a forest of exotic plants and trees that I had never seen before. If not for the mysterious gentleman leading the way, we would have certainly gotten lost. The light filtering down from multiple skylights reflected a mist that was being pumped in from a hidden source. Off to the left, there was a large aquarium filled with colorful tropical fish. To the right, there was an American flag on a pole.

With the aroma of vanilla incense in the air, in walked Faye Olay, slow, deliberate, and magisterial, appearing dignified to the point of saintliness. I immediately noticed her eyes, which reminded me of colors and patterns you see on butterfly wings: hints of grey, green, and brown blended in with oceanic blue. When she started to peel a Valencia orange and eat it, Brody interpreted this as body language intentionally aimed at him but Faye had codes, laws, traditions, long-standing friendships, ethics, and a reverence for the art of filmmaking.

Besides, she knew she was being groomed for her crowning as the next Queen of Hollywood.

Brody, on the other hand, was a stage play guy. A sandbox guy. A playground guy. A concrete jungler. A tar beacher. He had little interest in the "art" of filmmaking, feeling that Hollywood's job was to produce low-brow trash. Without warning, he started singing Cole Porter's "Anything Goes":

> In olden days, a glimpse of stocking
> Was looked on as something shocking.
> But now, God knows,
> Anything goes.
> Good authors too who once knew better words
> Now only use four-letter words
> Writing prose.
> Anything goes.

Brody believed that ethics are what separate man from beasts. It was through ethical principles that he manifested prosperity. But now, standing so close to this mythical woman, he whispered to me, "How did she acquire this level of achievement cleanly? Surely, there was a crime in her past. Or maybe the rumors I've heard have been embellished."

Brody had heard every possible variation of the same stories for years. They were stale and came across as shallow, devoid of meaning. Also, he was a sinner himself, so he gave people enough rope to either hang themselves or get back with the Lord.

Brody politely introduced himself to Faye.

"We have mutual friends," he said.

"Who?" she asked.

Whispering to her, he said, "Edward F. Albee, the scrap merchant from Lithuania, who started RKO. Wilhelm Fried, the Hungarian garmento, who launched Fox Films. Jesse Loewi, the Russian pharmacist, who founded Famous Players. Hirsch and Samuel Wonsal, the Polish janitors, who changed their names to Warner, and built Warner Brothers. And Shmuel Gelbfitz, the glove salesman from Warsaw, who changed his name to Goldwyn, and created MGM."

At this point, Faye's handler was trying to usher her away to her seat. She definitely had a confused look on her face, but Brody had his smile going, so she brushed off her handler and escorted Brody and me to her seats.

Once we were settled in, Brody said to Faye, "I always found it curious that all of Hollywood was run by a small band of men who began life from strikingly similar backgrounds."

Faye responded with her own golden smile: "You're full of charm, handsome."

Brody blushed. But keeping his focus, he said, "All Eastern European Jews…, poor, uneducated, laboring in lowly trades…, then, without knowing each other, they all entered the same business. It's almost like a signal went off in their heads, and they moved en masse to Hollywood at the same time. It's strange."

"Go on," said Faye. "I really adore men who don't give me a chance to talk."

Plowing straight ahead, Brody said, "When I was ten, I found myself under the tutelage of someone I thought was a warlock. But the old man was just a magician who knew a great deal about astrology, stargazing, planetary motion, and astrophysics. These were four distinct esoteric fields of study that no other child that I knew had any interest in, let alone knew anything about. My mind got dizzy every time I visited the old man in his engraving shop. The magician had a backroom that was always filled with conflicting aromas. Some were sweet, but mainly they were unidentifiable smells that couldn't please anyone with a nose. So I asked the old man about an awful-smelling concoction that was boiling violently on his stove. 'That, my boy,' he said, 'is a mixture of six fats. Horse, hippopotamus, crocodile, cat, snake, and ibex. It's for people who are restless.' Then he grabbed a small bottle, opened it, and poured a thick liquid into the pot to strengthen the dose. 'I'm using the tooth of a donkey crushed in honey,' he said."

All of that sounded nauseating in an otherworldly way to Faye, so you can imagine what it sounded like to a ten-year-old Brody, who had never even heard of a hippopotamus or an ibex.

"Then," Brody continued, "the old man directed me to a shelf that held all his healing drugs. Bottles of all different shapes and sizes filled with lizards' blood, pigs' ears, putrid meat, goose grease, asses' hoofs, tigers' tails, and, most surprising, fly dung!"

Everything Brody said was totally abstract and insane to Faye, but still she was curious—and boy, could Brody talk! He sounded like one of those church organs in a black neighborhood.

"Let me tell you," Brody said, "books! He had them all! Twelve shelves of them. Overflowing with books, some of which were older than the Massorah! One of the most interesting manuscripts was resting on a pew. It was a wild shuffle of what looked like torn pieces of paper. The old man explained that it was Egyptian hieroglyphics written on papyrus. Then he gave me a wooden stick that was two feet long and asked me to stir the other pot on the stove. While I was stirring who knows what, the old man launched into a story."

Brody told his story as if he were a Roman orator: "In fifty B.C., throughout the whole of France, Belgium, and Switzerland, there was an order of men who exemplified dignity. Those Druids were engaged in sacred ceremonies, conducted public and private sacrifices, and interpreted all matters of spirituality. They made decisions about all controversies. And if any crime had been perpetrated…, for example, if murder had been committed, or if there had been any dispute about an inheritance, the Druids decided it. They decreed rewards and punishments. The Druids didn't go to war, nor did they pay tribute to the Emperor like everyone else. They had an exemption from military service and a dispensation in all matters. The Druids never wrote anything down. They learned a great number of books by heart, adopting that practice for two reasons: they neither desired their doctrines to be divulged among the masses, nor did they want to rely on writing, since it occurred to them that dependence weakened their memories. They imparted to the youth many things respecting the stars and their motions, as well as the majesty of the Sun."

Faye was sucked in.

Brody continued his verbal assault, which he thought was a mental bouquet: "The old magician walked over to me and unwrapped a paper bag filled with bright green leaves that smelled like mint. He had me put each leaf in the pot, one at a time. There were thirteen in all. Then he continued his story: 'The most significant ability of the Druids,' he said, 'was hypnosis. With a single wave of their wand, they could send messages across the land, as far as a hundred miles away, and have people carry out the will of the magic wand. All they needed was the tree and leaves.'"

Faye looked puzzled. "*What* tree?"

"The old man pointed to the boiling pot that I was stirring, took the wooden stick from my hand, and said: 'You see, this stick and those leaves are from the Holly tree outside. The leaves make a delightful tea, and what I have in my hand is really a wand made from the wood of that tree.' He gave me back the wooden stick, and said, 'In your hand is Holly wood. And I can teach you its magic.'"

Brody opened his jacket, pulled out a stick, and said to Faye, "Here it is! Hollywood. It's a magic wand. And I want you to have it."

Faye took the wand as Brody said, "You're gonna be a big star, kid. You know why? Because you got the wand."

Brody got out of his seat and bent down on one knee. "Now," he said, "may I have your hand in marriage?"

Without missing a beat, Faye said, "Where's the ring?"

That was the only time I've ever seen Brody beaten at his own game.

The movie was okay.

When we broke out, I said to Brody, "Was all that stuff true?"

"You know," he said, "it doesn't have to be true. It has to be good. That was my Aunt Connie's wooden spoon."

I just had to know how long he had planned this.

"Brody," I asked, "did you make up that story?"

He got angry with me. "Look, man," he said, "did Moses make up *his* story? It's not *what* you believe, it's *who* you believe. So if you're naïve and believe in me, then you'll think the story's true. But it's not *who* you believe, it's what *they* can *prove*! So the story of the Druids came from a book by Julius Cæsar. I can prove that. But it's not what can be proved. It's how it's *validated*. And more importantly it was on October 6th, 1927, when the first words uttered from Hollywood came blaring out of Al Jolson's mouth: 'You ain't seen nothin' yet.' And if that doesn't shake your boots, you know what day it was on the Rabbinical Calendar? The evening of Yom Kippur, the Day of Atonement."

23

Artie Chews! Artie Swallows! Artie Chokes!

June 14, 1989, Part Four

Jack muttered, "Jeet?"

Alexis didn't follow his guttural Italian talk, so he repeated it louder, "JEET?"

"You hungry?" Alexis asked. "I'm hungry. Let's get something to eat."

"That's what I've been saying," Jack said.

"How about Chinese?"

Jack got up off the couch.

"Where's the kitchen? You must have something in the fridge."

"It's over there," Alexis said, pointing south. "You'll feel it."

Jack walked in the direction that she had pointed, heading toward an enormous refrigerator. When he opened the door, it was filled to the brim.

Alexis followed him in, went over to a cabinet, and got out a box of Frosted Flakes. Then she sneaked by Jack to grab some milk, sat down at the kitchen table, and poured the cereal into a bowl.

As Jack rummaged through the vegetable tray, he said, "Aha! Artichokes!" and pulled out six.

Alexis chanted, "Artie chews! Artie swallows! Artie chokes!"

"They're my favorite!" said Jack.

"Ugh! They look like broccoli and pineapple crashed into each other."

"Don't tell me you don't love artichokes." Jack was baiting her.

"Like maybe when I was a kid. I'm all about pizza, pickles, and pasta."

Alexis drowned her Frosted Flakes in milk. As soon as the liquid hit the cereal, she poured four soupspoons of sugar on top.

"Does your mom know you do that?"

"My mom's dead," said Alexis, in a don't-talk about it again kind of way.

"Guess what?" said Jack. "I'm a member of the dead mom club, too."

Alexis's eyes watered.

Jack nodded sympathetically.

Alexis crammed another spoonful of the Frosted Flakes into her mouth.

Disgusted by that obnoxious display and concerned about what a hopped-up-on-sugar Alexis might do, Jack grabbed the sugar bowl and dumped its contents into the sink.

"What an asshole thing to do!"

"We're gonna have artichokes."

After preparing four artichokes to cook, Jack trimmed an inch off the stem.

"Alexis, snap off the small bottom leaves."

When she had done that, he used a sharp knife to trim the thorns from the tips of the outer leaves. He also cut off the top inch of the artichoke to remove the thorns at the crown.

On the stove, steam swirled out as Jack lifted the pot lid. Sitting on the counter, there were a glass of freshly squeezed lemon juice, a bottle of olive oil, four crushed garlic cloves, and various spices.

Alexis was shaking a can of chicken stock, as Jack said, "You know, this is a seventeenth-century recipe."

"I think that's when my maid bought that chicken stock."

Jack opened the can, took a whiff, and signaled that it was good to go.

"You got a girlfriend, Jack?"

"Used to."

The water was now boiling on the stove.

Jack was standing there, frying up breadcrumbs. Turning himself into the economic statesman he wished to be, he said, "Lemme break it down for ya. There are only four ways a girl can relate to a man that really matter."

Alexis rolled her eyes as if this were some ancient secret.

"Lay it on me."

"As a mother, sister, daughter, and wife…. My last girlfriend didn't grasp that concept. She related to me as a psycho, a slut, and a lyin', backstabbin', cheatin' drunk."

Once again playing the provocateur, Alexis said, "What am *I*, Jack?"

He answered thoughtfully, "Too young to be concerned…. Actually, you're a daughter."

"Yeah, but I related to my mom so much more than my dad…. Besides, I'm also a sister!"

"But to another *girl*. I'm talking about how girls relate to *men*! …Is it because you related more to your mom that you became disenfranchised with life after she died?"

"Sorta. My mom and I had this crazy argument over how much eyeliner I was using. I told her I hated her. That was the last thing I said to her."

"I'm sure she didn't believe you."

"What was the last thing you said to *your* mom?"

Jack became foggy as he poured the chicken broth into a large pot. "Oh, I don't remember…, though I was with her when she died."

"Well, since that day, I've never said a bad word to anyone."

Jack sighed. "You called me an asshole five seconds ago!"

"Yeah, but I knew that wasn't gonna be our last moment together."

Infinitely wiser than Alexis, Jack said, "I see you've already grasped the art of rationalization. We're gonna have to let this cook for about forty minutes."

*

Jack and Alexis walked along the Gershovitzs' 125-foot-long rooftop, from which the view was glorious. Jack admired it while he could. Although Summer was approaching, there was a crisp Fall breeze in the night air, which gave Jack a romantic feeling.

"Ever wet toilet paper and throw it on the street?" Jack asked.

"No. Sounds exciting."

"Then, let's do it!"

Jack got a bucket of water, plunged a roll of toilet paper into it, and chucked it off the rooftop. The roll landed on top of a moving bus.

Copying him, Alexis threw hers as hard as she could. This time, the soggy paper landed on a man walking a dog.

Jack and Alexis ducked, and then giggled, knowing they were in trouble.

"We're in deep shit!" Jack whispered. "Don't you love it?! I can't believe it hit him"

Alexis was crying to keep from laughing. Then they both laughed harder, trying to keep quiet. When they slowly got up to look over the edge, they saw that the man was still standing there, looking around. As they ducked back down, they laughed even harder than before. Looking over at the remaining rolls of toilet paper, Jack finally wised up.

"We'd better quit while we're ahead."

When they headed back down into the townhouse, they went into the dining room to eat. Although the oak table was twelve feet long, Jack and Alexis sat next to each other at one corner.

Looking at the six artichokes on his plate, which he had breaded, Jack picked one up, and said, "Watch me."

He gently pulled off a leaf.

She pulled off a leaf.

"You can only eat a small section of this," he said. *"Alla salute!"*

When Jack put the leaf into his mouth and scraped off the bread as he pulled it out, Alexis did the same.

As she chewed her leaf interminably, Jack gazed at her mouth.

Subtle eroticism began to arise at the table.

When she stopped chewing, Jack felt an intense erotic charge and quickly turned away to stop a thought in his head.

After he simmered down, he pulled off another leaf, and she followed suit.

This went on until they saw the artichoke heart.

As Jack and Alexis strolled down Fifth Avenue on the Central Park side, they shared a cigarette.

At 79th and Fifth, Jack stopped walking and moodily pointed at a wall.

"That's where 'Lightning' Shawn Harper got killed. That mutha had a thing about racking up motorcycles. One night, there was a brand new Kawasaki standing right out in front of his place. Brand spankin' shinin' new. So naturally, he hotwired it for a joy ride. Within minutes, sirens were wailin', and the cops were on his ass. What he didn't know was that the bike had no brakes! He came flyin' around this corner, and kaboom! Splat! Brains everywhere! Most people think the cops planted the bike. So do I. Mayor Koch was gettin' rid of the vandals. Last week, he released wolves into the subway yard. Isn't that somethin'? What a sicko! My friend Cyan was chased by a foamin'-at-the-mouth wolf while he was taggin' up a train. Can you believe that?"

"What's his tag?"

"PNB260."

"Oh, I see that everywhere. You *know* him?"

"Know him? I *love* him! He's like my little brother. But Shawn..., what a waste. He could run five thousand meters in under thirteen minutes. Which would've, could've, and should've been the Olympic record, but no one ever recognized it because he did it running around the reservoir over there in the park. It's totally unfair."

Mustering up her version of empathy, Alexis said, "That sucks."

"You see," Jack said, "I was supposed to race him, but I never got the chance. So, I've been chasin' his ghost ever since. He was Olympic gold. I'm just the thoroughbred in the donkey show."

Being kind, she said, "I bet you would've beat Shawn, too."

Jack chuckled at the thought.

"I quit runnin' 'cause every guy in college can run just like me. I've never been beat here, though. And I've raced at least twenty guys."

Alexis took his hand, and they walked a bit until Jack realized what he was doing. Then he dropped her hand and pulled away.

"C'mon!" he said. "None o' that!"

"Whadaya mean? I'm the girl. Whadaya afraid of? I only do oral."

Jack smiled away the insanity of that statement.

As she started to stomp off back to her place, Jack grabbed her.

"No, wait!" he pleaded. "I wanna show ya somethin'."

On one of the smaller terraces on the fifth floor of the townhouse, Jack came across a hockey stick.

"Ya got any rope around here?" he asked.

"Sure."

"Well, while you're gettin' that, bring a fork, too."

When Alexis came back, Jack bent the fork into a hook, tied the rope around its handle, and turned the hockey stick into a makeshift fishing rod.

When he cast the rope off the terrace, both of them giggled as they watched the fork dangling over a pot of roses on the terrace below. When Jack caught the plant with the fork, Alexis almost peed in her pants with excitement. As Jack slowly reeled in the plant, Alexis helped out by grabbing it.

"Ya see!" said Jack. "This is why I love New York. Where else can you fish for roses?"

If Alexis liked Jack before, now she *loved* him. She didn't want to bed him, but would have loved a deep slow kiss. The ones she had only read about, or maybe heard about from the varsity girls at lacrosse practice. Jack could feel what she was thinking, but ignored the plea she was making with her body language. Pulling off two roses, he gave one to her and kept one for himself.

"Jack," she asked, "do you think we could be friends?"

"Of course, we can!"

"No, I know that. I mean, can we be *just* friends?"

"Sure. Most of the girls I know are much cooler than the boys I know."

"I was told that boys and girls can only be in love."

"Bullshit! I have a friend who's not my girlfriend. I never think about love with her."

"Maybe you're in love with her, and you don't know it."

"With Ramona?! Hell, no!"

"Maybe *she* loves *you*. Love is involved somewhere in there. It's what I've been told. By a trusted source, too."

"Sorry, Alexis. Ramona's just a friend. I know love. It's a bit different."

"Can I be your friend, Jack?" she pleaded. "I mean, a true friend? One you'll know your whole life?"

She was trying her hardest to do something with her eyes that he would notice. But when he turned his head to look at her, he didn't notice.

Then they heard the voice of Mr. Gershovitz, calling out, "Party's over, kids!"

"It's time to go, Joe College," she said, clearly disappointed.

"That's Jack Track to you."

24

Panic Attacks and Paper Airplanes

Rio de Janeiro, Day Five

Darius arranged for a zip line in the jungle in the afternoon. The hour drive there was already impressive and entirely scary. They were taking mud roads, inches away from bottomless drops. The driver was going far too fast with turns that were too sharp.

This caused Brody to have a panic attack. He popped a Xanax. Amongst this crowd, only Midori knew that Brody was professionally diagnosed as mentally ill since a child in 1975. However, because he grew up to poor parents he never was medicated for it until six months before the trip. He was a nervous system run amuck and had manic episodes his entire life but never deep depression. He was just always up and thrilling.

He dropped out of high school to work hard labor for $3.35 an hour. He couldn't hold a job for more than two to five months because the anxiety was that severe. Do you think his landlords cared he suffered about his anxiousness? He went twenty-seven years being bi-polar without medication and was forced to cope with it. He had to dropout of ninth grade regardless of extreme intelligence, because the terror of fight or flight made it impossible for him to attend school. Then, in the September before the trip to Rio, Brody had a full blown nervous breakdown, which included flopping like a fish on Fifth Avenue while people walked over him. He only heard the phrase "by appointment only" repeating in his head over and over.

He called Midori from his cell phone and said, "Come get me." She stayed on the cell phone while he was telling her where he thought he was. The entire time he was under the impression he was dying of a heart attack. Midori found him with a Bible opened on his chest.

She helped him up and they walked two miles back home. Where they realized he can't live like that anymore. But never once did he feel like he should "end it" because he was hopelessly optimistic that the pain, grief, hurt and damage would go away yet everyday he woke up and realized, "damn it" the problem was still there.

As he slowly calmed down on the ride from hell to the zip line, he decided to look at a sheet of paper his psychologist gave him entitled, "Challenging Negative Thoughts" and answered the questions that followed.

The first question was, "Is there substantial evidence for my thought?"

The bus ride was loud enough for him to talk freely, knowing only Midori could hear and not April and Paige who were sitting in front of them.

"I currently feel worthless," he said, "The evidence of this feeling has its roots when I dropped out of ninth grade. This worthless feeing was compounded by the fact, I was never formally trained as a business consultant. I simply lied about my credentials and learned on the fly how to use several different business software programs. These lies included pretending I had degrees in schools I never attended and expertise in areas that literally do not exist in business. I made up the phrase, "I've got my Masters' in organizational psychology in business management from Baruch." There was no such thing. A simple phone call would've exposed that. But I was working for people who were naïve and placed their trust in me because I knew how to charm them into hiring me."

The second question was, "Is there evidence contrary to my thought?"

"Technically, yes," he said, "All the companies that hired me as a consultant proved I knew what I was doing. Consulting cannot be counterfeited. You either can make the numbers and decisions work or not. But I had clever techniques to hide my weaknesses in understanding the full scope and function of each business I was working for."

The third question was, "Am I attempting to interpret this situation without all the evidence?"

"No I'm not," he answered, "and let me explain how I can prove this line of thinking. This worthless feeling is because I was living life as an academic fraud. This did not allow me to climb the corporate ladder. When there were positions to advance such as becoming the C.E.O. I couldn't take the chance of living that deep of a lie because in many respects what I was doing could've been already considered criminal. Everyday I went into a consultation, I knew I was living a lie, telling a lie, making up a lie to cover up my lack of education. I successfully conned people into hiring me. These people that hired me never vetted my background. They never called *any* of my references. If I was tested on any software program, at best, I would get a just passing grade. Eventually, I self educated myself so my cons got better and the work was solid. Although, the element of fraud? Now, that was impossible to escape."

The fourth question asked, "Will this matter a year from now?"

Coming down off high anxiety, Brody started making sense, "My decision to drop out of school because of undiagnosed mental illnesses with learning disabilities and anxiety has effected every single day of my life since May 4th, 1984. I've been bi-polar since 1975. The constant anxiety has been with me since October 14th, 1985. What a dumb question. Ask a black person if being black will matter a year from now? They can't change that. Ask an obese person if being fat will matter a year from now? Not necessarily because they may make lifestyle choices and lose weight. Ask someone who was raped last night, will it matter a year from now? Yes, it will matter. The only time it doesn't matter is when you dope yourself up with drugs or alcohol. I take synthetic medicines with precaution but I'm a goddamn guinea pig! When we get back to New York I'm quitting this life. I refuse to live lies anymore. I'd rather die telling the truth then living a life of lies. There's no such thing as one lie. It becomes an entire empire of lies. Lying is illegal. It is an affront to every fictional God in every fake religion. It's the commandment given by the Almighty Creator of the universe not to do. And to show you how deep this gets? On the occasions I found out I was being lied to, I would unleash hell on the liar. So that makes me a professional hypocrite. I'm saying this from experience. There's a reason why you're not to lie. It's a supernatural reason. This concept of lying that's contrasted against the truth is from the Author of Life. I've bucked up against a system that's beyond this universe. I've danced with the author of confusion. I am an iceberg of lies. I've told so many that I can't distinguish them from the truth."

The entire time, Midori was holding Brody's hands, not as his wife, but as his sister. She had been through all the jungle gyms of mania with Brody and it was all so endearing to her. Unpredictable and filled with variety, Brody was non-violent. He was just a broken down man.

"This Almighty Creator has been merciful to me," said Brody to Midori, "This exercise has been helpful but I've crossed lines and closed doors in which you can't turn back from. Most people don't know when they are lied to. No one can mark me out. Since 1980, I hold an invisible Master's Degree in lying and coping with anxiety."

She asked, "How do you feel right now, has the Xanax kicked in?"

He shook his head that it had.

He let go of Midori's hand, lifted himself over to the next row of chairs and sat next to April. Paige got up and scooted up front in a huff to Darius.

He grabbed April's hand and whispered into her ear, knowing full well the hot air of his breath would entice her, "If you have dreams and they're coming true, I say good for you. If you have a dollar you may wanna give away a dime just to see how it turns out in time. If you've made mistakes that you can't undo. If you didn't get a break you felt was due. I say drink yourself a cup of Brody soup, find your way to the nearest zoo. Look at the lions inside their cage and realize you got it made."

"Why do you speak in rhyme?" April responded.

"Because I find it more interesting," said Brody, "I once got a job because the man that was interviewing me suffered from anemia his whole life. I asked him 'what does anemia mean?' He said, 'It means I have lack of iron in my blood.' I asked him, 'Are you Jewish?' he said 'Yes I am. I'm Ashkenazi from the Ukraine.' Then spoke to him in Hebrew. I told him 'on the periodic table, iron is number twenty-six.' He looked at me with that crossed eyed vibe but said, 'What does one thing have to do with the other?' I said, 'The unpronounceable name of the Almighty Creator in gematria adds up to twenty-six. I told him he lacks the Torah of Moshe.' He looked at me and said, 'Is that true?' I said, 'Your anemia will be solved with diet but most likely you just need to go to your Rabbi, do a mikveh and ask him how to pronounce the name that is forbidden to announce.' He said, 'You're hired.'"

"Then what happened?" said April.

"A month later he came into my office and said, 'You're a mensch. I no longer have anemia because I did what you told me to do. And the Rabbi said he never knew about iron and the number twenty-six and wants to meet you.'"

"What happened next?" said April.

"I met the Rabbi and told him he shouldn't call himself Rabbi..., or Reverend for that matter because it means great one and..., yeah, that conversation ended badly.

"Brody, my dad's a reverend."

"My condolences. I'm sorry to hear that."

"I'm being serious," April laughed, "what's your take?"

"It's a moniker for people who want the respect that they don't deserve. I'm sorry but that's the truth. And the truth is what sets you free. First of all, the word reverend means to be revered. Why does your dad insist he needs to be revered? It's just an ego play. And the only way he could get the title is from another buffoon laying his hands on him and taking a fee. There's no criteria. It's academic doo doo. I'm sure if you ask your dad, he will insist the title is a burden but…, he must live with it."

April's shook her head in disbelief, she thought to herself, *that is precisely what my dad told me.* "You know Brody my dad feels *that* same way and I always say to him, 'why can't you be like everyone else in the room?' He just loved this man he called The Teacher. Isn't that absurd?"

"Oh, you're a child of a baby-boomer that was taught the Bible by Arthur Brown. Jesus Christ! I can't get away from this guy. Arthur Brown was a Biblically illiterate conman. He would insist the Scriptures were originally written in Greek and would reference the Latin Vulgate as if it was ordained by God!"

Little did April know that Brown was his personal *apparatus in spiritu sanctu.*

"He's a pure anti-Semite," continued Brody, "I hate to level an accusation against a dead guy but he had a book he called "the blue book", and he wrote that the 'Sabbath was the day of bondage'. You have got to be a moron to think that. The Sabbath was the day of freedom and rest but like I said, he hated Jews. And furthermore, he couldn't provoke a Jew to Jesus no matter what he did. He only attracted twenty-something baby-boomers. Period. And you need to bust way out of that shell because Brown put our loving, powerful God in a small box and kept him and his spirit trapped inside until he told you the secrets *after* you paid him."

They arrived at the zip line and got all geared up as a group. Paige, April, and Midori were all wearing white tee shirts and shorts. It was a sweltering day filled with ominous humidity. They climbed five hundred feet to the top of a mountain, with Paige's parents trailing behind.

One at a time, they each held on as they were pushed through the Amazon in some cases 1,000 feet above the forest floor. They were going at least thirty-five miles per hour when they landed smack onto a tree with a makeshift stage that can only hold five people tops.

Once you landed onto the next tree you needed to quickly move over to your left otherwise the fella behind would crush your spine like a crash test dummy. Being the genius that he was, Brody knew to bring the whole supply of Xanax with him but had it in his pocket covered by tissues because he didn't want to be seen with prescription meds.

This was the Brentwoods, World Class Christian Folk and major players in the secular realm. They are the American dream. Brody, far from the American nightmare, was the American disappointment. So he had to keep his stash under wraps. But guess who was else having a panic attack? Why if it wasn't Lesley Brentwood herself. The whole speed, power, and movement of the zip line had her breathing out of whack and presto, she was in anxiety. Swinging in before her was Paige, April and Midori, having the time of their life. However, the next tree was more difficult with a sensation that the rope was giving way. Now April was having a panic attack. Brody kept quiet.

Brody couldn't save them with his own blue pill supply. That was strictly his break-glass-in case of emergency supply. Right as he was about to suggest to April he could help out, a massive thunderclap hit with a vicious lighting strike.

Seconds later it was a complete down pour. By the time they got to the next tree, Midori, Paige, and April, were soaking wet. It was a 'can't believe this is happening' moment for Brody. The instructors announced to everyone that they must halt the rides and DO NOT TOUCH those small red frogs: You could die. Now everyone was in a panic. Finally, Brody realized this was getting out of hand, he had the cure and openly said, "I'm not ashamed to admit I've brought my mother's supply of Xanax because sometimes when I fly I get anxious due to turbulence. She gave me enough for all of us and I brought them with me because I had a feeling the heights would freak me out!"

"Thank God!" yelled Mrs. Brentwood, 'Hand them over!"

Brody went into his pocket and realized the tissues were soaking wet. He pulled the pills out and it looked just like a blue dye rag. All the Xanax were gone from the rain. Superman had failed.

The look on Mrs. Brentwood face was in a space between 'do I throw him off now' to 'why is April and Paige wearing leopard skin thongs?'

Darius winked to Brody and said, "There's something strange about this picture."

Brody responded, "I bet you wish you had a son."

He said, "You have no idea, gentleman. You have no idea."

Rio de Janeiro, Night Five

Everyone else was sleeping. That left Brody and April together again. At this point, the days were just long foreplays as they waited for everyone else to go to sleep, so they could enjoy the real trip.

They always met at the same spot: the day bed on the south deck, overlooking the ocean. Room enough for both of them to lie horizontal, facing each other, playing footsies.

As she folded a sheet of paper into an airplane, April said, "Brody, I'm going to throw this off the deck. Think of it as a time machine. As we watch it fly, it will take us a year forward. When it lands, I want you to tell me step two!"

April aggressively fired off the plane, which caught a breeze and descended onto some rocks, where a wave washed it away.

During its flight, Brody was figuring out what to say. Sometimes he wasn't as calculated as he needed or wanted to be. Closing his eyes, he slowly inhaled through his nose and exhaled from his mouth, but he couldn't find his point of entry. He did it again. Nothing. He did it a third time, and then fell into series of thoughts from his past that have been pin balling in his mind for years.

1. He could see himself being born on December 3rd, 1967, a Sunday. By that time, New York City had banned tattoos for six years. The lawmakers had decided that it was illegal for anyone to tattoo a living human being. Brody didn't have any tattoos. He only saw three groups of people who did: Hell's Angels, convicts, and Vietnam vets.

2. Brody got wasted on drugs and went to Dead concerts with a kid named Stone who was the son of Victor McGurk, who turned his loft in the Bowery into a clandestine tattoo parlor. According to Stone, it took his father six years to build a clientele. That's the definition of commitment and passion, of sacrifice and devotion. Victor was only one of five guys doing this in the entire city, one per borough. He was the man for the job in Manhattan.

3. When something is taboo, it glows like pyrite and tattooing had been a taboo art form ever since Abel was caught cheating with his brother's wife. Ironically, although tattoo artists in New York City had to keep a low profile, they left identifying marks on people's bodies. But when and if you found those tattoo parlors, you'd better have your money ready and not be faint of heart, because those spots were unclean—in more ways than one. Also, the artists weren't necessarily talented, and many couldn't spell to save their lives.

4. Lots of people miss the point of why Hitler tattooed the Jews during the Holocaust. But if you know your Levitical priesthood history, as Adolf did, you know that tattooing—the cutting of the skin, the branding of the flesh—is a serious prohibition among pious Jews. So this was not a numbering system to keep a database on who he was going to eliminate. Pretending to be Pharaoh, Adolf wanted to see whose God would prevail. We all know how that story ended.

5. Mark Twain had written an article about anti-Semitism, called "Concerning the Jews," which was published in the September 1899 issue of *Harper's Magazine*. Twain was retracting an incorrect point he had made in an earlier article, in which he had questioned why there were so few Jews fighting in the Spanish-American War.

As it turned out, proportionally, there were more Jews fighting in that war than any other people.

In his retraction, Twain wrote:

> If the statistics are right, the Jews constitute but one per cent of the human race. It suggests a nebulous dim puff of stardust lost in the blaze of the Milky Way. Within proportion, the Jew ought hardly to be heard of; but he

is heard of, has always been heard of. He is as prominent on the planet as any other people, and his commercial importance is extravagantly out of proportion to the smallness of his bulk. His contribution to the world's list of great names in literature, science, art, music, finance, medicine, and abstruse learning are also away out of proportion to the weakness of his numbers. He has made a marvelous fight in this world, in all the ages, and has done it with his hands tied behind him. He could be vain of himself, and be excused for it. The Egyptian, the Babylonian, and the Persian rose, filled the planet with sound and splendor, then faded to dreamstuff and passed away; the Greek and the Roman followed, and made a vast noise, and they are gone; other people have sprung up and held their torch high for a time, but it burned out, and they sit in the twilight now, or have vanished. The Jew saw them all, beat them all, and is now what he always was, exhibiting no decadence, no infirmities of age, no weakening of his parts, no slowing of his energies, no dulling of his alert and aggressive mind. All things are mortal but the Jew; all other forces pass but he remains. What is the secret of his immortality?

Brody wasn't into subculture; he was into subatomic culture. So when he awoke from his thoughts, he said to April, "Here's step two. We get matching tattoos."

April's eyes lit up, as if she had just been electrocuted and had decided to apply *more* voltage.

Brody held up his left hand. "I have a ring on this finger," he said, "which means that I can't break my covenant with Midori until she dies."

April's eyes brightened even more.

Brody took the ring off of his finger.

"See how easy that was?"

But then he put the ring back on.

April rolled her eyes.

"Don't mistake my offer as polygamy bullshit. What I'm saying is, the matching tattoos will be your pick..., but don't pick butterflies! The tattoos will be our wedding rings. That way, wherever you go, there I'll be."

April started crying, as if she had just been proposed to.

Had she been? Brody was in high mania. Fully elevated. Dancing among the stardust. Did he say, "Marry me"? Had they been bangin'? Kissing? Brody hadn't done a thing. Or had he?

Never one to make things nice and easy, he said, "Our first child will be a girl, and we'll call her Hannah. She'll be followed by two sisters, whom you will name."

Brody was desperately trying to heal a broken heart over the murder of his ex-girlfriend who was four months pregnant at the time. But he was compounding the hurt with bad judgment, which would later be compounded by more mistakes. He had no intention of letting April know he was in deep pain.

Brody hadn't uttered the name Hannah in years. He knew she had been alive in the womb because he heard her heartbeat. Life is a bloodline. Her birth would *not* have been the defining moment that started her life. She was not dead in the womb, waiting to become alive when she inhaled oxygen for the first time. That would have been the moment that made her live in this atmosphere, as opposed to living in Vanessa's amniotic fluid. She was alive from the moment she was conceived. The entire construction of her life was in her parents' blood at the precise moment of her conception. Brody talked to Hannah every day, growing to know her as the "squirmy" that moved around in the belly as she listened to Bach.

Brody never told his mother and father that the baby was his. He always regretted that. But somehow his bizarre proposition to April released the weight of pain and guilt and sorrow of having Hannah and Vanessa violently taken from him. It somehow lifted a lid off a boiling pot.

All the while, in April's mind, she had just gotten married, been impregnated, and delivered a girl named Hannah—all in one sentence.

You had to be in Brody's presence to know that he was light and love. Although, this fantasy would've never worked. There's not a sentence I could write or a story I could tell that could capture how fast life goes by. Life can be delusional fun. It can be children in a sandbox chasing bubbles. It can be powerbrokers making deals that squash countries in two seconds flat.

In Rio, on this fifth night, Brody finally felt that awful chasm growing between him and Midori. He felt a bond, a soul tie, being formed, which was going from the base of his spine to April's. He imagined that their love smelled like an orange peel.

25

The Conundrummer

Mid-December 1998

Brody was so deeply affected by people that if he heard anything remotely interesting about another person he would arrange to meet them. The girl's father that I was dating was a retired Marine that was prospecting for a drilling company. She told Brody that her dad used to drop micro-phonic buoys into the ocean to listen for oil and gas. Brody felt this was magnificent and wanted to meet him. So the three of us went to his house for lunch.

Whatever questions Brody had for this guy went out the window as we both found out above being a Marine, he loved taking in stray cats. We were in a regular five-bedroom apartment on the Upper East Side and the place smelt of urine. Toxic urine. How she wasn't embarrassed by this was remarkable to me?

Regardless, this smell and sight of a dozen cats parading around got Brody off his rocker. He could not focus and it turned out he was allergic. Brody's eyes were swelling up. He was sneezing in between every five questions about the nature of listening to the ocean.

At one point the man got up and started snapping his fingers directly into Brody's ear and asked, "You know what that is?"

"No"

"That's what shrimp sound like?"

"Interesting. What does gold sound like?"

"Like the Fourth of July!"

If Brody was normal, he would've just gotten up, apologized and excused himself from the situation.

To make the stakes higher, Brody was "witnessing" concerning the Gospel of Jesus to this guy because he was trying to connect the dots on how we all knew each other. Brody launched into a long-winded discussion about the Bible and the freedom of research and promoting the results of Biblical research.

I could see the ex-Marine signaling to his daughter, my girlfriend, as if he had been trapped on submarines on fire with a more comfortable feeling.

Brody went to the bathroom.

(By the way, the urine smell did not go away. I, myself, am thinking about pissing on some these pages to really bring the story alive but in lieu of that being a crushing blow to sales, just keep saying to yourself, it smells really awful, like poison has spilled and inhalation was causing you serious brain and lung damage.)

Brody came out of the bathroom, and went right back into his mile a minute routine.

Then comes another smell. This smell is familiar. It smells like crap. But so strong that as if were out in the open among us. My girlfriend's father announced "Damn, cats." He looked at his daughter because at this moment Brody was now fascinating him with comparative religion. He was telling this guy "who believes in what and why."

My girlfriend walked down the hallway and headed toward the bathroom and let out out a languishing scream.

She came screaming out of the bathroom.

"Daddy! Daddy! Get in here."

I thought *oh my, she found a dead cat.*

The ex-Marine rushed towards the bathroom. Brody was smirking then gave me that look that was asking me, "What's going on?"

Then I heard a sentence that I never knew could be formed.

"Check the cat's asshole!"

At this point, I went running down the hall to the bathroom, almost stepped on two cats and saw a large pile of crap in the kitty litter box.

The father scooped it out.

It was bigger than most of the cats I saw. He put it in the toilet, flushed it and went about finding the cat that had this large crap.

My girlfriend thought it best we all leave. I couldn't breathe, I couldn't think. I saw something horrible. The smell was putrid. We all said our cordial goodbyes.

Two weeks later, before one of Brody's Bible fellowships, he told me, "Man, wasn't that a trip?"

"Oh, you mean that guy's apartment! It was a piss factory."

Brody said without missing a beat. "The smell was bad but the dad can't be a good Marine because that was my own shit."

I was stunned.

"Dood, the guy couldn't see that was a human dump?" said Brody. "I scooped it out of the toilet and dropped it in the kitty litter."

"Why the hell did you do that?" I asked. "Are you serious? What an awful prank. I saw it! He thought his cat's butt ripped!"

"Benji, I was about to flush it but I couldn't resist. And there's no way anyone's going to publicly accuse anyone of crapping in their kitty litter."

"Brody, you don't see that as a problem and unbecoming."

"Not a problem. Unless you think funny is a problem."

"But it wasn't funny. That's demented."

"You know how much mileage I've been getting out of this story?"

"You're repeating this to people?"

"Benji, you're the last to know."

"You mean the Bible fellowship knows about this?"

The following answer explains Brody in a nutshell.

"Benji, are you stupid?!? Man, I'm telling you because I *knew* you could dig the humor in it!"

I laughed and laughed hard. But as I write this down I wonder if there was any wisdom in crapping into someone else's kitty litter. What was the pragmatic use for doing such a thing?

I wish I could say that was an abnormal thing for him to do, in a sense of avant-garde behavior, but Brody had several dimensions to his personality without it being spilt. He was just a walking conundrum. If he was a musician, he would be a conun-drummer.

The thing that drew me to Brody was his love for everything. It was genuine. You could not counterfeit what I was feeling or even seeing. And I'm one to know. By the time I had met Brody I had finished my stay at Hunter College. I had all my plans, with the wind at my sail, I was going to succeed. It was my God-given right. I'm going to write books. That's when my girlfriend at the time told me about Brody in Fall of 1998.

Early on, even when I was totally infatuated with Brody and his capricious ways of teaching the Bible, I had a sinking feeling this guy doesn't just have skeletons his closet. He was bone avalanche.

Upon spending more and more time with Brody, I used to tell my Grandmother about him. She believed somewhere along my line, he must've gained the supernatural ability to conjure up deception with a 'charming spirit' and it blinded his "victims." However, I assured my Grandma, he doesn't sit at the table with the scorners and mockers. He was not plotting out greed. He was not manipulating.

She said, "This ability starts in the sandbox."

Brody had this amazing thing where he could tell you something about yourself that would bring you a moment of satisfaction and clarity. Sometimes the message relieved you of an incredible burden and sometimes it nailed you to the wall and made you rethink your world.

So one day, after a Sunday brunch with my Grandmother, I asked Brody point blank, "What was your con? What happened to you in the sandbox?"

Brody answered as if he knew I was going to ask this question, "It really was a basic lie to get a girl into repeatedly whispering into my ear. We were in second grade and I sat next to a girl who I fancied. We were playing Chinese whispers. This is where a teacher, bored out of their mind, wanted to hear how a message got distorted through the whispering lips of children. So the teacher said one thing to the child and the teacher gets a kick on how it comes out in the end. In many schools, this was probably a futile exercise but in a public grade school buried in New York you got the United Nations! So heavy accents whispered, and translations misunderstood, you would get a real fine mix up. The girl I fancied relayed the message and I got a hard on. Her warm breath electrified my soul. At that time, I also happened to find a battery in the sandbox. The eight-volt kind. And I was experimenting with placing my tongue to get this sensation that for me was beautiful and calming. So the whisper of this sultry Latin voice was like that battery expect more potent. It was dangerous. So I did my best to pretend I couldn't hear. This went on six, seven times. I was so believable that the teacher sent me to the nurse's office to get my hearing checked."

Brody closed his eyes, slowly inhaled through his nose, and exhaled from his mouth five times, "I am innocent. It was with a pure heart I did this. But I turned it into a portal to how to get my way. The most recent one was a bit more urbane...I pretended to be a schizophrenic."

Now the irony in all of this was that Brody was every bit of a sociopath as a baker that burns their toast but his mission was much more dramatic. He was on a sublime mission from God.

He went on, "Pretending to be schizophrenic is even easier than it sounds. It just takes dedication to the role and being highly focused on the end game. The end game for me was finding the oldest psychotherapist practicing on Fifth Avenue. The logic behind this was a therapist who has seen it all before is probably no longer as sharp as they once were. Perhaps they have stayed on past their prime. But the Fifth Avenue address said, 'm-o-n-e-y.' And I felt maybe someone sitting behind a desk listening to decades of stories of legend *may* want to go out in a blaze of glory. After a few weeks, I marked out an old man named Doctor Edmund Rose. After three years and an investment of four grand on my part, I took him for two hundred and fifty thousand dollars."

"Brody! I can never tell if you're joking."

"Moses is the only man to write his autobiography and admit to murder. Then Paul wrote his and announced himself as the "chief sinner."

I had no idea what he was talking about but I sort of caught the drift. Brody didn't care what I believed, he only cared what can be proven.

Brody's West Village apartment was across the street from Marc Jacobs store, Magnolia bakery and Biography Bookshop. We went outside to get banana pudding

Brody always walked in an odd zigzag pattern down West 11th Street. He was purposely avoiding the cracks in the sidewalks. He took deep breaths of fresh cold air, pulled a yellow pill from his pocket, and popped it into his mouth. He stared at two beautiful girls currently shopping at Marc Jacobs store. They come out of the store and made their way to Biography Bookshop. Outside the store, there were three tables covered with paperbacks of every kind. The two girls were picking up various titles and after a quick glance they put the books down. Nothing was grabbing their attention and Brody was becoming upset by this routine.

Out of nowhere, Brody yelled, "Don't dismiss that! Don't you hear it calling you? I can! Yet you cast it off like morning dental floss."

The girls were immediately disturbed.

Then one of the girls picked up a copy of *War and Peace.*

Brody went into his inhalation routine and I tried to wave the girls to scram but they didn't notice me.

Brody screamed with vengeance, "I AM THE TUTELARY OF CONFABULATION!"

The girls tried desperately to become invisible.

"The answers, in which you so diligently seek, my child, are in those pages." He ranted on at full volume. "And yet that book was written in Russia in 1865! That's because books are a continuous magnitude of life where no part can be distinguished from neighboring parts except by arbitrary division. We are all connected by books and I am the defender of the faith! You may think you are who you are but you're not. You're Natasha Rostova! And all is ruled by a cruel determinism."

I thought to myself, *Can we all just die now?* But I grabbed hold of

Brody, who just fifteen minutes ago was teaching the Bible in full peace and said, "Brody, you're scaring me, man! Stop this joke! Apologize!"

He escaped my hold and went right up to the girls and said, "That book is about a girl who completely fulfills herself through marriage and motherhood. The book is telling you to be fruitful and multiply. And yet I stand here and see two of the most beautiful girls I've ever seen and you have no rings. It is not good for man to be alone. Please. Be fruitful and multiply. We need more like you."

I was now forcibly pushing Brody away from this scene and took him back up to his apartment.

Once we got in and Brody took a toad with four legs and placed it in a box with mirrors lining the four walls. The toad, amazed at its own appearance from every angle, broke into an oily sweat. He collected the sweat with an eyedropper. He then dropped the liquid into a jar and stirred it with a willow branch.

I'm saying to myself, *Holy shit! This guy has lost his noodle. This is not Brody. Who the fuck is this? I mean it is Brody but I'm scared. Why did I even go back into his apartment.*

"When the toad sees itself," Brody said, "it freaks out and this sweat is a drug better than LSD. But you got to let it sit in the sun for thirty days before it takes effect. I sell it for a thousand an ounce."

I immediately walked out of the room. During my time away with him, I found out he was the supplier of a drug named "Honey Reverie."

It was distributed by 260 all throughout the city to rich, white preppie kids. And 260 weren't even interested in building a drug empire. They would literally, take the money for the drugs, hands the drugs over, then beat the shit out of the kids and take the drugs and money back. Take the drugs themselves and head to Central Park flying high.

The duality and totality of Brody was he was a Bible teacher. He taught the Bible through and through but he lived in Manhattan and had them Manhattan blues.

At one point in time, the number one dealer of Honey Reverie was Don Tenenbaum. The money they made off of it was washed clean through Nicky Crowbar's Aunt's Restaurant. That clean money was invested into Ken Rosenberg's Art gallery that was to be named Endangered Species. These were enterprising guys. However, from that episode on, I wiped myself clean of hanging with Brody until he called me out of the blue five years later to talk about Rio de Janeiro.

26

Iron Sharpens Iron If You Let It

June 14, 1989, Part Five

If you lived in Manhattan your whole life, you have a friend usually ten blocks in any direction. Knowing he's headed back to UNC for the year, and that Hardcore Mordecai had him racing at the ungodly hour of three in the morning, Jack Track dropped by Hardcore Mordecai's spot on the Upper West Side.

Because of his line of work, Hardcore Mordecai lived in what they call an SRO a.k.a. Single Room Only where everyone on the floor shared a bathroom. These types of buildings were being torn down each and every day and he happened to be in the one of the last standing ones of the Old New York. In his late twenties, he had a mohawk but he happened to be a pious Jew the type that has a Kippuh stapled to his head. It made for a spectacular sight.

Mordecai opened the door and said, "Whatcha cookin' in Carolina?"

"Chicken wings and mashed potatoes."

"That's food..., in theory. Damn, you disappoint me, Jack! How about the lasagna? You make the freshman girls that lasagna, right?"

Jack broke the news, "Nah man. Nothing but shit ingredients down there. When the other guys cook..., they don't even lick their own fingers."

"Lachi," Mordecai said, "I'll send you a care package. Treat yourself to a Napoleon."

He pointed to a box of pastries from Ferrara's.

"One of the brothers," Jack said proudly, "gets this Cognac shipped in from his parents."

Mordecai liked the sound of that, "Fantastic. What else is happening?"

"I got this mad cool professor. She can really get—

Mordecai interrupted, "Profess her. Address her. Undress her."

"Now why you got dis me like that? College ain't your speed?"

"All of a sudden Jack Track goes to a fancy college," Hardcore Mordecai leaned in, "talking about your brothers frat and I ain't your speed. Perhaps you should unlearn what you've learned and spend some time learning what they don't teach you."

"You're a fool of not going to college. You would have loved it."

Mordecai reminded him, "I can always go back. Look, I'm gonna level with you. I don't know whose gonna win this race but whatever the outcome, this is truly the end of an era."

"But I don't run anymore, Mordy."

"I'm not asking you to win the New York City marathon. You just gotta keep the record from going to a Dalton kid. It'd be a sin!"

Jack reminded him of his subtext, "You mean to say don't let the record go to a monkey."

Mordecai snapped him a look and said, "Lachi, you either eat the matza or you don't."

"It's not my race to win anymore," Jack said.

Changing the subject Mordecai said, "I'm getting out of the drug game, Jack."

Jack didn't believe it for one tenth of one second.

"No, for real," Mordecai said, "I'm concentrating on becoming a botanist. Outside of my dick, it's the only thing that grows around here. Actually, I got this manuscript here and its gonna change my entire game around."

Hardcore Mordecai handed him a pile of papers entitled *The Uncrowned King.*

"Nice. When did you write this?"

"That's the beauty of it all," Mordecai said, "I didn't. A cat named John Kennedy Toole wrote it. Check it out. He won the Pulitzer prize back in 1980."

"No shit," Jack said, "So why do you have this?"

"Ole JKT, the dumbo cocksucker killed himself back in 1969! He wrote a book called *Confederacy of Dunces* then his momma got it published and the shit won Pulitzer. So it just so happens people thought he never wrote again but nah—I got this cousin who knew his joint and then bam! I got a copy of his last book that went unpublished. So I've been sending it out to publishers except with my name on it."

Jack was in disbelief, "That's so weak. Why did you do that?"

"It's my unique way out of the SRO banger. Dontcha get it. Crack is takin' over. I got girls, beautiful girls with their entire future ahead of them and one hit of this and its soulless hooker overnight. The cops have no idea what this is. In the lab it shows up as baking soda. Lawmakers are going full steam ahead with writing laws on the books."

Jack steered the conversation back, "But why are saying you wrote something you didn't?"

Mordecai admitted, "I changed his name because – he is dead and – it got rejected already like seven times. I may even off myself if it keeps getting rejected. But I really had to change his name on this shit because the ending was weak and the girls weren't strong enough so I made some tight changes. Don't give me grief."

Jack recapped, "I understand leaving this evil drug alone. But the new career is ripping off dead writers?"

"Do me this favor," Mordecai leveled with him. "Beat this punk. If you beat this kid then you can walk away knowing the memory will last forever."

Jack got up and found his way to the door as if the conversation and Mordecai's plan didn't matter.

Feeling slighted Mordecai said, "I heard that to get into your frat you were laid out with some tar and feathers and had to go into a dark room where someone spanked your bare ass with a paddle."

"Rumors."

"Rumors are premature facts, Jack"

"It's true. What's it to you?"

"Well geez, Jack, if I knew you were that hard up to be accepted and make friends. I would've made you put on a blonde wig and play with my balls."

"That's what Ken Rosenberg is here for!" retorted Jack.

The epitome of what a studio apartment can look like when you have no money to spend. But hey, this was a downtown apartment of Ramona, Jack's ex-girlfriend, self-proclaimed stylist—it may purposely look this way. Much has changed since they last saw each other. She was chain smoking, wearing ripped underwear that would look better on your grandmother, and her slippers made a clapping noise every time she walked. Jack motioned to her cigarette. She handed it to him. He lit his with hers. He took a long drag, "We should give cigarettes up for good."

Ramona threw him a glance that suggested she has heard better ideas.

"Remember when you were mine forever?" Jack said.

Jack handed her the rose he stole.

She smelled it and said, "Jack, it was more like a year. Want something to drink?"

Ramona took two glasses out from the sink. They sat at the busted up kitchen table with chairs that don't match and she grabbed a carton of milk from the counter. She poured him a cup of milk. There was not much left for her. Jack motioned to her asking if she wanted some of his. Ramona nodded her head. She opened a drawer, took out a spoon and got up to open the refrigerator. Then she took out a jar of honey, opened it and plunged the spoon in. Scrapping what little honey was left in the bottom of the jar, she dropped it into Jack's cup and stirred the milk. Once she was finished she licked the rest off the spoon.

"You hear I'm racing tonight?" said Jack.

"I'm privy to it."

"You coming?"

Ramona looked at her mess of an apartment and said, "I got some cleaning up to do." Pointing to his UNC gear, "So where can I get a sweater like that?"

"All summer long," Jack said, "people have been bustin' my balls about my colors."

"It seems like you're showing off,' she retorted, "like anyone here gives a shit about North Carolacky."

"Hey! It's where I go to college!"

"Go to school in the south of France *then* wave *that* flag. Maybe no one will bother you then. So whatcha learning over there?"

"I'm majoring in economics."

"I didn't mean what the books they making you memorize. I meant about yourself. Attend any Klan meetings?"

Jack was tired of hearing it from everyone. He has been sexed up by an thirteen year old and was simply looking for some action.

He slathered it on thick, "I found out I miss you big time."

Ramona knew his game, "Go sell it on the corner."

Jack took a sip from his milk, then looked at her empty glass.

"I'm gonna get ready for the race." Ramona said.

"That's the spirit!" Jack exclaimed,

Breaking his heart with a direct hit, "Not really. I wanna see you lose."

She got up, took off her shirt and headed into the shower.

Jack walked into the bathroom and was taken aback by the smell of mildew from the shower curtain. It was stained a piss yellow with streaks of dirt built up. The water came out in spurts. Ramona lathered up amidst these unsanitary conditions. It looked like the soap was dirty.

He removed his clothing and got into the shower. Ramona was briefly surprised but since they did this frequently in the past she was not startled. Jack put a dab of shampoo on his hand and rubbed it in her hair. She was obviously distracted and disinterested when Jack pulled her in close for a kiss. She was not passionate but she kissed him anyhow.

27

Jesus Saves but so Does Cannoli

September 27, 1991

Brody went to see Don for the first time at Riker's Island, a hell with ten thousand inmates in ten different jails.

Before he visited, he had just read Joseph Campbell's *The Power of Myth*, which is about who believes what, and why. But Brody had thrown it against the wall, because he's a seeker of absolute truth.

Looking up at the ceiling, he said, "If there's a God, an almighty creator of the universe…, if you exist, you *should* be able to hear me. When I see Don in jail, whatever he tells me will be the absolute truth. The whole truth, and nothing but the truth. The truth that sets me free. Whatever Don says, 'so be it.' I will dedicate my life to it."

As soon as the words were out of his mouth, Brody didn't give a damn about what he had said. He was just being his usual charmingly odd self.

When he was a hundred yards from the entrance of Riker's, he was nervous. With each step, he heard multiple radio stations, the squeaking of sneakers, and the clanking of steel, as if a railroad were being built. But he saw nothing. Everything was behind the walls.

Damn!

Before he got to see Don, he had fifteen minutes of paperwork to fill out. This was in addition to the application Don's attorney had given him weeks earlier to get on Don's visitor's list. In a waiting room, Brody was searched for contraband, which put him in a sour mood. The German Shepherd's growling didn't help.

Don was sitting behind thick glass, sporting fresh bruises.

When he picked up the phone, he said, "Well, the kid next to me killed himself last night because he was ass-fucked by a gang. I heard I was next if I didn't just give it up sweet…. How *you* doin?"

Brody went full-white-lip blood-pressure-elevation dizzy. When he shook his head to snap out of it, the phone slipped out of his hands because he sweated that fast. He tried to dry his palms off where he thought his legs were, but they were jumping as if he were on coke. The whole premise freaked him out. Brody wanted to bust through the glass to break Don out.

Don had been visited before, by his uncle, and seen the same reaction. I guess you get used to hell. I guess. But Don was cool, calm, and collected. As if he had something to prove.

"Brody, it's gonna be okay, man," Don said. "I was visited by Jesus Christ. Do you know who that is?"

"Sort of."

"He's the absolute truth, man. The whole truth, and nothing but the truth. The truth that makes you free."

Stunned by the exact wording he had used earlier, and by the deal he brokered with the Almighty Creator of the Universe, Brody said from the depth of his soul, "I've seen the light, and I accept Him as my Lord and Savior."

"Excuse me?"

"Huh? What do you mean?"

"Homeboy," Don said, "I was just fuckin' with you, man. I was pullin' a prank. I've bumped into guys in here who *think* they are Jesus, but Muhammad is up in here, too. But we really need Guccione Junior. Can you get him in here? Because he knows how to throw a fuckin' party? And all we got here is drama. I mean, you got to suck dick or kill a dood to survive in here. So let me make this clear to you. There are choices you make in life, choices you don't make, and choices that are made *for* you. You get where I'm coming from? When you see your momma smokin' a crack pipe, your own pipe dreams go up in smoke."

Still in his conversion to Christianity phase, Brody said, "The truth is a dying giant, and I'm going to nurse her back to health."

"Brody! Make me one promise."

"Of course. Anything."

"Visit me here next week, and bring me four boxes of cannoli from Venero's. Not from de Robertis, because Venero's gonna keep dicks out of my ass and mouth."

Brody winked at him.

"What does lasagna get you?"

"Quit fuckin' around, Brody! I mean it. Four boxes of cannoli."

"Why four boxes?"

"One for protection, one for the C.O.'s, one to dole out when I need to and one for the Latin Kings. I'm not here to encroach on territory. I'm here to make friends. And I use that term loosely. I'm swimming in-between slimy-paranoia and learning the underpinnings of what the fuck entertainment now means."

"Hey, Doby, you tell the good artists in there that Salvador Dali was supposed to come here in 1965 to teach, but the pussy chickened out. Apparently, he sent a painting, and it's hangin' in there somewhere. Go tag it up, 260."

Don put his hand on the glass, and Brody puts his against it.

"Next week," Don said, "four boxes of cannoli from Venero's."

"Don, the Lord will protect you. Two six zero for life."

"Two sixty," Don replied. "Till death do us part."

28

Opening Night at Palácio da Justiça

Rio de Janeiro, Night Six

On this particular night, the group did not go out to dinner, but instead decided to cook some food themselves and have a birthday cake for Paige. The night was festive, with music blaring. The Brentwoods left the place to the "kids" to have cocktails by themselves at a Flamenco concert. Darius told Brody to make sure that nothing got out of hand.

Act One: April and Midori

Midori, who was the de facto bartender, was making serious Mojitos. As Brody's woman, she knew how to get down. But she was really an angel-hippie bride way more than a femme fatale. So she was smoking a fat joint—the Brazilian gooey kind.

"Whatever's the normal amount of rum," April said, "double it…, no, triple it. I need to blow off steam. I feel like I've been in shackles, with Paige's parents treating all of us like kids."

"Oh, I don't see it like that at all," said Midori, in-between tokes. "They're protecting us from danger. Turn one corner here or there, and who knows? You gotta be sober in this type of atmosphere. I'm not one to get drunk. I just need a joint to unwind. I mean, I know what you're talking about, but I just see it differently."

"Married to Brody, you probably have to see it fifteen different ways."

"If you find what Brody does endearing, then it wouldn't matter if it's one time or two hundred. Once you get into a groove with him, he's jazz. They say jazz is dead, but what they mean to say is jazz is out of style. It's alive and well with Brody. He's free form. I like my men the same way I like my joints."

"You mean, short and fat?"

Midori giggled. "No, I like to inhale and then blow the bullshit smoke back in their face…. Wow! This is real fine shit!"

"I agree with you. I adore having a great buzz that lasts for hours. I never understood what Paige sees in coke. It's a fleeting high. I want to feel warm, fuzzy, not constantly vibrating. I need a great, monumental buzz. Something that reaches down and makes me feel like I'm being poured into a cistern. If I don't get the buzz I want tonight, I'll blow my chance to know what it was like to live in the Garden of Eden."

"I got you covered, April. With all the booze we've got here, I'll get you where you wanna go fast, and you'll stay there long. I can't believe we've already been here for six nights. Feels like we got here yesterday."

Act Two: Paige and Brody

While that conversation was going on between Midori and April at the bar, Brody was in the living room, chopping up coco with Paige. Brody broke out the cocaine because he felt it would be irresponsible for people to take globs of his prescription meds with alcohol. Once he had his lines all carefully laid out and good to go, Paige snorted three in succession.

"Look," she said, "I know you guys are mixing up the drinks and breaking out the coke, and I'm down for whatever, but you can't be messing with April. I see how she looks at you. She asked me how you shaped me into a sexual being."

Brody rolled his eyes in bewilderment.

"How did you answer that doozy?"

Casually, Paige muttered, "I asked her what she had in mind."

Brody threw her that give-me-a-break-already look, which pissed Paige off.

"I'm on the fuckin' outside looking in," she said, "with a fuckin' sunburn on my own fuckin' birthday! I know you, Brody. I know what you're up to!"

"Look," he said, "April's twenty year old from Wyoming, and practiced in Biblical instruction. I'm a hundred years old in New York seduction. We're not an item! Are you kidding me? What if your father sees me with her, or busts in on us making love? My life would be ruined in ten seconds flat!"

Paige had the gall to say, "If that happened, I would back you up! Just listen to me. Don't fuck April tonight. I mean, Mojitos and coke and pot and God knows what! I'm not stupid, Brody!"

"Who said you were? This is just another party, Paige. How many have we been to where nothing happens and everything happens? We don't cross lines. You're always telling me I saved your life, or I'm in your DNA. But all of a sudden, you tell a lie to a redhead from Wyoming, and now you're running scared. Where's Paige, the Queen Bee? The girl who's worth 41k an ounce. Can *she* show up tonight?"

But nothing Brody said could stop Paige from her plotting and scheming and preventing her being replaced by April. It was a love triangle from hell. That's what it was. No three ways about it.

"Brody," she said, "I hate to do this to you, but if you sleep with April here in Rio, on my time and my parents' dime, I'm gonna do my best to spread rumors and bring your house of cards down. What's that fuckin' word you always use?"

"*Intoxicating?*"

"No! The one that means next to last."

"Oh, *penultimate.*"

"Right. Don't sleep with April. It's our penultimate night in Rio.

This is your only chance to sleep with her, because my parents are gone. They'll be here tomorrow night. I know you, Brody. You would never sleep with her with my parents around."

Paige did another line of coke, while Brody nervously cracked open his bottle of Prozac.

"I'm deadly serious, Brody," she snarled. "Don't do this to me. My pristine word against yours. Please. You think I can't lay on the charm? You ain't seen nothin' yet! I'll have them believing you fuckin' flew into the Twin Towers once I get through with you! Don't sleep with April in Rio. Period!"

"Paige, I'm married man. And you're coming off like a girl with some sort of father complex. We're friends. Now and forever. Forever and now. You sound scared."

"Let me do a Brody on Brody. I'm scared because ever since you met me at twelve, you realized I arose quickly."

"Don't you mean *arouse* quickly?"

"Shut the fuck up, asshole! You heard me. I seem to be inept at everything, and the silver spoon jammed down my throat is now a coke spoon in a Chanel purse. For crying out loud, my parents had me in front of psychoanalysts before I saw my first soccer coach. And you saved me more times than you'll ever know. But ya know what trait I ended up taking from you? Jumping in the sack faster than you can say, 'jumping in the sack.' And guess what? Every single guy has told me I'm a terrible lay. Sure, I say to myself I crush it, but I must admit here and now, they all say I suck at it."

Act Three: Paige and April

Paige stormed off toward the balcony, where April, between gulps of her volcanic Mojito, was broadcasting that Midori should get another one up and running.

April was sauced. Through slurred speech, she said to Paige, "I wan' your bressing to shleep with Brody."

Two precious beauties. Friends from college. Looking for blessings to become mistresses. The world was backwards. Or was Brody backwards, and the world was forwards? Who could tell anymore? Everyone says that alcohol, especially the type they call "spirits," are truth serums. That never made much sense to me. I, for one, am what they call a happy drunk.

"Paige, I'm gonna shleep which him tonight."

All April was doing was confirming Paige's worst nightmare.

"Paige, do you hears me? I wan' Brody in side me."

April giggled uncontrollably as she took another sip. Looking out at the stars over the immense South Atlantic, she said, "He's got me, Paige…, look, hine, an' stinker. It's a crossed star deal, just like he wrote. But I want in. I wanna put on the brack mask and groves and rob the bank. Paige, I need your bressing. Otherwives, I may never have this chance again. Once we land in New York, everything will be over."

Coked up to the gills, Paige was restraining her anger.

"This is my fuckin' party, bitch! Godfuckin' dammit! Why did my parents even invite Brody! Ugh!!!!"

April was not having it.

"Bullshit, sis! If you don' give me your bressing to shleep with Brady, I'll tell Midori you blanged him! And you can bed your ass she'll believe me. I've got a f-f-feeling she already s-s-suspects. I see way she loogs at you."

Act Four: Midori and Brody

Midori was in a haze of herb as she flashed Brody that "I know you know I know what's up" glare.

Brody had seen this look from Midori ever since the first time he had laid eyes on her. But they were not swingers, and they were not in an open relationship. They were just madly in experience with each other.

"It's not exactly what you think," he said. "But it's pretty darn close. Think of it as a parenthetical moment that will end as soon as the plane lands."

Midori, a veteran of countless wars with Brody, both on the receiving and the sending ends, was resigned to agree.

"Brody," she said, "I've seen you pull rabbits out of your hat, heal a diseased man, but I've never seen you dizzy on two pieces of trash like this. Is it the Brazilian air? I mean, that waitress was a perfect bombshell, and I saw her give you that 'anytime, anywhere' look, but you ignored it. You've snapped thirty photos of April, so she's got you wrapped around her finger. And whatcha gonna do when Midorimania runs wild on you?"

Brody's usual feeling of joy was stolen from him. He felt like he was playing a losing hand, and there was no way out. He had gone for temptation and was fully trapped.

Watching him in contemplation, she said, "Brody, they couldn't handle you even with a full set of instructions. This is low-hanging fruit. You're getting lazy. Put an end to this!"

Brody flashed a fearful smile as he watched Paige storming off from April. Walking away from Midori, he waved Paige over to the other deck.

Act Five: Paige and Brody

On the northern side of the house, there was a view of the deep jungle. It was scary for a guy who had grown up thinking that roaches were the worst.

Paige, who was coked up in that insane can't-think-straight way, had just heard April say that she wanted to bang Brody. He was a rainforest, and she was gonna chop it down.

Brody knew this was a high-wire act and was prepared for anything.

"There's a meat cleaver in this house," Paige said. "I'm gonna get it and cut your—"

"Paige!" Brody shouted, interrupting her in a fever pitch. "Grab ahold of yourself. I'm not having some May-to-December fling with your friend. I haven't even touched her. You're not seeing things clearly. I'm all about *you*. And you only. Always have been and always will be. But for God's sake, I'm not here for you *or* April. I'm here for reasons beyond your imagination. You only see birthday cake and your own expectations. But my point of view says, 'Stop thinking about yourself!' You think I was gonna come all the way here and ruin your party? You gotta admit there could be a nasty panther somewhere in there that would be more than happy to eat us alive. It's the goddamn Brazilian air. Have you had the tangerines? They'll give you heart-attack-level blood pressure. Midori's high, April's passing out drunk, you're coked out, and I'm not contemplating suicide, but I'd rather kill myself than have you chop me to bits. So please calm down. When have I ever led you astray? Tell me I'm wrong. You've turned your own life into a mess, and you don't think I know how deep we're connected. You say, 'Brody, you're in my DNA.' And I gotta ask, does DNA mean Do Not Attach? Because all you do is go for months ignoring me. I'm shocked I'm even here. I'm the Keeper of the Corny. The Custodian of the Senseless. I got no plans to deal with a potatohead from Wyoming. Christ almighty! Stop with the coke! It doesn't treat you kindly."

Brody practically had Paige hypnotized. If he had said, "Jump off the roof," Paige would have jumped, and then asked from her hospital bed, "How'd I do?"

Instead he said, "You know, Paige, when April asked you how I shaped you into a sexual being, if you had any decency, you could've said, 'You know what? I lied. But here's the truth. It was a healthy, paternal, mentor relationship. It was everything and anything it needed to be on any given moment, because he actually gives a shit about me. It was an extraordinary relationship, and he told me, when I was sixteen, that when I turn twenty-one I was gonna kick him across the sands of time. And here we are. And I told you I slept with him because sex sells.

And long boring stories about salvation and redemption hit the dustbin. And there are people who literally spend their weekends reenacting the Civil War, instead of singing songs that never have been sung before.'"

Paige took off her shirt to reveal a tattoo on her back. A gorgeous piece that he had never noticed before because her father Darius would not allow such things.

"Whadda think?" Paige said.

It was an image of a spider making a web.

Brody said, "I got your tattooed back. Always had. Always will. I never cared what they thought 'bout us. I had your back. And when you went away, it was because you had to cover someone else's back. I understand that now. I didn't then. Because we all need someone to lookout for us. Because we don't have eyes behind our head. But we've always been partners. Cohorts in time. We're not fifty-fifty. That's a split. We're one hundred percent ownership of misfit power. I got your tattooed back."

Paige hugged Brody. Then he walked away as April entered the arena and drank *another* Mojito.

Act Six: April and Paige

With a sense of dread that Brody had been right all along, Paige realized that there was never a reason to lie, but in her coke binge, she still couldn't bring herself to tell April the truth. Nevertheless, she was briefly inspired to tell April about a part of Brody that April would never experience.

"Take it from me, April," she said. "You suck one dick, you suck them all. But walk through Central Park with Brody, that's where he's so different from everyone else. He grew up in poverty, you know. Ran with a crazy gang. Half of them are in jail, the other half are dead. He literally gave a different name to every tree on every street in New York, from First Avenue to Fifth Avenue. He had to drop out of ninth grade, but wanted so badly to be cultivated that he read every book, one by one, on every subject, whether he cared about it or not. Every moment was an adventure for him. He can't really dance, but he's read every biography of every ballerina. Who does such a thing? He was saved by the Public Library. I'll have a lifelong friendship with him. You'll be a shooting star."

"A shootin' tar hash nothin' at all to do wit' stars! It's asteroids fallin' into our atmosphere, burnin' up…, amazin' streaks of light. Your metaphoria wasn't thought through thoroughly. I have no probrums bein' an amazin' streak of—"

At that moment, April vomited over the railing.

"All you wanna do, Paige, is tear me down…, tear me an' Brady apart. What's it to ya, anyway? *Maybe* there's no *us*, but I have a gut f-f-feelin' an' I t-t-trust it. You act like you're above it all, Your Highness, but you're as low as a weasel. How many times at Vassar did I turn my back on you for one loushy sec, and you were wrappin' your legs aroun' my date? Jus' cut me some slack. Couples split up all the time, Paigey-Waigey. It's called divorce. Brady and I are fallin' in love. It jus' happens."

Wow! Paige thought. *And I thought I was delusional! She thinks she can replace Midori?*

With renewed confidence, Paige said, "Alrighty, April, I'll give you my blessing, but with one asterisk. You can't sleep with Brody here in Rio. You can do it back in New York. I'm sure he'll put you up in some dump motel, and you can have all the fun you want. But nothing here. Okay? And let me add this: if you sleep with him here tonight, I'll place a curse on your soul."

Confident about her own devious plans, April said, "Okay, P-P-Paige. Thank you. Fair enough."

Act Seven: Paige and Midori

"Paige," Midori said, "I'd like to tell you something. I've given my body, soul, and spirit to God. And my father was a pastor. He died six months before I met Brody. After he died, my faith died. But Brody taught me that faith is meaningless. It's all about proof and what you do. He's proven time and time again that humanity is frail, and God is real. I've heard rumors. But rather than discuss them, I know you know what I'm talking about. Regardless, if they're true, I forgive you."

Paige went into shell shock because the rumors were lies. Midori was really forgiving Paige for lying about sleeping with Brody. Inside, Paige's coke-fueled mind was screaming, *This can't be happening to me!*

"I'm forgiving you," Midori continued, "because I need to be forgiven myself. I'm not a piece of merchandise that can be bought and sold. I'm not a precision tool. I'm not a board member, shareholder, or president. I'm just a girl who had a pastor as a father. And by forgiving you, I'm seeing the best of what God has to offer. Because it's painful for me to do it, but I'm feeling the pain leave me as I do it."

Was Brody the luckiest sonovabitch on Earth, or what? In one fell swoop, Midori was forgiving the girl who had lied about an adulterous affair with her husband, who in turn had just given a "blessing" to another woman to have an adulterous affair with her husband.

If any woman—besides Midori—was ever going to play games with Brody, she had to be at least ten steps ahead of him, because God's mercy shined on him more than on anyone else.

29

Born on the Bridge, Die on the Bridge

June 14, 1989, Part Six

Nicky walked around in the background of the Limelight, admiring the girls dancing. His attention was grabbed when he heard his name being shouted, "Crowbar!"

He was surrounded by kids looking for drugs and screamed, "NickNick, help me out over here."

Nicky pushed his way through the crowd. A couple of young girls pestered Hardcore Mordecai about the assortment of drugs he dealt. On the streets, he goes by the name "Healer". The dealer named healer. He lied to the girls that the place was crawling with narcs, "I'm being watched". He said this so he could have a private conversation with Nicky. He escorted him into the V.I.P. section and handed him a joint.

Hardcore Mordecai rhetorically asked, "Why am I pushing drugs to kids? What the hell happened to me?"

Nicky said with emphasis, "Not going to college could be a reason."

Mordecai shrugged, "Lachi, I went to Hebrew college in Minnesota. Just for a couple of months. After that I came back."

"Why did you come back?"

"When you're born on the bridge, you live on the bridge, you die on the bridge."

Hardcore Mordecai waved a bag of drugs in front of Nicky, "Besides, no Rabbi's gonna make this kosher."

"Well, I think I wanna die somewhere else."

Aghast Mordecai said, "What do you mean? I heard you're helping out Charlie Parmesan at the restaurant."

Nicky shook his head, "Nah. I'm off to California for school."

Even more upset, Mordecai said, "Whatcha thinking, Lachi? Now's the time you can really live life, bro. No strings attached. Don't go to some stupid college. The things you can do right here. Lachi, look at me."

"I'm looking mio fratello."

"If I were you," Mordecai said empathically, "I'd stay. But I wish you the best. Remember, you always do what you can't help doing."

"That's what we say."

"Hold it. Did you tell Jack about the race?"

"He wasn't too thrilled about it."

"No problem. He'll come around."

Cyan and Ken were looking at a brownstone plotting.

"We got to be real fast about this." Ken said. "In and out. Ten minutes tops."

Now they were now directly in front of the entrance door to the brownstone.

Ken looked at a list of names next to buttons. Ken pressed the "Rotondo" button, waited anxiously. Ken pushed the button again. They waited again. No answer. Just to make sure that no one is home, Ken pushed the button again.

Cyan pondered, "We do rather hurt someone else than help ourselves."

"This no time to get soft. You getting soft?"

Cyan protested, "I'm all saying is the secret of being happy doesn't lie within this apartment."

"And your point is?" Ken said.

Cyan reframed his idea.

"Life is not about 260. It ain't even about us. It's about giving a wake up call to someone. Tell them the city isn't a perfect place."

Ken pushed the button. He's positive that no one was home. Ken put the key in the first door and they entered the hallway.

They put on their disguises. Ken wore a propeller hat with X-Ray glasses and Dracula fangs. Cyan was wearing a Frankenstein mask. Quietly, they walked inside the apartment. At that precise moment. The next-door neighbor opened their door to go outside not suspecting any trouble.

Startled, Ken pushed Cyan into the apartment and he closed the door. No matter how much you plan you always have to be prepared for the unexpected. This left Ken to sweat it out in the hallway with the neighbor.

In his always charming mode, Ken said, "Good evening. Masquerade party. I see you weren't invited. Unless you're coming as mister boring normal."

The neighbor giggled.

Cyan opened the door and the boys looked as stupid as can be are just staring at the neighbor hoping for the best.

The boys closed the door. The neighbor's instinct tells him to wait a second. The neighbor now concerned makes a phone call—presumably the police.

The boys were in the living room of the apartment. They were thinking. They get to work rearranging the furniture! These guys we're not there to steal a thing. They're just pulling a prank. They moved the couches and the TV. They changed the painting on the wall. They moved the plants. Etc. They were working fast. Ken moved a small occasional chair next to an accent table away from the large overstuffed sofa. They saw a long empty wall. Cyan and Ken carried a long narrow table and placed it against the wall. Cyan grouped pictures over the table. Cyan gestured for Ken to move the large sofa from directly against the wall about a foot or so away and put a plant that as been by the window behind it.

On another wall, Ken positioned a mirror on the wall. They moved a small bench from another room in the living room and place magazines, journals and newspapers under the table.

The boys stood together and admired their work. Cyan took out a disposable camera and snapped a picture and said, "I have to take a leak before we jet."

Cyan walked down a hallway and peeked into the bedroom.

He became astonished.

His eyes widen then he took a step back.

He had seen a vision.

It was a completely bare white wall.

There were no paintings hanging on it. To Cyan it appeared to be a large canvas. He muttered, "Oh my God."

Cyan walked into the room towards the wall. Ken took notice and followed him.

He said, "This wall. I've dreamt of a wall like this."

He pulled out his spray can and just as he was about to tag it up, he paused and said to no one in particular, "We will meet again, my dear wall."

30

Art Is Not Priceless

March, 1997

Standing in awe of Picasso's 1955 painting, "Les Femmes d'Alger (Version 0)" was Ken Rosenberg staring intently at its use of color and shapes.

He was in the Upper East Side apartment of Victor and Sally Ganz. The Ganzs were legendary art collectors and in their apartment was masterworks from everyone to Jasper Johns, Louis Eilshemius and of course, Ken Rosenberg's philosophical arch nemesis Pablo Picasso. The paintings were priceless but headed to auction in a few months time. The rumored numbers were ten to twenty-five million a piece: an unfathomable concept.

Ken's father, Barry, was an attorney who had connections and told him about this private collection hanging in an apartment and its once-in-a-lifetime opportunity to see it under these circumstances.

"What circumstances could those be?" Ken asked his dad.

"The way the market for modern art is headed means it will be less likely you'll ever had a Ganz type collection in an apartment. This is not a posh home. Ganz bought fifteen Picassos for a few hundred grand back in the 50s'. It's just not a feasible idea anymore. These paintings are worth millions now. And who can afford a million on a painting?

These aren't trophy pieces for a Czar. This is an art lover who happen to get his hands on Picasso's."

"Dad, you're such a romantic, a few hundred grand back in the 50s is probably close to a million in todays dollars!"

"Will you quit being a wise crackin' wisen heimer?" Barry said. "I'm asking if you want access to something few people will get. Stop busting my chops. You know how lucky you'll be to see all of these in one place! Mark my words!"

"I wasn't busting your chops," said Ken, "I'm saying if you think the guy who bought these paintings had some sensibility about artistic statements, he wouldn't have bothered with Picasso. Picasso screams investment just like he screamed NO to war but YES to young women. Sure there's so much too love but there's so much more to fight for and he stayed away from that game."

"Ken, what in God's name are you ramblin' about? Picasso is Picasso. John Huston is John Huston. These are heavyweights of artistic expression like Charlie Parker. Ganz had an eye for talent. If he lived to see your stuff he would have bought it."

"Picasso may have been the real deal but the baby-boomers have turned him into a blue-chip stock. But buying a quarter of million dollars of Picasso's in the 50s was an investment. Sounds like one, smells like one, feels like one which goes to show that it was an investment, dad."

"Kenny! I'M IMPLORING YOU TO GO! This would be like walking into a book. This isn't Warhol soup cans! You wanna talk trends and meaningless pop art. Fine, let's talk Warhol but this is Picasso! And I don't care that he was a pacifist. Your mother drives me nuts with that shit."

Here was Ken standing in front of the Picasso, with a No. 8 pencil wondering *should I tag this? An unnoticeable tag so I'm attached to Picasso or should I tear it to shreds and show Picasso that is life is about getting your hands dirty?*

Ken did no such thing. He just stood and admired the painting. It's substance. But his mind was always drawn to *Guernica*. He wanted to make his mark on someone else's art. An unwittingly collaboration of two artists, worlds apart.

Pablo lived to the ripe age of 91 and died a few months after Ken was born. But Ken feels the pull. The tug of destiny.

Ken Rosenberg, graffiti artist, known vandal, was about to get his first big break. Eric Daniels was going to buy four of Ken's largest canvases. Little does Eric know that two of the pieces are plagiarized from Cyan Laurent and another is from Don Tenenbaum. His lone original was the one that caught Eric Daniels's eye and it was Cyan that invited Ken to his first Eric Daniels SoHo ready-for-action art orgy back in the Summer of 1989 but Cyan wasn't able to make it. But there's no better first impression than knocking the person out.

Royce's loft space gallery was artfully arranged to be scuzzy but nobody was actually scuzzy. It was all twerpy decadence but suggested a silk tact. It was essentially a painting party for adults. Ken saw how everyone started their paintings with Picasso or Jean-Michel Basquiat ideas first.

However, Ken started his paintings with the premise that "no one other artist existed." That's American ingenuity. However, he noticed the lazy famous artists would pop in like a delightful cameo just to let the local talent know what's what. But Ken felt their art wasn't welcome because they too, started all their ideas with someone else's. Ken strove for originality that's why his plagiarizing of Don and Cyan was more of stealth homage than man trying to take credit for something he didn't do.

So now Ken decided would *not* be the time to make a mark, when he could be making a name for himself. A cooler head, a higher self prevailed but he knew there would be a time when their worlds would collide.

The piece that had to come down was *Guernica*.

May, 2003

Guernica belongs to the world. Painted by Picasso but an international painting. A masterpiece the world over. You just got to see it to immediately understand its symbolism. Back in 1974, Tony Shafrazi spray-painted the words KILL ALL LIES over the painting. When the Museum security apprehended Tony, he yelled, "Call the curator. I'm an artist."

The big mistake Tony made was not realizing the varnish on *Guernica* made it impossible for spray-paint to stick. Tony's tagged was easily cleaned off. The whole point of being a vandal is to be prolific and to make sure it's hard to scrub off.

Ken's idea was much more vicious. He was set up to take a sword and slash his tag like he was Zorro. But Ken had no political agenda like Mr. Shafrazi. He just wanted to make a point: a long overdue point about Picasso being heartless and not willing to fight for what is right. Picasso wanted to paint to get laid is exactly how Ken saw it.

Ken was in front of *Guernica* with Don and Brody. The three unlikely amigos. They just stood there, and did nothing.

Brody broke the silence, "It's not worth touching this up. This thing is priceless. They can prove you banged up something worth five hundred million."

Don freaked out at that price point. "Are you fuckin' kidding?"

Brody said, "Not one bit. There are multi-billionaires in Germany and Russia that would get into a bidding war over this puppy. Ken, it's not worth it. I think we can only afford to spit on it."

Ken rationalizing his idea from being Zorro to plainly spitting on it was a cop out.

"Saliva? That's your big send off."

"Hey, it has our DNA in it. You wanna talk about leaving a mark."

31

Ballad of a Boyfriend

June 14, 1989, Part Seven

Enjoying pasta Nicky was interrupted in between bites by a waiter. It was his cousin Sonny, "Hey Nicky. Do me a solid. I need you to stop by Kristi's joint."

"That's outta my way," Nicky responded.

"Whadda crazy. I asked for a solid," upset Sonny said.

Resigned to the fact he had to do a solid, Nicky said, "What do you want me to do?"

Sonny reached into his backpack and pulled out a small wooden box. The edges were painted a reddish-gold.

At the center of the box was the word Psalm and he said, "Tell her that Sonny loves her. And give her this."

He opened it up and showed Nicky that it was filled with hand crafted drinking coasters. On each coaster was a psalm written over small pen and ink drawings, done with astonishing skill and imagination.

Nicky was astonished, "Geez Sonny. This is beautiful stuff. Plus you got the psalms on it. Real nice touch."

Touched by emotion Sonny said, "Thanks, bro. There's nothing like using the psalms to get with the ladies. Look man, I gotta scram. Make sure she gets it. I would've given it to her myself but I got an unexpected ride down. Thanks. I owe you one."

Nicky reminded him, "I'll owe it to you tab."

Nicky went to the brownstone at 94 Macdougal street and rang the buzzer number five. He waited for a moment and then heard Kristi say, "Whose is it?"

Nicky announced, "Kristi. It's Nicky Crowbar."

"Hey Nicky. What's up?"

"I've got a package for you."

The door buzzed Nicky in and he walked up five flights and got to the door. He knocked. Kristi opened it up. He walked in and smiled at her.

"I'm guessing Sonny sent you." A disconcerting look came across Kristi's face.

She walked Nicky into the dining room where a candlelight dinner was prepared, "I'll be right with you."

She walked into another room and Nicky heard her whispering "Sonny's cousin Nicky is here with a package from him. What should I say?"

A man's voice also whispering said, "Tell him to tell Sonny that it's over. It's what is best. It's the truth."

While this was going on Nicky couldn't believe his ears. He was really taken back by this arrogant display. Nicky became incredibly uncomfortable. Kristi walked back into the room, "Sorry about that. I had to get a few things."

Nicky was peeved that Kristi was acting as if Nicky didn't know what was going on. From his bag, he pulled out the wooden box with the detailed psalms made just for her. He puts the box on the table. She asked, "What is it?"

"Coasters…with the psalms written on it."

All the while Nicky was giving her the evil eye.

With an unthankful attitude, she said, "Oh coasters."

Abruptly, Nicky made his way out the apartment and she followed him. She opened the door and before he left she addressed her cheating ways, "Crowbar, doncha tell Sonny what you saw."

She thought for a moment. "Wait, maybe he should know."

Nicky was still giving her the evil eye as he walked down the stairs without saying a word. He was thinking about this whole affair with each step taken. It's getting under his skin. He stopped and ran back up the stairs to Kristi's place.

He knocked on the door; she opened it up and Nicky walked in and took the wooden box back. He turned to her and gave her the evil eye. He was fuming. She watched him and knows what she has done.

✶

Nicky brought the coasters to Tony, Sonny's father and reframed the package to save face for Sonny.

Nicky said, "It's coasters with the psalms on it. Sonny hand made them for you."

Tony was metaphorically floored by this display of art. Apparently from the looks of it this was an unusual thing for Tony to receive anything like this from Sonny. They did not have that type of relationship.

"So this is really from him?" Tony said. Nicky nods his head.

"Wow. Nic, have a seat. You want some coffee? Have a cup of coffee."

Tony poured a cup for him, "Nic, did you know about this?"

Nicky stumbling, "Uh...yeah for a few weeks. He told me about it when he started working on it. And I told him, man, I sure wish we all could do something like this for our poppas."

Tony said, "I know *you* love your father!"

Beaming Nicky said, "Sure I do, except I never made him something like this. Matta of fact, all the guys knew about it and they were so proud of him. Everyone respected Sonny for putting the time in to make a gift for his father. Everyone said, 'man, Tony raised Sonny right. Especially in these days when lots of kids are screw ups."

Proudly Tony said, "Tell me about it. Well it wasn't easy. Especially with the divorce but," Tony raised the box, "it was all worth it. This is really wonderful."

Tony thumbed through the first coaster. The great, beautiful one that had the psalm on it that Nic saw. Now a second coaster comes into the scene. It read: You cunt whore. You lied to me. I know you are sleeping with Harry. I hope you die. How can you betray me like this? You sleazy two face.

Tony's face looks deeply disappointed. Nicky said, "What's the matta?"

He handed the coaster to Nic and said, "Nic, these are not for me. Not unless I'm sleeping with Harry."

Scrambling like an egg, Nicky said, "Oh no. That's just a mistake. They are for you. Look at the next one."

Nicky picked up the next one and it read – You lousy lay. You were all teeth. I lied when I said you gave good head. You sleazy cunt rag.

32

Childhood Drawings

June 14, 1989, Part Eight

Cyan had just finished a painting that looked if it was made by a small child. A cookie cutter house with a tree and a dog. The colors had a crayon palette. Unbeknownst to Cyan, a police officer was behind him writing a citation and said, "You ain't an artist, tough guy."

With a previously rehearsed speech, Cyan said, "There are few people who continued to draw after their childhood who were not interrupted by academic training. People who went on to perfect childhood drawing."

Cyan pointed to the wall.

"You're a vandal, buddy. You're affecting the neighborhood."

"Thanks for the lecture," Cyan said "gimme the fine."

He scoped the citation and with arrogance said, "Fifty bucks, that's all."

He reached into his pocket and pulled out a crisp one hundred dollar bill, "You got change?"

The cop took the bill from Cyan's hand, "Tell ya what. I'm gonna keep this and I'll let you tag up here tomorrow."

The cop walked away. Because a cardinal sin was never approach a cop with any type of aggression. Cyan, muttered under his breath, "Asshole."

Orbit Wayne walked into the dark room where Cyan was drawing. He was sitting on a couch in front of a fish tank, "Am I disturbing you?"

He said, "No. Not at all."

She walked towards him and sat next to him. He took a toke from a joint. Orbit opened one of his books and she saw a drawing of a skeleton in bra and panties wearing a blindfold. The skeleton was holding a rake mowing a field. Orbit was put off by the imagery, "What is this?"

"I have a hunch that death wears sexy underwear."

"What are you drawing now?" She inquired.

"Just finishing something up for Ken."

"Let me see."

Cyan closed his book and walked over to a mirror, "It's not done yet. You'll see it soon enough because it's gonna be the first painting Ken hangs up in his restaurant."

Orbit was half impressed.

"Come here," said Cyan, "I want you to see something."

Cyan pointed Orbit toward the mirror, "You're so beautiful. You're definitely the most beautiful you've ever been. It's because you've changed. I wasn't aware of it until I put these on."

Cyan put on the Groucho glasses.

"Do you wear those stupid things all the time now?"

Cyan huffed at the notion, "Before you would only sneak at a peak at people with quick glances. It was as if you were afraid to look into people's eyes. But now you gaze openly, unafraid it's like you want to know everything and you can feel them without touching."

Cyan touched her lips, "Your lips are relaxed and soft. Before they were tense and you always were frowning."

Orbit smiled at the memory.

"You always hid behind mounds of make up," Cyan said, "now you have this wonderful pale complexion."

"Stop bullshitting me Cyan Laurent."

"I'm not!"

"You're talking about yourself. All of you artists are selfish snobs."

Cyan leaned in for a kiss then seductively twisted her pearl necklace that hung around her neck. The string broke! Scattered pearls everywhere. Cyan was speechless. Obviously, he didn't mean to break it and Orbit was aware of that but she lets out a freak of frustration. She kneeled on the floor and meticulously picked up one slick pearl at a time, all the while rejecting to be overcome by the desperateness of it all. The pearls have found their way behind the legs of chairs, under the refrigerator, in the far corners against the baseboard, under the counter, by the saddle between the kitchen and the living room, several made their way into the bathroom. Her fingers pluck them up, every last one and she drops them into a bowl.

Cyan defeated said, "Will ya be able to re-string them?"

"Yeah. I've done it before."

Cyan thumbed through a book, a brown book edged with raised letters on its cover that said "poems" against a picture of the star of David.

"How long will it take?" Cyan said.

"Not long. Not long at all."

Orbit carefully flattened the string and puts a bead through it. She went for another bead from the bowl and asked, "How long have you been drawing?"

"I suppose right outta the womb. And if all goes according to plan I'll probably be drawing something in my coffin."

Ken told me you have "the gift."

"That's because I once drew him a picture of some girl then word spread among the dejected that I could draw. But it's nothing you can fall back on. It's not like I can simply paint a pole with red and white stripes and set up a barber shop."

"Aren't you going to art school?"

"Nah. I'm off to Stanford. I like the sun and chemistry more. Besides I'm French, drawing comes easy. It's the perfect art. You start with a hard, immovable, lifeless canvas until you make it come alive. A painting has more life in it then some of the people I hang with."

"Then why jerk around with tagging walls?"

"I've seen paintings from thousands of years ago. The artist made himself immortal by making that piece. So the way I see it - the quickest way to immortality is to draw it."

"Graffiti is hardly immortal."

"I suppose you're right."

All the while Cyan was working on his piece for Ken. He finished and held it up to the light. Orbit never saw what it was.

He said, "It could've been a wee bit better but it'll work. You got a pair of scissors round here?"

Orbit opened up a drawer, fiddled around and pulled out a pair of scissors, "Whatcha doing?"

"You'll see."

Slowly, Cyan folded his painting in half then folded it over again. He then flattened it out and then folded it in another direction. He flattened it again and then *cut* it in small pieces with the scissors.

Clueless and surprised Orbit said, "Why?"

Matter of fact, Cyan said, "I decided to make it a puzzle. If he really likes my work then he'll be sure to take the time and put it together."

Orbit laughed! The painting was shredded.

"Help me out," said Cyan as he threw all the pieces into the air!

Orbit picked up the pieces as they were falling to the ground and placed them in a bowl.

33

Salute to Paula, the Savior of Street Souls

May, 2003

Cleopatra's Needle was not a gang that you run up on because you ain't afraid of scraping and knuckling up. This was ancient. Sixty-nine feet high. Two hundred and four tons of stone and God knows what else. It was mammoth and its got hieroglyphics with esoteric messages…, but its still man-made.

Now the needle was surrounded by a bunch of guys that will pull out the heat over small shit. They will let the semi sing. They are dramatic on automatic. They know underneath this thing was a big pile of stuff. So they're loaded up with the shovels and they got that strong rope they "borrowed" from the Cirque du Soliel. They had a metal detector on hand from a local pawnshop. This was a bunch of different ethnic types. We're talking Puerto Rican's drinking Jamaican Rum and Jamaican's pounding Puerto Rican rum. Both groups getting bombed. They're taking down history.

A time capsule was buried beneath the obelisk that included an 1870 U.S. census, the Bible, Webster's Dictionary, the complete works of Shakespeare, a guide to Egypt, and an early facsimile of the Declaration of Independence. But most importantly, a box was placed in the capsule by the man who orchestrated the purchase and transportation of the obelisk. It was said he'll probably be the only person in history ever to know its contents.

Unfortunately, no one had the foresight of Don Tenenbaum. They most certainly didn't know about Brody Shaw and they didn't know about Paula Bagley.

Paula was the founder of Chimerical Fortress School established in 1969 that ran from nursery to third grade. Brody entered it free of charge because his family qualified for below the poverty line living. As for today, it costs fifty-five thousand to get in and you have to apply when you're a fetus. Paula's concept was to provide high-end day care to children that either were abused, handicapped, homeless, or in some cases, all three. The rest of the crowd was the Crème de la Crème of the Upper East Side that was paying a hefty sum of eight grand a year. This was essentially a social experiment welfare program for children. The school had 130 children but a staff of twenty-two. If you know your New York City Public School history that is a remarkable ratio. In addition, it had a cadre of health care specialists such as doctors, nurses and social workers. Even psychologists were on hand. The school was located inside a Spanish florid *plata* cathedral on a quaint, peaceful block lined with town houses. The entrance was a wide-open garden with flowers that bloomed in different seasons.

Paula Bagley was an impassioned, pioneering crusader who fought vigorously on behalf of the disadvantaged and disabled youth. She was famous for saying, "Childhood ends quickly, in many cases, it ends quickly in death."

When she discovered the predicament of the city's thousands of homeless children, who tag along behind their unemployed (and ill-equipped) parents from the streets to dreary shelters to seedy welfare motels, she began rescuing them.

Bagley had single-handedly taken several families out of the hotels, found them apartments and enrolled their children in her school. Sometimes she sought them out; sometimes they turned up at the school the way sometimes stray dogs do.

Bagley was not afraid to get her hands dirty. By getting an up close and personal look at one of the city's emergency shelters, she saw homeless families sleeping on broken chairs as they waited to be assigned to other shelters. Horrified by what she saw, Bagley had a life altering moment.

Instead of getting married and raising her own children, she would dedicate her life to quietly and persistently taking care of children that were without hope. Her ultra-brilliant decision was to match these castaways with these well-to-dos.

Bagley was a highly educated person from affluence. She could have made an entirely different life for herself but chose to be a caretaker. What she out to do, is not something colleges offer. She had to learn everything from scratch.

But the vision of seeing, criminally dirty children with infected scabs, begging for food hit her like an unseen lightning bolt. She was electrified from head to toe to help at any cost. God knows what these children had experienced.

After her first year of taking in children and assembling the staff she made an observation that she will take to her grave. "It is not the handicapped, abused and disadvantage children that gained the most from this. It is the children from the stable homes. The ones with no cares in the world grow without measure in love, patience, joy and being thankful for their reality. The gifted children randomly born into opulence see humanity in another lens and become truly kindhearted. And by God, the parents were acutely aware of this."

In so many respects, 260 was indirectly her socio-experiment in all its tapestry beauty. It was not rich and poor for 260, it's rich in God's Mercy and poor not because of your ball busting efforts but because "The Man" has been stepping on the hose. And they are all hyper aware of this. They are the outsiders, the commoners, the rank unbelievers of society and its rules. No matter how you earn your money, whether you earn it, hustle or jive-talk for it. You will not keep it around 260.

Paula was a modern day Robin Hood, watching these behemoth corporations robbin' the hoods. She must have known deep down back then this would be a never-ending battle she will not win. But there's so much too love. There's so much too fight for.

Although five years older, this is where Brody Shaw originally met

Ken Rosenberg. Years later, Rosenberg would remind Brody for laughs that his dad was on his family's "welfare program."

This was the crew that was going take down Cleopatra's Needle. The plan was not a calculated one. It was more similar to a hit and run, a classic smash and grab except dealing with ancient history.

The first part was to shovel a four-foot ditch around the obelisk. Why four feet? No one knew other than it felt right. Once the ditch was completed. They tied the ropes to the obelisk and hooked it up to thirty-five dirt bikes. They also came equipped with half sticks of dynamite. Once the obelisk came tumbling down the idea was to take the buried treasure.

"Easy peasy. Lemon Squeezy," said Ken.

Once the shovels started cutting through the grass, it was obvious this was not dirt surrounding the obelisk. It was silt. After the first two feet of digging through the silt, the gang started finding small containers embedded therein. Each box was found by the metal detector and was filled with unidentifiable trinkets but everyone was excited. The legend of this buried treasure may be true after all.

The quick robbery and toppling over a structure was now looking like a excavation and a group of 260 were concerned they were unearthing not only mounds of ash and soot but now they maybe stepping over dollars to get to pennies. Perhaps the contents of these small containers were the treasure itself.

It was dark and no one was doing a database of the find. This was robbery. Pure and simple. No one had the time to think it through. There was an implicit trust among 260 that everyone would return what they found to the main table at 260 Elizabeth Street and things would be catalogued and divided up fairly. No one in 260 even has empirical knowledge of old time trinkets. To be fair, Aristotle's students published two studies on loaded dice and probability. Be confident 260 knew all about broken dice and the chances of doing this without getting caught.

Taking down the Needle wasn't a fate turning on the roll of rigged dice. This was all matter of fact. A proclamation of devastation.

"Any pious Jew" Brody hissed, "will tell you this Needle is akin to having an enormous Nazi flag flying high over the city in the name of antiquity. In this day and age, it would be labeled as priceless historic art. Although, if you dialed back the clock, the Egyptians enslaved our Hebrew brethren. These are not symbols of freedom ringin' free. These are stark reminders of a dark past of enslavement. And Twain was right, you just try and go up against Jew Squad and you'll find out who has got God on their side."

But that was slightly misleading, the purpose of the take down was to steal (thou shat not) the treasure. However, with a public relations man like Brody on the scene, this was a war and 260 were taking its booty over the victory.

Once the silt was removed, the integrity of the obelisk was no longer. The bikes would simply make a run and the obelisk would tilt and another group of 260 would swipe what was underneath.

That's precisely how it went down.

When you see the Needle now, you can tell it had been moved a few inches but like the exhibit of Caveman Poetry, no one has noticed. People's lives are to busy. Each member swore to secrecy what they ended up finding.

Brody fenced all the other stuff to the black market for hundreds of thousands of dollars. Legend had it he put out a few pieces here and there on special occasion. The amount of treasure of that exquisite and vast.

Each member was paid a percentage of the intake and Brody Shaw's reputation was in tact. He paid on time, paid what was fair and he took care of things. He was hyper-empathetic and trusted.

34

The Validation of Jack Track

June 14, 1989, Part Nine

90th & Fifth. Reservoir Track Entrance - 3 A.M.

The party spirit prevailed. A banner tied to the gate announced the BIG RACE. The crowd, three or four clusters of kids – maybe four hundred in all were behaving as if they were performing in a burlesque circus. A lot was riding on this race but it resembled a festival.

In a top hat and coattails was Hardcore Mordecai with two sex goddesses by his side. He spoke through a megaphone, "Welcome to the Big Fuckin' Race, y'all."

The crowd was ecstatic.

He continued, "Tonight's event stars a freshman from Dalton who currently holds the track record of twelve minutes and fourteen seconds. Say hello to Walter McDaniel!"

The place went wild.

Hardcore Mordecai was flush red from a bump of coke said, "As you may know *that* time crushes the Olympic record but they won't feel it. So what do we have to say?"

The full force of four hundred New York kids with energy to start an earthquake yelled, "Fuck the Olympics."

Hardcore Mordecai got the good coke that night because he was buzzing straight down to his toes, "That's right, fuck 'em. Walter may have broke the record but he has yet to break the man."

The place explodes louder than before. It was a Jack Track crowd. The full platoon of 260 and they ain't afraid of no one.

A chant goes up, and if you don't tell me they couldn't hear this all the way down by the Twin Towers. "Jack! Track! Jack! Track! Jack! Track!"

Hardcore Mordecai waved the chanting down and screamed, "The undisputed. The undefeated. The unquestioned. Jack Track!"

Jack and Walter swaggered up to the starting block. There was something comical by Jack in comparison to Walter. Jack doesn't look the part anymore. He was out of shape. Walter, tall, lean, confident. Both boys get down into their stances.

"If I really gave a shit" Jack said with attitude, "I'd blow you out from the gate. I could make it seem like you were walking to the finish." Jack took a sip of bottled water.

"Quitja beggin'" Said Walter knowing how this was gong to end.

"Scratch that," said Jack "I'm going make you seem like you were crawling."

Little did Walter know, that Jack just had a bump for real good coke. The kind that makes you get all sorts of bursts.

With a grin, Walter let Jack know his mind games are not working, "How do you run?"

"I crush the snakes and spare the worms. How do you run, Walter?"

"Fast."

Jack's jaw tightened as he took a deep breath. Hardcore Mordecai had the stopwatch in hand. The tension built. The crowd was hushed.

Hardcore Mordecai went into count down mode, "Ok. Are you guys ready? On your mark. Get set. Go."

Both guys roared off the starting line, people were cheering. They ran forward faster and faster. Walter and Jack were now disappearing around the first turn.

Jack shot through and moved up.

Walter went wide and Jack took the inside and moved up some more.

The boys running hard, side by side. On the right of them was spacious greens. On the left the water and the glorious view of Fifth. All the buildings look like diamonds or stars. An important counterpoint to the concrete jungle of the daytime.

Jack sped up and got behind Walter to use him as a windbreak.

Walter was now separated from Jack about five yards. He's on a mission. They are approaching the straightway and Jack kicks it into high gear and caught up with Walter. Strain was starting to show on Jack. For Walter, it's all too easy.

The boys running a quick, steady pace. They're both concentrating on the track ahead.

Jack was going all out. He was in terrible pain now ten yards behind at FULL SPEED.

Walter turned around to see Jack losing steam. He was really pouring it on now.

The crowd was cheering Walter on.

A few black kids are hi-fiving each other in their excitement.

Hardcore Mordecai was looking through binoculars and thought *shit! I'm gonna lose some heavy bread.*

Running a good fifteen yards behind Walter was Jack. The crowd was starting to feel bad. Jack was holding on to his right side. But he continued, running pathetically but yet defiantly.

In an effort to make his friends think he had a chance. Jack dug deeps inside and ran like hell. Jack was gaining on him. Walter sped up instinctively.

Jack was now eating Walter's dust. His face registered the emotion of losing his identity.

Jack running for his life, his pride, his dignity. Oh God, he was about to become Jack Wack. Trying to make it close or least make it an honorable finish he was now at full gas. The rhythmic motion of his legs were nearly a blur.

Jack had once again caught up with Walter. He was a bit surprised.

Walter, all too easily, jumped ahead of Jack by a serious distance. His feet pounded the dirt at lighting speed.

One step after another, then all of a sudden Walter took a nasty spill!

He cried out in agony. Walter can hear Jack's footsteps coming along hitting the dirt and gravel. Walter can't believe the turn of events. Jack had no time for compassion. He booked by Walter not once looking to see if he was okay. Jack had put at least twenty yards between them. An insurmountable lead.

Walter got back up. His bearings a little loose. He shook it off and started to run again.

Hardcore Mordecai appeared satisfied that Jack was ahead but he had no idea what had taken place.

Jack knew he'll win but he also knew it took a freak accident for it to be possible. He saw the crowd in front of them. They EXPLODED at the sight of the legendary Jack Track coming to the finish line.

A man was waving a checkered flag.

Jack raised his arms in victory.

Cyan, Ken & Orbit were running towards Jack. They knock him down. Hardcore Mordecai runs up and jumps on them.

Everybody was shouting. The crowd was cheering. Several Roman Candles had been ignited.

Jack was happy but felt empty and wanted to tell someone but Jack was not a party pooper.

Walter heard the roar of the crowd. He pounded his fist into the dirt.

Jack's arm was being held in victory by Hardcore Mordecai and he was beaming but Jack couldn't shake his feeling. He knew he lost badly.

Hardcore Mordecai was high on coke, but this victory was making him feel like his was kissing God, "Now and forever. Our winner. The winner. Jack Track!"

Cyan was in a glorious mood, "You the champ! He'll probably never run his mouth again."

"He was beating me, Cyan! He was winning!"

Cyan was struggling with what Jack was saying, "What?"

"He fell. The dumb idiot fell. Twisted his ankle. He was easy four seconds in front of me when it happened."

Jack stopped cold, "He would've won!"

Cyan was still not getting it, "What?"

"Don't you get it! I'm over, man. I've been over. He was blowing me out."

Now swimming in his second lap in denial, Cyan said, "Nonsense!"

Jack got so angry, "You didn't see it. Believe me when he hobbles over -he'll explain it himself."

"You won the race!" Cyan said in delight. "So what if he fell. Staying on your feet is a part of the gig."

Jack was upset at reality! Not perceptions! He held Cyan's shoulders and grabbed them, "Get off my dick. He was beating me."

Cyan wrestled himself away and said, "No one cares, man. You crossed the line first. You'll always be the man. No one can take that away. You're Jack Track."

Jack calmed down, as his heart rate was naturally dropping, "Look at you in those Groucho Marx glasses! I can't believe you get laid."

"Hey, you wanna pair for North Carolina?

Jack smiled and slapped him five, "Okay Cyan Laurent. You call it like you see it. I won the race."

"Examundo. Egg salad. Exactly! You won."

Jack's confidence brimmed back up, "No one beats me. No one. No one beats us. Two sixty all the way."

They watched the sun rise then went their separate ways.

35

Only Drink the Expensive Shots

Rio de Janeiro, Night Seven

April strolled in seductively like a panther, since she had blown her chances in the Garden of Eden by passing out. Now came her shot at redemption. She was wearing no makeup. This was her body language talking: I'm naked, unafraid, and vulnerable.

"You sitting next to Midori on the flight back?" she asked Brody.

I've been sitting next to Midori my whole life. Sometimes I think we met in kindergarten. I can't remember...a time before her. Or when I do, I just assume she's always been there."

April started crying. "Brody," she whimpered, "I'm not ruining your life with Midori. If I read Shakespeare, our story must be in there somewhere. This is destiny, Brody. You don't have kids. Do you guys own property?"

"No," said Brody, "although it's death, not destiny, that will do us part. Are you the Grim Reaper?"

He placed his fingers on her bottom lip.

"You sure don't feel like him."

He sniffed the nape of her neck.

"You sure don't smell like him."

Speaking through tears, April said, "I'm not death. I'm life. You're life. We're life. We've had splendid nights, one after the other. Together.

Don't you see? There's someone else for Midori. Somehow things just got mixed up. It's just one big mix-up."

"I fall in love too easily," Brody said, tearing up. "And so do many. I'm running out of poems, April. I told you to give me a year. You'll head back to Wyoming, meet Prince Charming, and forget all about me!"

"Like Captain Ahab forgot Moby Dick?"

"Hey, that's my line, sister!"

Wiping away her tears, April winked at him.

"Can you keep a secret?" she asked.

"I *am* a secret."

"I figured you'd say something like that. But can you really keep a secret?"

"Sure. But let me share my theory about secrets. This is how they're kept: You tell one person, and then hope that person is dead within an hour. Otherwise, you're foolish to think secrets can be kept. Now, here's my caveat. Did someone tell you not to repeat this?"

"No."

"Okay, I'll keep secret what you're about to tell me."

"Paige gave me her blessing to sleep with you…, but not here. She said you'll bring me to some dumpy hotel, like I'm a piece o' trash.'"

"That sure sounds like Paige…, giving you her blessing to be my mistress. Geez. Let me set two records straight. First, you and I are not real, never were, and our relationship was all wrapped up in an interesting illusion that lasted for seven nights. This whole thing is not fair to you, April. I dragged you into it and got carried away with your assets and my definition of them. Obviously, you played a part, too, but I really think from the bottom of my heart that you've been subconsciously looking for a way out of this mess. I know you've got a great deal of respect and admiration for me. I believe everything you ever said to me or felt about me is true. But none of that is logical, and that part is entirely my fault. At the exact time that I wanted to dig deeper, and expressed my desire to dig deeper, you pulled away. Then, when you wanted to go deeper, I pulled away. The more I asked, the more I demanded of you…. My God! Midori's the only one who's obligated and happy to meet them. You're practically a stranger."

"Stop right there!" April yelled. "You want to be free, to just cut the cord and fall in love. But you don't have the courage. You're gutless, Brody. All talk. No action."

Brody liked what he heard.

"Fight back, April! Fight for it!"

April counterpunched: "Can I just be a friend? Of course not! You say we need a year. I say we need a night. We owe each other a single night."

Brody ducked and bobbed: "I have no doubt you will succeed in life. I have all the confidence you'll make the right decisions. But I want you to be free of this. Losing this type of relationship in your life will make it easier. Life is tough as it is. But we need a year to go by where there's no contact. Where we both can live our lives without the impression we owe each other anything. There's always been an undercurrent of deceit between us. Nothing good comes out of such relationships. Trust me, I know. I was going to write a detailed account of my past to prove that, but I don't want to lump you in with those categories. We met, we were attracted to each other, you inspired me in ways you can't imagine, we opened a door that should've stayed shut. We went as far as we could under the circumstances. You want to be a mistress? You want that on your soul? Don't get involved with a married man. It's poison. I swear to you that, whatever I said, whenever I said it, was inspired, and I meant every word. You have so many blessings awaiting you directly from the Lord. I don't want to interfere with that anymore. I'm releasing whatever hold I may have had on you. You don't have to dream about me anymore. You're knowing and growing. Ultimately, this is a natural extension of our relationship. We were never ones to play games with each other. We were serious about us, but I don't want to hurt you. Not now. Not ever. You're a bright girl with so much to offer. Stop wasting it on me. Our paths will cross again. I know they will, but for now let's set sail."

April screamed: "Enough of the backtrack! Saying one thing and doing another. It's show-and-tell time, Brody. Show me the cards you're holding. Do your breathing thingamajig and set yourself free. Otherwise, you're just like all the other punk-ass guys, with just a better game. I'll even blame all of it on these Brazilian avocados and yuccas, for crissakes!"

Brody closed his eyes, slowly inhaled through his nose, and exhaled from his mouth two times.

"I'll meet you somewhere, Feline Daisy," he said softly. "It'll be a surprise. I can't wait to see the look in your cream-colored eyes. I'll want to hold you in my arms. I only hope you don't think I'll bring you harm. I'm sure you'll be angry, and say "Why are you here?" I'll lie about a dying aunt who lives near. Then you'll stare right through me, we'll be walking along in the Mission in the rain—"

"How'd you know I was going to San Francisco?" April said, grabbing him by the arm.

"The same way I knew you thought you lost your virginity to me. I just knew. I can't explain it. Look, I'm not Houdini. I'm in a trap, and there's no easy way out. Do you even know what sacrifice means? Do you even know what devotion is?"

"I'm willing to learn," April said with humility.

"Exactly," Brody said with master-class authority. "You need to live to learn. To figure out what all this is. You need to find out if I'm who you think I am. This goddamn Brazilian rain! Have you tasted the almonds they put out every morning? They're pure joy. You're eating pure Almond Joy."

"Brody, it's not the food. It's you. It's me. It's we. You're magical. Cosmic. I want to dive headlong into this."

"Into what? Midori's been in the foxholes with me. She ain't scared of nothing. She'll shank a demon. But I get the feeling you'll book on me at the first sign of trouble. You don't know me. And I'm not interested in teaching you what it's all about. I'm not about to show you where the bodies are buried and going back into the past. I don't want to relive history. I want to *make* history. What do you want? Besides me? You're in a class by yourself, April. You're telling me that once we land, there won't a billion guys ready to take my place? What's gotten into you?"

Once again through tears, April said, "You, Brody, you! I'm not ashamed. I know it's true. There will never be anyone like you in my life again."

Brody hugged her.

"Oh, sweetheart, that's *so* not true. I'd leave Midori just so you wouldn't feel that pain, because Midori's already seen the Grim Reaper. She's seen him up close. She's danced with him. But I'm not even a prototype of what's coming your way."

Still sobbing, April said, "Why aren't you listening to me? You're mine!"

"I could be. But I get a sinking feeling that this illicit love can only end in heavy tragedy. I'm talking pallbearer type. For *what?* Ten showers? Forty orgasms? A hundred breakfasts in bed? Happiness comes and goes, and you go looking for it. And then you can't find it. And then the whole thing sours, and you walk. And I'm *what?* I'm stuck making a pleading phone call to Midori. 'Take me back!' 'No, thank you.' First of all, April, you haven't even thought this through. Ten minutes after I dump Midori, she'll have me replaced. She don't chase. She replace. And you can bet your fine-looking ass that it'll be with a much better, much bigger, much richer man. And sure, he may not tickle her funny bone, but you know what's gonna give her the big laugh? The last laugh. And what are *you* offering me?"

April went silent.

"Even the whiteface monkeys stopped dancing on the roof," Brody said, picking up the pace of his rant. "Even *they're* interested in how the scales have to be tipped into balance. Give it to me straight, April! I'll leave my devoted wife for you. I'll divorce her right on trip back…. But I hear a big train comin'. You ready to throw yourself on the tracks for me?"

April was angry now.

"You said to give you a year. And then you talked about matching tattoos, Fatso! And you said I would have Hannah and two other girls. You *said* that! And you meant it, too. You said, 'I'll be the face of Christianity for the next twenty-two years.' I want that, Brody. That's my destiny. You're the destination. I'm not a helpless plaything, and you know it. You may be happily married, but you must be awfully miserable to not mean everything you said."

"I meant every word, April. Somewhere in Vienna, there was a violinist who said, 'I played with Mozart.' A philosopher in France who said, 'I dined with Voltaire.' A soldier in Mississippi who said, 'I fought alongside Grant.' A teenager in New York who said, 'I tagged the Statue of Liberty with Wiz260.' Perhaps, young lady, we can get you a badge with lettering on it that says, 'I danced with Brody.'"

"I would wear it proudly."

"I know you would, April. And the more pervasively sensual this is becoming, the more lowdown and dirty it's getting. The whole thing is turning me on. And I can see that your thighs have already moved three inches further apart from where they once were. I'm a grown man, married to a grown woman, but I can't, for the life of me, stand up to you with any sort of determination. You're the best show in town. You'll outdo us all. And I hate to admit it: you beat me at my own game. You win."

April flashed a tremendous smile.

"I *knew* it all along. What's the second record you want to set straight?"

Brody cracked his knuckles.

"I'm tellin' ya, Paige is a dummy. I don't go to dumpy hotels, and I definitely don't cheat. I break hearts and bones. Point-blank. You see, Paige only understands money or the sound of a swiping credit card. She has no concept of favors. Absolutely none. She doesn't know the value of holding somebody down. Or a connect. Or a juice card. Or an in. According to her spoiled rotten pea of a brain, there's no value to anything but cash. For her, if it's not in Marc Jacobs's store or some boutique in SoHo, it doesn't exist. She doesn't understand the macroworld, microworld, underworld, or black market. She only sees what's right in front of her nose. She's a spoiled brat. To answer your question, April, we won't be meeting in a dumpy hotel. We'll be meeting at Chateau Marmont, because the valet owes me a favor. *Capeesh?* And we'll be fine dining, because the sous-chef owes me a favor. And we'll be driving in any type of car you want, because an old buddy of mine just got a job at a luxury car dealership on Rodeo Drive."

"What did you ever see in Paige, anyway?"

"Paige was a young girl who gave me sage advice. She said, 'To go real far, you'll need to be nice.' And I countered with my experience that you gotta be able to step on some heads, and you gotta be able to go through some reds."

Finding that answer unsatisfactory, April said, "But what did you *see* in her? What was it? Has she turned into what you originally saw? You know, they called her 'Abercrombie and Bitch' at Vassar."

"I would respect that if they said it to her face. But behind her back, that's meaningless…, just a poor reflection of an envious mind. But I don't think I'm answering your question, am I?"

"No."

"I'm hyper-empathetic. In other words, I'm in a constant state of elation, and I never crash. In the psychiatric field, there's something called bipolar, or manic depression. The shrinks mainly see people who crash from being the life of the party into depressive or aggressive states of mind filled with phobias and anxiety. They have no peace and become paralyzed with fear. Couple that with drugs and alcohol, and some can commit suicide. But that's not me. I'm not bipolar. I'm unipolar."

"You're not crazy, Brody. You're wonderful!"

"I got news for you, doctors have diagnosed me as bipolar. And technically, clinically, I am. And there's a major stigma attached to it. Especially among Christians, because they paint Jesus as an instant healer."

"Isn't he?"

"We can't talk about that now."

"Brody, I've been meaning to ask you…. What's that breathing thing you do?"

"It's an ancient technique. There are twelve forms of meditation in the Hebrew Scriptures, but I'm reluctant to call it meditation because that may be misleading. For now, we can call it that. Reading, writing, speaking, and breathing are the four that I've mastered. The breathing has intention: getting the proper amount of oxygen in, and releasing the proper amount of carbon dioxide. Essentially, what I'm saying is, breathe in eight on the periodic table and exhale six. Or breathe in the Messiah and exhale the Evil One. Or inhale the good and exhale the bad. Although, come to think of it, plants use the carbon dioxide. I'm pretty sure the Chinese stole this concept and called it *yin* and *yang*, but I can't prove that. I suspect it, though. If you do it right, you get addicted to breathing. Think about that. We're already addicted to breathing but this stuff makes you high."

April laughed at her own observation and said, "But do you ever stop to take a breath when you speak?! I love your notion…addicted to breathing. Technically, we're all addicts to oxygen. However, you're saying by not doing it right, we're not getting high off it thus humanity uses other drugs."

Brody did not respond and put the conversation back on its track, "Getting back to Paige, she opens umbrellas inside. And to me that's daring and appealing. And I do that, too, because I'm such an anti-authoritative asshole. The problem for my whole life is that I confused real authority with fake authority, and just put a blanket over all of it. And I guess I still do. Paige plays in the rain till nothing's dry. And I love watching her smile as she tells me her dirty lies. Paige comes from a world in which all that matters is two seats in the orchestra. And I come from a world in which all that matters is entertaining whores. And somehow it works. I'm reading a book right now concerning toxic relationships. It says that you'll know you'll be getting into one if the first question you ask is, 'What do you do?' instead of, 'What are you doing?' But none of that will matter a damn when life shows you the door…. So getting back to the breathing, let me show you how it's done."

36

Bad Things Happen to Good People

The legendary Chateau Marmont: A hotel and bungalows of misbehaviors. The unofficial motto: Where good things happen to bad people.

Check In: 3 P.M.

Brody managed to finagle the one-bedroom penthouse. It can set you back $3,000 a night but you're renting pure uncut Hollywood history. The room was anchored by a hardwood floor and décor that screamed, "I'm important." How many men have paraded dissatisfied housewives through this room to see them transform into sensuality amplified? They probably were wearing strap-ons without an ounce of liquor in them. *That* is how powerful this room was. Brody told me, "It felt like a battlefield with the ghosts of the innocents lingering around."

But with Brody in the room, April kept thinking to herself, *if we can't be together forever, then we can't be together at all.*

"Brody, my god, this is stunning."

"Not more than you."

Brody thought to himself, *if you can't get laid here: kill yourself.*

Brody had all the tricks up his sleeve. And he revealed each one like a magician throwing knives at you while you're tied upside down to a spinning wheel.

First up was a trip to Studio City for a custom fitting of a black jumpsuit with a plunging neckline. April was an A cup breast size but had the most remarkable set of freckles across her chest that that became the true attraction. It was an ethereal tattoo: a constellation that lit up your consciousness.

April did not have many choices in what she was going to wear. Brody had told her to just wear a sundress with no underwear and he would take care of everything else.

Next up was shopping for an assortment of shoes then a bathing suit for tomorrow. Later, he took her to a salon on Rodeo to get her hair and make up done for the evening.

Brody had a look in mind: L.A. sex kitten combined with Pharaoh's daughter. However, with April Graves, her unmistakable beauty much like the sound of Coltrane's tenor was a force. She was blessed. She did not need any get-up. Brody put her in this costume, so to speak, so she would enjoy the get-down that much more.

At the table over dinner, Brody said, "The Christians you've grown up with are passé. They are replicating their past. They have cannibalize their passion that once was. All you've been around are the elements of lights that used to shine bright. You sing the same songs, you hear the same teachings, and do the same events. And it's being mistaken for the genuine soul of what walking in spirit really is."

He was saying that out of habit and anger. Here he was across from April Graves knowing without a doubt they would be making love and he would be devouring her. She knew it would be a night she'll never forget. However, Brody can't stop being Brody. He was caught up in a web of deceit. The married man going outside his marriage to experience a fiery red-head in more ways than one. And he was still not sure if he was going to be her first. He only knew he won't be her last. Dinner. Drinks. Champagne. Dessert.

During the dessert he said, "I want to recite a poem that I wrote for you."

"Of course," April said while teasingly dipping her strawberries in melted chocolate and whip cream, "I'm sure it will be your best."

Brody launched into his poem: "She gave me green eyes, the best eyes to have, until you see a pair of blue. She gave me widow's peak, some crooked teeth, when I kiss its only true."

The DJ set started at 9 P.M. Dancing: Get Up, Close, Get Down, Closer.

The party goes on but Brody can barely hear the music or even the sounds of people all around them. His eyes have locked onto hers.

April had slightly reddened cheeks and Brody was not sure whether it was from the Merlot or whether she was thinking of what he was. He knew which when she glanced around and gave him the sexiest look in the universe.

He felt himself stiffen up in his pants. Her eyes beamed seeing the lust in his eyes.

She then spun away from him and walked out of the lounge.

Her hips swayed making his erection somehow even stiffer and he marched after her nearly shoving everyone who got in his way.

Instead of the elevator, she took the stairs. April Graves was gifted with a physique but she spent hours and hours on the Stairmaster. Unless a fifty-pound weight was on her, walking up to the penthouse in Castle de Sex, she wouldn't break a single bead of sweat. Brody, however, was gasping for air, his heart racing because of the view. Her hips swayed. Her long legs extended and Brody was fully hypnotize. He had a hyperbolic vision: he thought to himself *she's the garden of Eden.*

Back in their one-bedroom penthouse:

He finally kissed her. And there her lips interlocked with his. He felt like he was simultaneously waking up from a dream and going into another.

Then Brody pushed his tongue in rather than kiss her properly.

A delicious rush that overpowered all other sensations: Her tongue, dancing with his. He felt her saliva inside his mouth. Then her teeth biting his lip as she pulled away. Brody was left open-mouthed, wanting more. Always more.

She slipped out of the jumpsuit: Topless with heels.
She looked like the Feline Daisy. The Dirty Rainbow.
She fingered herself. She swayed.
Dropped to his crotch. Unzipped him.
Unhurriedly, he sunk his cock in, inch by inch.

Salt. Musk.

He went pass her red pouty lips.

Now in her mouth. Back and forth.

Sexual haven.

He stood her up.

He turned her around.

Eats her.

Nectar!

He glided his cock on her pussy lips.

She was way wet. Much too wet.

He went in.

He fucked her.

Fuckin' fucked her.

She looked from behind.

What a gaze. He was left star struck.

The room was dimly lit from the moonlight.

A neon light flashed outside.

A small lamp illuminated the corner.

He saw her brown skin and the tan lines that she got from earlier in the day.

He moved her to the bed.

He got her on top of her.

He thrust.

Grabbed her throat.

He thrust over and over.

Hearts thumped, lungs flailed, apprehension wrapped her body in sweaty tremors as he left her and thrust back in.

She got on top.

Pure beauty.

April Graves ringing in full glory.

Brody laid back and thrust upward.

Sugar rush. Blood rush.

In sync. Harmony. One.

She bent forward.

He bit her lips.

She slipped off him and sucked his cock.
Slowly.
She got back on.
A goddess among women.
Energy picked up.
They were both breathless.
Heart rate through the roof.
She was right where he wanted her. Needed her.
He fondled her nipples. Her skin was warm.
The door to the room opened up.

"I had given a key to a prostitute," Brody told me, "A high class escort. Hollywood style. Wearing a sliver slip. I won't describe her. Your type. My type. The world's type."

And here we go down the Brody rabbit hole. It can never been a straight line. The book you're reading is called *The Do-Anything Kids* but I hadn't spoken to Brody since I wrote his biography (behind his back) entitled *A Friendship Dare*.

It was a collection of all his antics since a child. The manuscript never got published but to my great surprise Brody got hold of a copy because he just so happened to know an agent at Random House and it was "big hit" there but never gained traction. They rejected the book. And so did everyone else.

I once remembered Brody telling me, he had all the respect in the world for Moses because when he wrote his autobiography he included that he killed a guy. And that it always upset him that Dali didn't go to Riker's and Picasso never tagged up the Two Line. And the Apostle Paul beat him and everyone to the punch by saying he was the chief sinner. Whereas, everyone else was off to the races to tell you they're the chief winner.

So when Brody invited me to Mang's Chinese Restaurant it was to clear the air about the injustice of airing out his dirty laundry without letting him know I wrote *his* memoir because maybe, just maybe he could've helped write it.

Brody continued, "Just like you're thinking I arranged a three way.

April's thinking I arranged a three way. I can see the kink go off in her eyes. The eyes tell all. But sadly, gladly, madly, badly, this is Chateau Marmont where good things happen to bad people and bad things happen to good people all the time. So two other girls follow the whore inside."

Brody can hardly contain himself. I've never see him in this condition. And I've seen him in a lot of conditions. He was measuring out his sentences. As if he wanted me to memorize this. Like he wanted me to picture it.

"She giggled and abruptly stopped grinding me. I explain this is Gemma. A host. She throws parties. And April was buzzed from the alcohol and the room was dark enough not to care. And her body was glistening from sweat. Nipples erect. But now I can tell she was a tad uncomfortable at what's going on."

To be honest, I'm a tad uncomfortable at what's going on.

"Gemma opened her hand bag and broke out several lines of coke. And I hadn't seen April since Rio and I asked, 'Have you ever done coco?' while I asked this, Gemma gently helped her off of me."

Brody lit a cigar, took a few drags as if he was conjuring up his memory bank.

"Everyone does the powder. A big shot of adrenaline! World conquering primo stuff! We've moved an inch closer to the edge. Then get this? Gemma said, 'Ladies! She's all yours!' The three girls drop their pants and reveal their own moist pussies. Gemma grabbed April off the bed. I make eye contact with her. I see she was struggling with the idea she was a now a lesbian fuck toy."

I stop the story in its tracks. I get the feeling Brody was testing my will, "Brody, what's the point of all of this jive ass baloney?"

Brody paid absolutely no attention. Then I figured it out. He has been feeding me another book the entire time but was going to leave me with this bizarre ending. The ultimate joke and instead of leaving well enough alone and letting everyone off the hook, he wants me to feel pain. His pain. Their pain. The trip from hell disguised as the trip from heaven. Okay I got it. Let me have it.

Brody looked at me with a cold, dark stare that sent a shiver down my spine that I can feel right now, he said, "Listen here boy, sticks and stones may break your bones and names will most definitely hurt you but you wanna be with the best, you gotta beat the best. Let me tell you what I gotta say, like I did the last time. Unedited. Like I did the last time. And then you can *try* to cash in like the last time. And change the names for the safety and holy sanctity of others, Asshole."

Brody took a drag of his cigar.

"Gemma forced April to her knees and held her arms back. Every girl made out with her. She felt her chin wetting as her saliva coated her face; the rhythm of tongues going in and out. Gemma pushed her head back and forth. Her massacre ran down her face. The punk rock Pharaoh's daughter gave way to a flush red face, watering eyes and globs of her saliva ran onto the carpet. It was a sight to behold. She got pushed down onto the carpet. Her eyes went wide in excitement. Immediately, a girl strapped on a dildo and went inside with no trouble at all because she was soaking wet. I made her wet! Although, this girl is fucking her much harder than I was and makes her arch her back. I see her body contort in doggy style. The coke had her moving along. The Feline Daisy, The Dirty Rainbow: the wet dream. A fever dream. And I wanted to see her fuck and cum. So I made the necessary arrangements. The whole thing was hypnotic. Her hair started to mat down because of the sweat. She looked so good. I was hard as iron. They lifted her up off the floor. Even in the dark you saw her pussy was dripping wet. Then get this? April goes completely unchained and took over the party. She announced to Gemma, 'I'm gonna fuck you up good.' And she went to town on these girls. It was insane! It was a long while since I looked eyes with her. And even longer since I was in her. But then I joined in and her she felt so good and swollen and extremely warm. I just stared into her eyes and I thrust up. I decided the best way to end this night was for her to swallow my cum. She agreed. I came so hard. Her mouth filled up with all my cum. She swallowed. We got into the bath together. I put lavender Epsom salts in. She dried off, I had her snort another line: just to pick herself back up. We drove down to Ventura Boulevard to get some espresso. April: au natural. Cannot be fucked with. A pure ten. The top was down in the convertible. Got fresh air. I talked but she kept quiet. Morose. No longer excited and panting like when we were out. More introspective. We drove up to the Hills and visited a friend."

Brody's *story* about April was finally over. I looked at his finger and there was a wedding ring but was he married to Midori? Did this episode turn April into a wildly insecure nut for coke? Did she die that day doing it just once? One can imagine Brody beating his chest like a monster having its way with a weakling. Who wins in these scenarios?

37

Let There be Rubidium

June 14, 1989, Part Ten

A light drizzle was spraying the concrete and making puddles. Cyan was carving the candle he stole from the apartment with a knife in the fashion of a sculptor. He was in deep focus.

Walking towards Cyan was Reggie lighting matches and throwing them into the air. His version of fire flies.

Cyan was spray painting on the back wall of P.S. 357's schoolyard.

Reggie finally caught up with Cyan.

With his blood boiled and static energy flying, Reggie called out, "The sign says post no bills."

Either Cyan didn't hear him or he was not paying attention but he continued to paint.

Reggie pulled out a pink Spalding High-Bounce Ball. He threw it on the ground and it bounced high up into the dark blue sky. Once the ball came back to earth, Reggie had a handgun pointed to the Cyan's back.

"No one expects to be erased in a playground, without apparent reason."

Cyan turned swiftly around. The gun was now pointing at his heart.

He was trained on Reggie's eyes as if to telepathically say, 'please don't shoot'.

Cyan heard his own heartbeat as if he was having an echocardiogram. Then the whole world went silent. He was so scared that he lost his hearing.

Rather than a fight or flight panic, Cyan went tranquil. He watched the ball bounce to the exact beat of his heart. They both stared, never wavering, until after a while, a slow, sly smile slid across Reggie's lips like a contemptuous serpent. Cyan relented.

He smiled back, with a little warmth and seethed, "I'm starvin' and when you hungry you can't crack a smile. I checked your background. Who run with you? WIZ260. That's a rich Jewish kid. Doby260! Nonsense. Why didn't you check my background before you went crossing me and my crew out? If *anyone* you rock with spent one day with us, trapped in the cage with us, they come back tamed as fucked. Dangerous as a chained up pup. I let the piece go buck, until my wrist sprained and my finger is cut. Your hostile actions don't mean a thing to us. I hit the angel dust. Get my anger up. Turn into a juggernaut, do you in point blank range. I'll see you soul flying – and I'll still be flying. Even your guardian angel is gonna get dumped."

A trepid smile came across Cyan's face.

Reggie whispered, "Bang. You're dead."

Reggie pulled the trigger.

The unmistakable sound of gunfire.

Cyan stumbled back against the wall, slid down and went limp. He groaned and rolled over with his left foot twitching.

His dark red blood was running backwards in his veins.

Reggie ran away, right by Cyan's last piece. As far as what he painted no one will know. It got painted over the next day because the blood splatted on the wall. All that was left was a message that said, "Let There Be Light."

On a big grass field that had just been soaked with a good amount of rain, Ken was carrying boxes of grapes from a truck and walking them towards a giant empty vat in front of a barn.

A hand-powered crusher was positioned perfectly on the top of the vat. As Ken reached the vat he poured the grapes in. Charlie Parmesan was already sweating as he cranked the crusher handle. Ken then stacked the empty crates neatly out of the way. There was already a stack of fifteen crates. Charlie and Ken removed their shoes, socks and pants and slipped into the vat.

Charlie started to mutter under his breath then raised the volume so everyone can understand, "We're ready! Alla Salute!"

That was the signal to start stomping. It was a glorious time and Ken seemed to be having the most fun. The aroma! My God! Feeling the caps break. What a sensation.

A car pulled up and out came Nicky. He walked triumphantly towards the vat. He decided moms can be wrong and college was not his calling.

Once he was close enough he removed his shoes, socks and pants. Ken had been too busy stomping on the grapes to notice that Nicky had arrived when he said, "Yo! I thought we're gonna do this together?"

The mood was much different than the last time they were together. There was no longer any physical or emotional distance between them. Ken's eyes moistened with gratitude as he laughed, "You ain't see nothing yet!"

Charlie Parmesan shouted, "Get workin'!"

Nicky jumped into the vat. They hugged in a passionate embrace. Nicky stomped, Ken laughed joyously and followed suit. Hanging on the barn was the painting that Cyan drew that Ken had spent three hours putting back together then framed it.

It was a painting of a silhouette of a man and woman eating.

The Dead Fuckin' End

Acknowledgements

I thank from the depth of my heart, Bing Sespene, Spike Alden and Meigi from Solarium House Publishing for taking a daring chance on me.

My relationship with my editor, Dr. Paul Weisser will always be remembered as one of the great times of my life.

I also had an equally pleasurable time listening to the incomparable Kristan Cunningham read a draft and point out things I would not have otherwise seen.

Special Thanks to Trevor Murray & Jesse Husband for their valuable feedback.

This book would not be possible without the support of Koali Gillingwater and Robert Alper.

I would also be remiss not to mention the journey of this book was connected to my happenstance moments with Rich Cohen, Chanan Tigay and Shep Gordon.

The influences to this book are countless and many, if not all, are musicians, writers, actors and painters that I met along my way growing up in Manhattan.

About the Author

Christopher Giarratano will come as a new name to readers. His style is unorthodox because he weaves a story rather than telling it straight. His versatility is striking. He writes assuredly about primitive Italians, reformed Jews, slum children, wealthy WASPS, the mentally ill, dumb Bible scholars, intellectual women, and visionary graffiti artists. His grasp of these characters comes from deep inside.

His Italian name is somewhat misleading, because his mother is an Ashkenazi Jew who married his Sicilian father and settled in the West Village of Manhattan. On both sides, this union was considered treacherous, but he was the blessing of that rebellious love.

To sit and talk with Mr. Giarratano, you are taken aback by his personality, which is seemingly capable of multiple alterations. He is incredibly funny but also possesses a profound soul. His writing style is unrestrained and unexpected thus this enchanting debut novel is for the reader to unravel.

www.ingramcontent.com/pod-product-compliance
Lightning Source LLC
Chambersburg PA
CBHW020835260626
47169CB00003B/1004